G000278976

The Water and ... .

Tamar Hodes

Hookline Books

'Highly recommended'
Nick Broomfield

'Well-turned storylines, excellent character development, and a generous portion of the world as lived in the 60s make this a very fine treasure of a book.'
The San Francisco Review of Books

'An enchanting, entertaining read.'
Cohencentric

'A read that deserves recommendation.'
Book Traveller

'Leonard Cohen fans, creatives, and anyone who loves Greece, will enjoy this story. You'll want to book a trip to Hydra to find your own muse.'
Windy City

'A haunting, unforgettable work.'
Rebecca Smith

'An evocative portrayal of an artists' community.'
Bryony Doran

Published by Hookline Books, Bookline & Thinker Ltd
7 Regent Court
Chipping Norton
OX7 5PJ
www.hooklinebooks.com

First published 2018, Hookline Books, UK
Second Edition 2019, Hookline Books, UK

All rights reserved. No part of this book may be reproduced or stored in
an information retrieval system (other than for the purposes of review)
without the express permission of the publisher in writing.

The right of Tamar Hodes to be identified as the author of this work has
been asserted in accordance with the Copyright, Designs and Patents
Act 1988.
© Copyright 2018 Tamar Hodes

A CIP catalogue for this book is available from the British Library.

This book is a work of fiction. Names, characters, places and incidents
are either a product of the author's imagination or are used fictitiously.
ISBN: 97819164410374

Cover design by Jessie Barlow.

This book is a work of fiction based on historical fact. Names, characters, events and places are either products of the author's imagination or used fictitiously.

For all the maids, nannies, and countless others, often neglected, who make it possible for artists to pursue their dreams.

On an island, eventually, you are bound to meet yourself.
Charmian Clift, *Peel Me a Lotus*

Preface

In April 1963, my parents took my brother, seven, and me, three, to live on the Greek island of Hydra. My father had been commissioned to write a book on the politics of the Middle East, and we needed to live somewhere cheaply for a year.

Among the artists and writers already living on Hydra were Norman Peterson, an American sculptor so poor that the only way he could heat his home was to keep a felled tree in the main room and set the branches alight when needed. The Australian novelists Charmian Clift and George Johnston wrote when they weren't fighting or drinking. Their three children witnessed some difficult scenes. As Max Brown puts it in *Charmian and George: The Marriage of George Johnston and Charmian Clift* (Rosenberg, 2004) 'the victims were the children.' American writer Gordon Merrick and his partner, dancer and novelist Chuck Hulse, were able to live openly as gay men. However, the most important resident was Leonard Cohen. He was in his early thirties and just about to become well-known. Unlike the others who rented houses, he had bought his, with an inheritance from his grandmother.

In the evenings, the writers and artists would gather at the Douskos Taverna (still owned by the same family) and, beneath the pine tree through which a wisteria released its sweet scent, they would drink retsina and discuss their work, ideas, philosophy and music by the light of the kerosene lamps. Leonard Cohen would strum his guitar and sing his songs. The local Greek people were surprisingly tolerant of these bohemians for two reasons. Firstly, it was their nature to be easy going and also, economically, it did them much good. The artists employed them as maids, cleaners and odd job men. Sponge-divers sold their wares and boatmen ferried passengers to and from Piraeus, the port of Athens. As there were no cars on the island (and still aren't today) everyone travelled by donkey and 'the mule boys', as they were known, were paid to accompany the riders. The Katsikas brothers owned the local store, and it was in this shop that Leonard Cohen first met Marianne Jensen. She was living on Hydra with her novelist husband Axel and their young son, but the marriage was an unhappy one. Axel had other lovers, and Marianne felt lonely and neglected.

During his period on Hydra, Cohen wrote many of the songs which would later become classics: *Sisters of Mercy*, *Suzanne* and *Bird on a Wire*.

Years later, my parents would often talk about the time we spent on Hydra. I had published a novel, *Raffy's Shapes,* and a collection of short stories, *The Watercress Wife*; there were also stories in anthologies and on Radio 4, but I always thought that the period on Hydra would make a fascinating novel. Many books documented this time but I felt a fictional version would allow a writer to go behind the facts and sit at the table with the characters, eavesdrop on their conversations and hopefully understand their desires. As E.L.Doctorow said, 'The historian will tell you what happened. The novelist will tell you what it felt like.' Fiction is a passport which allows one to slip into the lives of others. Leonard Cohen said in a 2005 interview with Kari Hesthamar for Norwegian radio that '...to write about Marianne and Hydra, it would take a novel...'

There were so many issues that interested me: how in such a liberal society, the women and maids were still responsible for domesticity and the children; the way that the youngsters had freedom but were, in some people's eyes, quite feral; the extraordinary tolerance among people practising Judaism, Christianity and Zen alongside the local Greek orthodox natives; whether freedom from work helps creativity; if focusing on your writing or painting is self-indulgent; whether being a muse is a blessing or a curse; and whether you can escape your demons on a Greek island. Charmian Clift thought not and wrote in *Peel Me a Lotus*: 'On an island, eventually, you are bound to meet yourself.' I was also very interested in the tension between excitement and risk versus stability, and whether children's need are different from those of adults.

For many years, I thought about Hydra and read extensively about it. Then several events happened which compelled me to write my novel. My father sadly passed away in 2013; he left me his journal about that time; my mother died the following year and left me a signed first edition of Cohen's poetry collection *Flowers for Hitler*. Marianne died in 2016, four months before Cohen; it felt like a groundswell beneath me, pushing me to write my book.

It has been a fascinating process, trying to plait fact, fiction and memory into a coherent whole. At times, I felt exhilarated by it; at other times, upset by the exploration of the relationships which fell apart. Leonard Cohen admitted this in Kari Hesthamar's 2005 book *So Long Marianne*: 'Those relationships on Hydra were all doomed. We didn't know it at the time, but they couldn't withstand what life imposed on us.... None of those relationships survived, except in the sense that we honour them and we recognize the nourishment of those experiences.' The island was both magical and tragical. Without giving away the plot of the novel, there was laughter on the island but there was also pain.

I also became very interested in islands, in the way that they seem to be an escape but actually they are places of confinement. You have to face reality, as there is nowhere to run. My husband and I love visiting Mediterranean islands and I really enjoyed describing Hydra – the birds, food, flowers and goats. It felt to me as if Hydra was a character in the novel with an identity of its own.

I could not help but think about *The Tempest* when I wrote this novel. Prospero may feel that he has left behind his problems and his past, but actually it is on the island that he is forced to confront the truth as all his history is revealed. When he says to Caliban, 'This thing of darkness I acknowledge mine' he is eventually admitting that he was also partly to blame for what happened.

My main concern was how to represent my parents, whom I loved deeply, without being disloyal to them. My only option was to reinvent and fictionalise them as Jack and Frieda Silver. Some of the events actually happened; some did not. I asked my brother's permission to reshape him into Gideon and I modelled the little girl on me and gave her my middle name, Esther. Many writers face this dilemma: do you have the right to tell your story when it is also the story of other people?

Luckily, I found a publisher, Hookline Books, who loved the novel, and most of the reviews have been positive. *The San Francisco Review of Books* wrote: 'Well-turned storylines, excellent character development, and a generous portion of the world as lived in the sixties make this a very fine treasure of a book. Recommended.'

Writing is a strange activity, full of paradoxes: it is solitary and yet it is a form of communication; it is deeply personal but can also be universal; it is specific and general; it is liberating and entrapping; it is joyful and upsetting; it can be comforting and unsettling, and it takes so much longer to write than it does to read!

Whether *The Water and the Wine* works as a novel, readers will have to decide for themselves.

Tamar Hodes, 2019

Like its artistic inhabitants, Hydra was creative. It painted the earth with purple orchids, wrote itself into the history books and even made its own music: the hum of chatter in the air; the clink of coffee cups at the harbour café, and the light bells on the donkeys as they ambled along the cobbles. Cocks crowed their rough chorus and the single bell chapel at the Monastery of the Virgin's Assumption added its tinny percussion on the hour.

~

Leaving the boat, the Silver family felt as caught in the island's magic as the shiny fish wriggling in the yellow nets. Frieda held Esther's hand but Gideon walked on ahead. Jack, tall and bearded, thanked the boatman, Mikalis, and his good-looking, shirtless son, Spyros, who had tied the rope to keep the boat steady. The family took their luggage and followed signs to Douskos' Taverna, where wicker tables and chairs were arranged beneath a dark pine. A thin wisteria threaded itself through the tree, releasing its subtle scent into the spring air.

Jack shook hands with the owner of the bar, greeting him with *Kaliméra*, and handed over a piece of paper. The publishers had given him an advance for his book and arranged the family's accommodation. Douskos was swarthy and dark, stockily built, his white shirt and trousers immaculate. His wife, Polixenes, was sweeping away dead leaves, broken glass and candle wax from the previous night's revels.

Douskos gestured for the family to sit and ordered drinks for them, while he went outside. Then the family saw her for the first time: The Gardenia Dwarf. A tiny old lady, her body and head cloaked in black, a white bloom just discernible, tucked behind her ear. Like her daughter, she was sweeping the stone floor, but the large broom looked unwieldy. She mumbled something which the Silver family did not understand.

They finished their drinks and went outside where three donkeys were waiting, flat wooden saddles on their backs for carrying loads, the 'mule boys' sullenly at their sides. The cobbles beneath them bubbled in the sun. Douskos looked expectantly at Jack for some coins; once received, he vanished.

Frieda, short, her long dark hair plaited and wound round her head and Gideon, thin, with wiry glasses, travelled on one donkey: Jack and Esther, small, slightly podgy, mounted the second, and the luggage was strapped to the third.

Slowly, they climbed the hill to Kala Pigadia, passing a skinny, bearded man picking up litter from the side of the path. A goat chewed wild rosemary in his gummy jaws. The donkeys were slow and hesitant, the boys hitting them with sticks when they almost halted. Esther didn't like this treatment of them and snuggled up to her father for comfort.

'It's alright, sweetie,' he said.

It was the second time that day that she had cried. On the ferry boat from Piraeus, a man had come on board, handcuffed to guards. His clothes were tatty and his face unshaven.

'He's a prisoner,' Jack told Esther.

She was unsettled by the sad expression on the man's face and the way he hung his head in shame. She was eating pistachios that her mother had given her, cracking open the brown shells to release the yellow-green nuts. When she tried to feed the prisoner one, he took it. He was like a bird bending his head, and Esther kept on feeding him, the guards letting her. When they stopped at the island of Poros, the man was yanked off the boat. He caught Esther's eye as he left and she started to cry – until her dad told her a story about Peter the butterfly who lived in his beard but who flew off on his adventures around the world.

The trek across the island was uncomfortable, the donkeys swaying as they ambled, the saddle hard beneath Esther's cotton dress, but eventually they arrived. They gasped when they saw their house. White-washed and gleaming, it perched upon a hill. It had a blue door with a bronze lion's head knocker and shutters, which cast broad stripes upon the walls. As they later discovered, there was little electricity (an hour in the morning and an hour in the evening) and no running water, but there was a well in the courtyard as well as some manic chickens and a goat to provide the family with eggs and milk.

The large balcony wrapped itself around the house like a sash. Terracotta troughs of red geraniums perched precariously on its ledge. On one side it looked out onto the harbour – where half-melon boats bobbed slightly in the occasional breeze – then to the sea beyond, where leather-skinned fishermen drew in their catch. On the other, they could see red-rooved houses clinging to the hillside as if they had grown from it; on the Kamina ridge was an old windmill with a house attached.

Gideon and Esther ran excitedly around their new home. It was simply furnished but bigger than any house they had lived in before. The children fought over which bedroom to claim but finally settled it with Gideon taking the bigger, with room for his rocks and stones, and Esther's having a wonderful view over the town. She unpacked the few clothes she had, together with some books and dollies, which she arranged tidily at the end of her bed.

On the balcony, Frieda served the meal that had been left for them: a Greek salad and warm pitta. They liked tearing it, dipping its spongy pieces into hummus and tzatziki. Grapes gleamed in the bowl, glassy globes bursting with juice. The April sun was warm and gentle, casting a glow over the food, making it shine.

'So what are your first impressions of Hydra?' asked Jack.

'I love it.' Esther was often effusive. Gideon remained quiet as if reserving judgement.

'It's beautiful,' said Frieda, looking out dreamily over the harbour. 'I think we will be very happy here.'

Jack drew his chair nearer. 'I'll tell you the story of Hydra.'

'I thought hydra meant water,' Gideon said.

'Yes, it does as it is surrounded by water but there is also the Greek legend. Hydra was a snake-monster with many heads.'

'Ugh,' said Esther.

'It lived near the Fountain of Amymone. The peasants could not go to fetch water because they were afraid of the monster, but no-one could kill it. Every time a head was chopped off, two new ones grew in its place. Hercules, the great hero, was called in to destroy it and he asked his nephew Iolaus to help him. Each time Hercules cut off a head, Iolaus sealed the wound and so they killed the snake-monster.'

'Good,' said Gideon.

'Hooray!' said Esther.

'And that's why "Hydra" refers to a situation which is problematic and needs clever solutions.'

Jack and Frieda exchanged a silent glance.

Just as they were wondering about taking a walk to the quayside, there was a knock at the door. A large woman stood there, dressed in a pale lemon overall, her dark hair tightly coerced into a bun.

'Evgeniya!' she pointed to herself, and Jack nodded knowingly. Yes, she came with the house. She stepped forward and hugged Esther who lost herself in the large folds and contours of the maid's comforting body. Evgeniya immediately started clearing away the dishes and helping as if she had known the family all her life.

A while later, the door was knocked again. Frieda opened it to a beautiful young woman carrying a baby. Frieda led her onto the balcony and introduced the family. Marianne, a Norwegian, lived on the island with her husband, Axel, and her baby, Axel Joachim. Both mother and son had bleached-blonde hair and shiny blue eyes. She put the baby on the balcony to play with his toy giraffe and drew some almond biscuits from her bag.

'These are to welcome you,' she said shyly.

'How kind,' said Frieda.

Evgeniya brought coffee in tiny gold cups and Gideon had juice. Esther tried the goat's milk but could not stomach it. They all shared the biscuits. Esther brought out some wooden animal figures and Axel Joachim played with them. Gideon arranged his collection of rocks on the balcony and scrubbed them with an old toothbrush and foamy water until they gleamed.

'Are there many artists on the island?' Frieda asked Marianne.

'Yes, a fair number and it's growing all the time. My husband is a writer. That is when he is not distracted by his lovers. The present one's Patricia.'

Jack and Frieda looked awkwardly at each other.

'I'm also a writer,' Jack said. 'I have a commission to write a book about the Jewish-Arab conflict.'

'That's interesting. I would love to write but I find it so hard. Trying to express myself truthfully when I am not sure what my feelings are.'

Esther bounced Axel Joachim on her knee. He was chuckling, the wooden giraffe in his mouth.

'Among others, we have Charmian Clift on the island and her husband George Johnston. They are from Australia and are both writers. Feisty people! Plus, we have Norman; he's a sculptor. He makes amazing structures from litter he finds on the ground.'

'Oh yes, I think we saw him on our way here.'

'That's him. John Dragoumis, who has shell-shock from the war: he does beautiful charcoal drawings, and then there's Carl, another painter.'

'I'm also a painter,' said Frieda. Just saying the words excited her. On the kibbutz, she'd had to fit her art between caring for the chickens and picking oranges, but here, this would be her identity.

'What do you like to paint?' Marianne drained the last of her coffee. Her skin glowed in the soft light.

'Flowers, fishermen, harbours, anything. I'm hoping to rent a cheap studio on the island.'

'Ask Douskos. He knows everything and everyone, especially when some drachmas cross his palm.'

They all laughed.

'Yes. We met him today,' said Jack.

'And The Gardenia Dwarf? That is his widowed mother-in-law. She lives a few roads from here. She grows beautiful gardenias, shiny like no flower you have seen. The scent of her garden is so sweet. She will sell you a bloom for a few coins.'

Frieda's face lit up. 'How lovely.'

'Most evenings, we meet at Douskos' Taverna and drink ouzo and talk about art and life. You must join us. We never arrange to gather. We just turn up and there are always interesting people there.'

'It sounds wonderful. We'll come along,' Jack said.

'Do you take your baby with you?'

'Sometimes, or we have a maid, Maria, who watches him. Most people leave their children asleep in bed and check on them every now and then. It's very safe here. Come and join us any time. I must go now. Axel Joachim needs his nap.'

She scooped up her beautiful boy and left.

As they were unpacking, Frieda said: 'She was so beautiful. Why would her husband take lovers when he has a wife like that?'

'We are in an artists' colony,' said Jack. 'You have to forget all your bourgeois conventions now and embrace the free culture here. We aren't in South Africa any more. There are no boundaries on Hydra. I thought we wanted that?'

'We do but it frightens me. Letting go of the rules. Being free. And, anyway, I don't remember your background being so bohemian.'

5

'It wasn't but yours was...'

'Mine was... what?'

'Very conventional. of course, you're going to find it hard to adjust to the creativity, the openness here.'

'You're so patronising, Jack, the way you speak to me. My parents were in business, the same as yours. Groceries, shoes, what's the difference?' She stormed off, unhappy at how they always used each other's backgrounds as weapons.

But as the afternoon progressed, a serenity fell on the family home. There were no more arguments, either between Gideon and Esther or between their parents. What they did not know was that the biscuits contained more than ground almonds. Marianne had used an extra ingredient which she often added to her cooking: hashish.

That night, Jack and Frieda made love for the first time in months: cautiously, trying to draw the other close, in an attempt to start again. Their lovemaking was always unsatisfactory: him too eager, her too unwilling to say what she wanted and shutting herself to his demands. But at least they were together, feeling slightly optimistic, marking what they hoped would be a new beginning.

The following morning, the sun varnished the island in a warm, honey glaze and the eucalyptus' smooth leaves shimmered seductively. Marianne, in a striped, pleated skirt, cotton shirt and simple sandals, had left Axel Joachim with Maria and gone to collect her mail from the post office in the Katsikas brothers' store. It was also the day for the *Athens News* to arrive and she needed groceries: olive oil, rice, feta, a string of onions, potatoes, candles.

She swung her deep basket as she walked, thinking of Axel and their lives and wondering in which direction they should go. Every time they tried to live and love, it fell apart. She wondered how long she could stay with him when his heart was with Patricia, and she worried what effect their dysfunctional marriage would have on their child. She thought about her own childhood: problems with money, problems with health and problems in her parents' marriage. She had dreamed of so much more for her own son.

The island had sprung into full beauty as if the flowers had been poised beneath the skin of the earth, waiting for their cue. And when that signal had come, they had burst forth, uncontrollably: the blood-red tulips dotting their random beauty across the ground; the camellias, white and pink, like sugared candy sweetening the air; the gorse bushes, their yellow flowers an antidote to their prickly leaves, and the air, benign.

Inside the shop, Marianne marvelled at the range of products that Nick and Antony Katsikas had in stock: sacks of ground almonds and flour sagged shapelessly on the stone floor as if they had no intention of ever moving; boxes of dried fruit; barrels of retsina stacked sideways to form a pyramid; octopus tentacles and sheep testicles hanging up to dry; tins of tomatoes and bags of sugar along with household items: baskets, brooms and pots. There was also fresh vegetables: potatoes, aubergines and onions, smug and fat in their papery skins.

As she paid for her goods, framed through the doorway of the store into the yard behind she saw Charmian and George seated at a table. They waved to her.

'Hey, Marianne. Come and drink with us.'

Charmian embraced Marianne as she approached and George drew out a chair for her. He looked thinner than when she had last seen him. As usual, he had a drink in one hand and a cigarette in the other. His hair looked lank and greasy and he had not shaved. Charmian looked as elegant as ever in a wide-brimmed straw hat and a long white kaftan but Marianne noticed that the hem was edged with dirt. She was drinking whisky. Opposite her was a man Marianne had not seen before.

She sat down, releasing her heavy basket, and feeling her cheeks redden.

The sun lit the stranger's tanned face and dark hair and he looked casual, in chinos and a linen shirt with rolled-up sleeves, and yet it seemed as if he had always lived on Hydra, was comfortable here.

The stranger felt his body tingle as he saw the beautiful woman, her flaxen hair tied back into a ponytail with an elastic band, her satin skin catching the light, the simplicity of her and yet her otherworldliness as if she had arisen, like a mermaid, from the sea. He found it hard to move his eyes from her.

'This is Leonard,' said Charmian. 'Isn't he a delight? He's staying with us until he finds his own place.'

'Pleased to meet you,' said Leonard, in a husky, growly voice. 'Come and share the sun and wine with us.'

Marianne remembered her beloved Momo's words: 'You will meet a man who speaks with a golden tongue.' Maybe this was him.

'Where have you come from?' asked Marianne.

'Originally Montreal. I was in London and couldn't bear the rain so I travelled here.'

'You just packed your bags and left?'

'When I went into the Bank of Greece to cash a cheque, the teller looked tanned. I asked him where he had been and he said, "Greece, it's springtime there," and so I came.'

Marianne laughed at his impulsiveness. 'So suddenly?'

'Of course. What is life for if it isn't living for the moment?' Leonard's voice was velvet gravel and deep. Marianne felt her body burn as if he had lit a fire inside her.

Leonard felt it too. He had noticed her wheeling her son (the same bleached hair, the beautiful eyes catching the Greek light, the same delicate half-smile) in a pushchair around the island and wondered who she was.

'Len's a writer and singer,' said George proudly, coughing and smoking at the same time.

'Put that fucking fag out before you kill yourself, George!' barked his wife. 'No-one wants to hear that racket.'

'Go hang yourself, Charm!' he yelled back.

Marianne smiled. She had become used to their fights. She and Leonard exchanged glances as if to say: here we go, again.

'Charmian and George are kindly putting me up,' said Leonard.

'Or you're putting up with us!' George laughed.

'I've been doing that for years, sweetie,' Charmian quipped. 'Why shouldn't he?'

'Shut the fuck up, Charm dearest, in the nicest possible way.'

'I've just bought a house in Kala Pigadia,' said Leonard, trying to improve the mood, 'and I'm waiting for the sale to go through. Where do you live, Marianne?' Just saying her name made him happy.

'In Kala Pigadia, also.' Marianne blushed. 'It is beautiful, near the communal wells and the monastery. You can see the whole of Hydra spread out from there. I think you will like it.'

'Marianne has a husband, Axel, who is an arsehole,' laughed George, too loudly.

'Well, we all know how that feels,' Charmian couldn't resist. 'Believe me.'

Marianne noticed that Leonard was drinking water and that he had written in a notepad and even on the paper tablecloth. She sensed his discomfort at his friends' public spats.

'You're a writer?'

'Trying to be. I'm not in the league of my friends here though.'

'Nine books in ten years. Forty-three countries covered when I was a war correspondent,' boasted George.

'Shame we can't find a forty-fourth one for you to visit, darling.'

'How's your novel going, George?' Marianne asked.

'First in the David Meredith trilogy done. He's my alter ego. Bill Collins is going to publish it. They're getting Sid Nolan to do the cover. Sid's great. We're both sons of tram drivers. Did you know that? The man's a wonderful painter.'

'And Cynthia, his wife's a good writer, too,' said Charmian.

'Oh yeah. Cynth. And it was Sid who introduced us to Clarissa Zander who first gave us the idea of living on a Greek island.'

'No, we heard the islanders of Kalymnos singing on the radio,' Charmian contradicted him.

'Actually, Alex Grivas told us about taking Prince Philip round the nightspots.'

'Well, anyway,' Marianne interrupted them, 'we're pleased you're here.'

'It's been great for my writing. I'm onto the second book of the trilogy,' George looked at his wife. 'That's gonna be explosive.'

'Just leave me out of it. Your novels are getting more uncomfortably autobiographical as the days go on, George, and I don't fucking like it.'

'What else is there to write about but real life, my darling wife?' He poured himself more retsina. 'You do it, don't you? What's *Mermaid Singing*? Fantasy?'

In the middle of another coughing bout, George drew a cigarette from the pack, threw it to his lips where it stuck, lit it and then blew a series of perfect smoke rings into the air. Charmian rolled her eyes at this much-performed trick.

'If I'd wanted to be married to a dolphin, I'd have gone to the fucking aquarium.'

George laughed, coughed and clapped his imaginary flippers in the air.

'Do you write about real life?' Marianne asked Leonard.

He looked up from his notes. 'Writing is at once the deepest connection and the greatest escape,' he said. 'When you write you are both at the heart of life and away from it. The writer is absent and present.'

'Len speaks in riddles,' said George. 'Jeez, the man's so deep, only a few people on the planet can understand him.'

'Better than writing those potboilers that you churn out!'

'Ouch, that hurt, Charm! That really did!'

'Good. It was meant to.' She downed her whisky in one and filled up her glass again.

'At least my writing covers the bills.'

'Almost.'

Marianne had had enough. She wanted to be alone with Leonard and find out more about him.

'I need to go,' she said.

As if understanding her thoughts, Leonard jumped up. 'May I help you with your groceries?' he asked and lifted her basket.

'Bye George. Bye Charmian,' they called. 'See you soon.'

Outside the sky was brazen and it was a relief to be in the fresh air.

'How do you stand living there?' she asked, as they perched on the low quay wall and watched the red and blue boats settle after a busy morning. 'People here call them The Hat and The Skinny Australian.'

'It's really hard,' he said, looking out at the wrinkled water. 'More than anything it is sad. They are both so talented and they had such a love story. He was married before.'

'I know. To Elsie, and they have a daughter, Gae, back in Australia.'

'But as soon as they start drinking, they can't stop and they are so nasty to each other.'

'I worry about the children.' Leonard could see that she was compassionate.

'Me too. Poor kids. I feel for Martin, the eldest, as he is very sensitive, a good writer himself, and he can see what is going on and he tries to protect Shane and Jason. But the strange thing is, no matter how ugly the night before, seven o'clock the next morning, they are sober and back at their writing again. That's when I start writing, too, so the house lulls into serenity.'

'I bet you can't wait to have your own space.'

'So true. Peace and quiet and time to write.'

'Poetry? Novels?'

'Yes. Both, and songs, too, although of course lyrics must stand on their own. I play the guitar. I was in a band, the Buckskin Boys, when I was at McGill. The name was chosen because we all had buckskin jackets; mine was my dad's. We weren't very good, Country and Western, but now I just sing on my own. I haven't been on Hydra long but I sense something in the air which is creative and dangerous.'

'Dangerous?'

'Yes. As if it could both revive and destroy you.'

Marianne nodded. 'I know what you mean. Axel and I came here full of idealism and hope and now our marriage has shattered on the rocks. He takes lovers.'

Leonard shook his head. Why would a man do that if he could have a woman like this by his side? The light caught her eyes and they shone bright blue, as if they had been cut from the same material as the sky.

'He must be crazy.'

Marianne smiled modestly. Maybe she had disclosed too much but she felt so comfortable with Leonard, as if they had known each other for years.

'Who knows?' Her eyes filled with tears. 'Maybe I am to blame, too? Or maybe it is Hydra?'

They sat for a few moments, reluctant to leave the warm wall and each other.

'I have to go now,' she said, rising. 'My son needs me.'

She picked up her basket.

'Can you manage?'

'Yes, thank you. You should come and join us. Most evenings, people gather at Douskos' Taverna and discuss art and life. You would enjoy it. You could bring your guitar.'

'I know about the evenings but I have avoided them. George and Charmian often go and the house is peaceful then. The kids do their own thing, I do mine, but if I know you will be there, I will certainly come along.'

Marianne blushed.

'And do please come and see me in my new home. I move in hopefully next week. I have written my address and slipped it in your basket. Goodbye, Marianne.'

He watched her leave, saw how her dress floated about her legs as she walked, and knew that his life had changed.

She knew it too. As Marianne climbed the hill, she felt her heart flutter and all she could think about was Leonard. She dipped her hand in the basket and there, among the mud-encrusted potatoes, was a piece of paper. Beneath where Leonard had written his address, he had sketched a bird, its wings opened wide. Marianne smiled and rubbed her finger over the drawing. She could not stop thinking about his dark hair, his deep eyes, his chiselled face, the way the sun lit his skin when he smiled.

The island hummed with spring and surely [...] open now than when she had walked down to Kat[...] before.

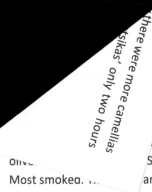

...there were more camellias
...tsikas' only two hours

...skos' Taverna, the friends sat in a circle, their
... Loops of coloured light bulbs were draped
...e cheap necklaces. Terracotta bowls of shiny
oliv... Some people drank retsina, others ouzo or wine.
Most smoked. ... an atmosphere of warmth and animation.

Jack and Frieda felt shy as they approached the circle but to their delight Marianne stood up and beckoned them over.

'Hey everyone, this is Jack and Frieda, just arrived from an Israeli kibbutz.'

There was a sound of welcome, chairs were drawn up and drinks poured for them.

'Let me introduce everyone. This is Charmian and her husband, George, from Australia. Writers also, like you, Jack. And John Dragoumis, a painter like you, Frieda. And Norman, Norman Peterson, the artist I told you about.' Yes, Jack and Frieda recognised him from earlier: he was the man picking up litter at the roadside, presumably objets trouvés for his work. 'Oh, and my husband Axel.' They saw a thin, intense man with short blonde hair and glasses. He did not smile. Marianne scowled: 'And Patricia Amlin, an American painter. Ah and here is Anthony Kingsmill, another painter.'

'How many fucking painters does an island need?' George shouted drunkenly through a smoky haze.

'We can never have enough, surely?' Charmian lit another cigarette. 'We have to balance out the fucking writers here somehow.'

'True, my dear,' said George sarcastically. 'The painters and the writers have to fuck. Just kidding. Hiya, Jack. Welcome, Fried!'

'And, also, here are Chuck Hulse and Gordon Merrick,' said Marianne. 'Or as Axel always calls you, Chuckandgordon, whichever one of you he means.'

The men smiled. 'We're cool with that,' said Chuck.

'Author of *The Strumpet Wind*?' said Jack, his eyes alight. 'That was amazing. I read it three times.'

'Thank you,' said Chuck. 'And are you the man who wrote that wonderful book about Buber?'

Jack smiled proudly. It was a dream come true to be surrounded by creative people. He saw copies of books by Robert Graves and Yeats on the table, presumably lent and shared among the community.

'I loved the part about the existential test that all individuals face at some stage of their lives and how we are never the same again,' said Gordon.

'Not only individuals are tested but also nations,' added Chuck.

'And what he has to say about responsibility and truth and the I-Thou relationship as opposed to the I-It.'

'Thank you,' said Jack, flattered. 'I am so pleased that you enjoyed the book. Buber was a wonderful man.'

'And this is Leonard Cohen,' said Marianne, trying not to appear too pleased that he had, at last, joined them. He looked up and smiled before bending his head back to his guitar which he strummed quietly beneath the conversation.

John Dragoumis beckoned for the young couple to come closer. Newcomers were sometimes fought over on Hydra. 'Have you heard of the *I Ching*?'

Jack was interested. 'Heard of it but never seen it in action.'

'It's a way of discovering who you are using ancient Chinese philosophy,' said John. He was plump and friendly with a white beard, open leather sandals and dirty toenails.

'That's my copy,' said Marianne proudly, 'with an introduction by Jung.'

George said, 'The *I Ching* insists upon self-knowledge throughout.'

'We know that, thank you, George.' Charmian scowled. 'Throw the coins, would you? You said it was my turn to have my question answered. Here we go. Is Hydra the right place for me?'

'Jeez, Charm. Take it easy.' George tossed the coins and let them fall onto the table. After six turns, he drew the hexagrams while everyone gazed on with interest. 'Right, let's look at the pattern. Okay. So unbroken lines. Chien. The creative. Light-giving. Strong. You need to best develop yourself so that your influence can endure.'

'What damn chance have I got of that, with you and your bloody books and three children to care for?'

'You asked me to look it up, Charm, so will you let me finish?'

'Maybe we should leave it,' said Marianne nervously. 'Let's talk about something else.'

'No!' Charmian swung her bottle in the air and it smashed against the taverna wall. The red wine stained the white bricks. From the bar, Douskos and The Gardenia Dwarf looked up but ignored it. They were used to these foreign artists and their fiery tempers. They would sweep the glass up later. 'It's my turn to have the limelight, do you understand? I want my damn question answered.' She belched. 'Should I remain on Hydra? Is it doing me any bloody good?'

'Right,' George continued. 'Cool it, Charm. The Chinese dragon is dormant in the winter but in the early summer it is active again and is creative and a force for good. So just be patient, will you? Your time is coming.'

'Well, I wish it would hurry up and arrive. I'm sick of being a nobody.'

Frieda noticed how thin Norman Peterson was, his ribs visible through his creased, batik shirt. 'I think we saw you by the roadside,' she said. He turned politely to answer.

'Yes, probably. I collect objects. Bottles, paper, wire, string. I make sculptures and try to sell them.'

'I like the randomness of it,' said Jack. 'Buber believed, of course, that whatever or whoever we come into contact with is significant.'

'Even wire?' Norman smiled modestly.

'Of course,' Jack said. 'It is the little encounters that nourish the soul. I'll lend you some books about him and also about the founder of eighteenth-century Hasidism, Baal Shem Tov. I think you'll find him interesting.'

Norman nodded gratefully.

'We've been reading John Cage's book, *Silence*,' said Gordon, breaking his. 'He also uses the *I Ching*, in his compositions. He is fascinated by chance and randomness but in a paradoxical way he puts a lot of planning and structure into his work in order to make it random.'

'Yes,' said Chuck, 'do you remember the talk in New York that we went to?'

'What was that?' John put his hands on the table to try and steady them: his tremor was bad this evening.

'At the Artists' Club on Eighth Street and what he said was dependent on chance. That meant that there could be – and there was – a lot of repetition and Jeanne Reynal stormed out saying that she loved John, but she couldn't stand it.'

'He's interested in Zen as well, isn't he?' George said. Charmian was sulking.

'Sure.' Chuck and Gordon always seemed to agree with and listen to each other.

'Thanks,' said Norman. 'I didn't know my picking up of scrap had such deep philosophical roots. I thought I was just a cheapskate and a thief!' And everyone laughed.

The conversation rolled along easily: philosophy, art, politics. Norman said he was pleased to read about how President Johnson was trying to end segregation in America.

'It's very noble,' said John, 'but is it achievable?'

Back at home in the early hours, Jack checked on the children and saw that they were asleep.

'What fascinating people,' he said to Frieda, his eyes shining. Below them, Hydra had settled itself for the night, its houses low in the unremitting darkness.

'It was so stimulating, having interesting people to talk to. I really missed that on the kibbutz, that intellectual debate. So much of our time was focused on how many avocados we'd picked or which goat was dying or whether we should replace the tractor part. All my life I've wanted to be among people like these. It's wonderful. I'm thrilled that we came to live on Hydra, the best decision we ever made. It will be so good for us.'

'Well, for you, it will be.' Frieda was unpinning her plait, letting her crinkled hair fall.

'What do you mean?'

'No-one asked me my opinion. I couldn't get a word in, you were all so full of it: Jung, Cage, Buber. The men dominating, as usual.'

'Rubbish, Frieda. You could have said whatever you wanted to. No-one makes a gap for you in life. You just have to join in. Marianne and Charmian did.'

'You never gave me a chance. Look how Chuck and Gordon treat each other, with respect. But it's all about you and your books and never about my painting. Did you mention me? Did you include me? Of course not. The bottom line is that you don't take my work seriously. You never have. You think I'm just a nice girl from the Cape who paints fruit and flowers as a hobby, but that you are the serious artist in the marriage.'

'When have I ever said that? You have such an inferiority complex.'

'You wonder why? Because you don't admire me. You don't value what I do.'

'You're talking crap, Frieda. You need to discover who you are yourself. You can't expect me to validate you all the time. Leave your bourgeois past behind. Shed it like a skin.'

'My bourgeois background, Jack? What was yours – bohemian?'

Frieda suddenly felt a deep longing for her mother and her childhood home: the pale irises and dovecote in the garden, the mulberry trees whose leaves they picked to feed the silkworms.

She thought of Kibbutz Timorim, where she and Jack had met, located on rough terrain in Galilee. There was little there, just fifty young people from all over the world, bursting with enthusiasm and idealism. Together, they started to create a community. The buildings were small and primitive and in those days the youngsters lived communally. They had some goats, cows and chickens and a large terrain. They grew oranges and lemons in shaded groves, avocados and dates, clustered like jewels at the top of palm trees.

It was easy to see why they had fallen in love. They had come from similar backgrounds whose traditional codes they had both rejected. Five years between them, they craved excitement and believed deeply in the state of Israel. Neither was religious: their Judaism was more cultural, social, a strong part of their identity. As the kibbutz thrived, their marriage struggled. They hoped that a year on Hydra would, like the well in the courtyard, refresh and restore them.

'You're impossible,' said Jack. 'I'm heading for the couch.'

The next morning, Esther and Gideon awoke to find their father asleep in the living room. His large frame was awkwardly angular on the narrow settee.

'Why are you here, Abba?' asked Esther.

Jack jumped up and forced a smile. 'It was just a bit hot in the bedroom, sweetie. Now who wants a story?'

'And breakfast on the balcony?' said Frieda, putting on her bravest face.

iv

And so the Silver family settled into their new routine.

Gideon, aged eight, attended the one-room school on the hill, Jack went to his study to write, and Frieda painted in a studio she rented by the quay. It had an easel, a table for her paints and a blue chaise longue. Through the large windows, she could see the boats rocking on the water and occasionally she would see an avocet. She admired his thin, carved body, his slender legs, his bill, sharp and upturned, and the way the sun illuminated his perfect, feathery back. Through the wooden door, she could smell the bread baking in Demi's rough ovens. Each day she bought a crusty loaf, stamped with the wooden imprint of each family, and it was still warm by the time she arrived home.

Esther loved spending time with Evgeniya, her smooth, dark skin and her wide smile. Each day she wore an apron the colour of sugar almonds, pink or lavender blue. Her dark frizzy hair was pulled into a tidy bun. When Esther cuddled up to Evgeniya, her large body was all soft hills and valleys, curving in and out, providing plenty of places for the little girl to nestle in and find refuge. Evgeniya smelled of lemons and wild flowers.

Esther spent the mornings at nursery where she played with the other children. Building with wooden bricks, playing in the sandpit, and spats over who had the best doll first were similar to the events in the kindergarten in Israel and so Esther slotted in well.

While Esther was at nursery, Evgeniya would sweep the wooden floors and do the laundry on the washboard in the marble sink. Then she would fill the iron with hot coals and press the clothes. She would also prepare dinner, maybe crumble feta cheese over sliced tomatoes and olives or grind hummus from chickpeas, garlic and olive oil before scooping it into a pottery bowl, pitta bread arranged around it like the petals of a large flower.

Evgeniya collected Esther at lunchtime and led her slowly home, passing the dry and papery bougainvillea clambering along a wall. Esther's small white hand pressed into her smooth dark one, they might spot a gecko scurrying along a ledge or a bright butterfly alighting upon a tree. As they walked the uneven paths, they would see wild narcissi and anemones strewing their colour among the tall, dry grass and the camellias, their waxy, glossy leaves catching the light. Although Esther spoke no Greek and Evgeniya no English, there was no mistaking the maid's pointing at something delightful with her finger, her squeals of delight, or her genuine embraces. Sometimes they would sit and cuddle on the balcony, Esther pressed into her ample bosom, and she would plait ribbon in Esther's hair and sing songs with words the child did not understand.

Often Evgeniya had more work to do, sweeping, carrying buckets of water into the house, cooking and laundry. Esther was quite happy to play with her dolls on the balcony, dressing them in the clothes that Evgeniya had made, brushing their hair and bathing them in the plastic tub she had given her, half-filled with water, not enough to be dangerous but enough to make it realistic.

At about three, Gideon would walk home from school. Then later the parents would return and eat the meal Evgeniya had prepared. They might spend some time together but then each return to their own occupations: Jack to his study a few minutes' walk away to carry on with his book; Frieda to her studio to paint; Gideon would arrange his rocks and fossils on the balcony and label them; and Esther would tell her dolls stories, or sing them songs, cradling them.

But some evenings the family spent together. Jack would tell them stories and the children liked to see if Peter the butterfly was at home in their father's beard: he never was. He was always travelling in Italy or France or Spain and that would lead Jack neatly into a story about the butterfly's recent adventures.

Or the family would sit at the table on the balcony when the dinner plates were cleared away and Frieda would bring beads and threads to make necklaces with or open her paint set where the colours were set in blocks like a bright ice-cube tray, and they would all have a go at painting the view from the terrace, egged on by her encouraging words.

Sometimes, she brought out her flower press, its alternate layers of green blotting paper and cork, held down tightly with a wooden lid and four butterfly screws. When the family went on walks around Hydra, they would pick flowers and bring them home to press. Forgotten about, weeks later, the press was opened and there they were, dried and flattened and ready, to make cards with or stick on letters sent to grandparents in Israel and South Africa.

Esther loved these evenings when they sat together, focused on the task, making their own circle, their backs to the world elsewhere. But Gideon often left the table and returned to his rocks and fossils.

'Do you not want to join in with us, Gideon?' Jack would ask.

'Leave him,' said Frieda. 'He likes to be on his own.'

By this time, Evgeniya would have returned to her own home a few yards away to care for her husband, Nikos. People said that they had a son, Costas, who was a waster. Both men had lost their fishing jobs due to their excessive drinking.

Nikos was large, unshaven and always seemed unfriendly. He wore loose trousers and a vest. The family could not believe that someone as wonderful as Evgeniya could be married to such a misery. There was a smell of drink on him no matter what time of day. A few times, he came to the house when Evgeniya was looking after the family. On one occasion, he arrived in the afternoon and they shouted at each other in the kitchen. Esther couldn't understand what they were saying but she could hear angry voices and the sounds of something smashing.

Much later, when the children were in bed, Jack and Frieda sometimes went to Douskos' Taverna to talk about philosophy and art and, as time went on, they felt more and more comfortable there.

The family began to feel rooted, making connections with the shop owners, friends and school. They also registered with Dr Benedictus who had a surgery by the harbour. His plump, smiling wife was the receptionist and their daughter Keri was Gideon's school-teacher. The surgery was whitewashed and from the windows you could see the boats and the gulls, so that going there made you feel better even before you had seen the doctor. He was a white-bearded man with warm eyes. Whatever condition anyone presented him with he nodded in recognition: he had seen it before and in a more acute form. If he hadn't, he referred you to the hospital in Athens so all eventualities were covered.

A few yards away from the Silvers' house, Marianne and Axel were struggling. Their house was right by the two wells so there was always fresh water for them. Their home was adorned with Tibetan rugs and straw mats hanging on the walls. Their carpenter Francisco had made Axel a worktable and there he sat at his typewriter. At first their lives on Hydra had been idyllic. Marianne would read Axel's writing, marking with a red star where she felt the story flagged. She too was writing, doodling, filling journals with her thoughts and dreams, sitting in Kamini on the rocky beach and pouring her heart onto the page.

All this had changed when, not long after returning from her father's funeral in Oslo, Marianne was walking barefoot back from the beach, sandals dangling in her hand. When she returned to their house, she saw a petite, dark-haired woman in her living room.

'This is Patricia,' said Axel. 'My lover.' Marianne's first thought was relief that Axel Joachim was at Magda's house.

'What? You said that this would be a fresh start, that from now on...'

'I know what I said. But I can't be tied to one person, like a dog on a lead. Marianne, I love you, I will always love you but I need to be with Patricia.'

'She can't live here.'

'Yes, she can, and she will.'

'Are you crazy? We're all going to live together, the three of us?'

Patricia shrugged her shoulders and left the room. They could sort out their own problems.

'Listen, Marianne. You are the paranoid, neurotic one who has to own people.'

'Believe me, Axel, I do not want to own you. I don't even want to touch you.'

'You are not my jailer, you little witch. I will sleep with whoever I like.'

'Then why did you marry me? Just to betray me?' Her face was red, her normally pretty features twisted in anger and fury.

'You don't want a husband. You want a prisoner.'

'How dare you?' and she lunged at him. He grabbed a clump of her blonde hair and pulled it until her scalp stung.

'Let go of me, you bastard,' and she kicked out at him. He pushed her back and she fell on the stone floor but not before she had spat in his face. She saw an ugly globule of saliva slide down his cheek. 'I wish I had never met you. I wish you were not the father of our precious little boy.'

'Why don't you fuck off then back to Oslo where you belong? This island is too exotic for you and your little rules. Hydra is all about freedom and that's what I want.'

'By freedom, you mean do exactly as you please with no responsibilities or regard for anyone else. You are the most selfish man I have ever known and I wish I had never met you.'

'Really?' said Axel, coming up close to her face and spitting on her as he spoke. 'I feel exactly the same. I need someone who understands and nurtures my artistic needs, not a little housewife in an apron putting the dinner on.'

Marianne wiped his saliva from her face and leapt towards Axel. Her fist caught him on his face and his skin reddened.

'How dare you speak to me like that? You think you are a genius and I am nothing. It's the other way around. You are a deluded man, a dreamer, who is worthless. I am better than you. You are the dirt beneath my feet.'

'You fucking little bitch,' he shouted and shoved her against the bookcase. She felt her back hit the wooden structure and the sting as he slapped her hard in the face.

For a moment she could not see clearly but she shook her head and her vision cleared. Her cheek smarted.

'Only a coward hits a woman,' she snarled. 'You are a piece of rubbish. Our son deserves better.'

'Better than you,' he shouted. 'You are a useless mother, more interested in yourself than others.'

'You'd know all about that. I hate you,' she shouted and ran out.

Wiping away her tears Marianne felt bitter. The island was pure and clean and hopeful: everything that her marriage to Axel was not.

She had no choice. They would have to continue to live in the house together: Axel and Patricia, Axel Joachim and Marianne. It was an uneasy arrangement, in which no-one would ever feel comfortable.

She thought of Momo and her warm optimism. What would she say now about her granddaughter's life? And what would Marianne give to feel her loving arms around her?

'You have come, Marianne. I wondered if you would.'

'You gave me your address,' she said shyly. 'Why would I not?'

Leonard was framed by the wooden doorway of his whitewashed home as if he were a portrait. His dark hair, open shirt and linen trousers seemed, at the same time, casual and sophisticated. His heart thumped when he saw Marianne, in a blue cotton dress, leather sandals, her hair tied back, her face slightly reddened by the sun.

'Your house is so beautiful.'

'Thank you. I haven't finished unpacking yet but come in. Let me show you the view.'

He led her up primitive stone steps past large, empty rooms to a wide terrace, tiled in ochre. Marianne gasped when she saw the landscape: mountains rising majestically from the ground as if they had no intention of ever stopping, and the white, red-rooved houses strewn haphazardly across the island like children's blocks. In the distance, she could see the coloured boats in the harbour and the birds wheeling in the canopy of the sky, stretched wide and hopeful.

He stood so close to her that he could smell the light floral perfume she wore and imagine the softness of her skin.

'That is Mount Ere, two thousand feet high, and there is the Monastery of the Prophet Elijah. Every year at Passover, which is coming soon, Jewish people leave a cup of wine for the prophet Elijah and open the door so that he may enter. You should come and join us. I never dreamed that I would live beside a prophet. *And now our feet are standing inside your gates, O Jerusalem.*'

'You're Jewish?'

'Yes. But I have shed the traditional Judaism of my childhood. This island allows you to make your own rules.'

'You speak as if the island was a person?'

'It is.'

'I love your home. So you've left Charmian and George for good now?'

'Yes, what a relief. I don't think I could take their acrimony any more. My grandmother left me a small inheritance so I bought this house. I knew about Hydra many years ago as my friend Jacob Rothschild's mother married the painter Ghikas and they have a house here.'

'Oh, of course, everyone has heard of Ghikas. How amazing.'

'Mind you, when I arrived and went to visit Jacob's mother, she didn't know who I was and said that Jacob had never even mentioned me!'

'Oh. Where is that house?'

'A seventeenth-century mansion, forty-seven rooms, on the hill, overlooking the harbour.'

'Yes, I think I've seen it in the distance but never been there. But you are happy here, even without knowing many people?'

'I feel that I can write in this place. I sense that Hydra has the power to transform people. When you come out of the sea here you are covered in plankton, your body shining as if you have become someone else. Writing requires you to release that part of you that is reluctant to show itself but is there nonetheless. It takes courage. It is hard.'

'Like being in love? Like allowing yourself to be exposed, to be vulnerable, to let others see the person you usually hide?'

'Yes. Writing is nakedness. You are born that way but your whole life you cover up. Writing insists you peel those layers off. As Jung said, "The privilege of a lifetime is to become who you truly are." But you have to be ready for the task. No-one else can do that for you.'

They looked into each other's eyes, his dark, hers blue, and the Aegean sun seemed to light them from within. Marianne looked down shyly.

'Do you have a routine here?'

'I get up early and write and there is a beautiful silence, a genuine one, very welcome, not like the moody silence between Charmian and George.'

They both laughed.

A thin maid, older than most, with grey hair and dressed in black and white checks, brought out a tray.

'Marianne, this is Kyria Sophia, my wonderful helper who takes care of the banalities of life so that I can be free to write about the banality of life.' The women smiled warmly at each other.

After the maid had gone, Leonard poured them each coffee in white cups. The porcelain caught the light and glinted.

'You say you write, Leonard, what are you working on at the moment?'

'A novel, poetry, lyrics for songs. I get up at seven each day and work until lunchtime. It is cool in the morning and there is a purity in the air, a cleanliness that helps me. If I am stuck I look to the sky, the place which demands the most of the birds and stars. How could I let it down? How could I not honour it by offering it the best words that I can? You cannot deliver smudges to the heavens. It is the home of angels.'

Marianne loved the sound of his gritty voice, listened carefully to each word he said, did not want to miss a syllable. She was calmed by the gentleness of his ideas, so different from the fury of Axel. 'I want to write but I cannot find the right words.'

'There are no right words, just language and music and you have to pluck at them, like you would do grapes from a trellis.'

'You make it sound easy, but which words do you choose?'

The coffee was strong, the sun gentle, and Marianne felt at ease with him. She thought: when I write, I struggle, yet I can speak so easily to you.

'It is something to do with the light, the way it pours freely here upon you, connecting you to the truth. You cannot lie in this white sun. It will not let you. It will catch you out.'

'So writing is telling the truth?'

'A version of the truth. It is like religion. It asks you to commit yourself to a certain kind of honesty.'

'It sounds like you are quite religious?'

'I was brought up in Montreal, going to synagogue with my parents, but it was too rigid, too routine for me, too inflexible, bound by rules. Here I light the candles on Shabbat because I want to, not because I am commanded to, and then I meditate. On Saturdays I go to see Demetri Leousi, an islander here. Do you know him?' Marianne shook her head. 'He learned an old-fashioned kind of English in Istanbul so we can talk. Also, in New York he fell in love with a Jewish woman so he sees Jews as special, not to be feared. He says that I am the first Jew to own a house on Hydra and he sees that as a gift.'

'So you have created your own rituals?'

Leonard laughed. 'Yes, I have replaced my parents' traditions with my own. That is the irony. But there is so much about Judaism that I love: the juxtaposition of pain and joy. Even in a wedding the bridegroom stamps on glass to recall the destruction of the temple in Jerusalem. The symbolism. The imagery. The poetry: *the mountains skipped like rams, the hills like young lambs*. I love the psalms. But tell me about you. How do you come to be on Hydra?'

'I was born in Oslo but my father and brother were both ill with tuberculosis, and my mother had enough to do. So I spent most of my childhood in Larkollen with my grandmother, Momo.'

'And what was Momo like?'

'Wonderful. She told me stories about princes and the sea. She made me curious about the world and encouraged me to travel. She fed the birds bread each day and when I was little, I would make too much noise and frighten them away so she taught me how to be still and listen so that the birds would come to me.'

'And did they?'

'Yes, they did, and the longer I stood still, the longer they stayed. And we collected white shells, and I carry them with me to this day, wherever I go.'

'And Axel? Where did you meet him?'

'At a party. He was so handsome and charming and had so many ideas for the books he wanted to write. I was working in an attorney's office and then as an au pair and I was bored with my life when in came this interesting, angry young man. He had read Jung and books on philosophy and the symbolism of dreams. He asked me to go to Greece with him. My parents weren't happy. I was young and we weren't even married. We rented a room in Athens but then on a boat we met Papadopoulos.'

'The candy millionaire?'

'Yes. He told us to travel round the islands and disembark at Hydra, the most beautiful of them all. So we did.'

'So like me you have fallen upon it by chance?'

'Yes, maybe everyone on Hydra has done the same. They have stumbled on its beauty and do not want to leave.'

'And do you? Want to leave?'

'I don't know. We married and like it here but Axel and I, we are rocky. He has lovers. At the moment it is Patricia who he has brought to live with us.'

'That must be painful for you?'

'Yes, it is, but it does help Axel to write if he is happy and it is good for our little boy to have his father around.'

'I can understand that. My father died when I was young and it has left a scar.'

They paused, comfortable in silence.

'Would you like to see where I write?' he asked.

He led her down to his study, a cool white room with windows deep-set in thick walls. The desk was simple, a green Olivetti typewriter and several sheets of paper and that was all. In a raffia wastepaper bin, she saw crumpled balls, discarded poetry, she imagined. A guitar leant its shoulders against a fireplace, dormant in the spring.

'It is so tidy.'

'I have to have order if I am to create.'

He moved her through to another room, where again it was simple: a bed covered in a white cotton spread; a table piled high with books; several fat candles, squatting in a hollow alcove.

Leonard eased her onto the bed and then he kissed her: first her high cheekbones and then her mouth, releasing the band from her hair so that it fell free like a bird fanning its wings in the sun. She was all softness and light, kissing him back with a mixture of gentleness and passion. He slipped the sleeves of her blue dress over her shoulders and saw that her eyes were the colour of cornflowers.

Beneath her dress, she wore no underwear and he lifted the skirt and felt her skin, warm and receptive beneath the material. The more he kissed her, the more he wanted to, needed to, and she responded, undoing the buttons on his white shirt, then unzipping his trousers and feeling him stiffen at her touch. He took a dark nipple in his mouth and heard her cry out and they lost all sense of time and place as they immersed themselves in each other. When he entered her, it was as if this was what they had waited for all their lives. They could not tell where one flesh ended and the other began: the silkiness of her, the smell of him, the hair flaying on the bed, her legs, his skin, their mouths. They cried and licked each other's tears from their faces.

Afterwards they lay naked in the cool room and rejoiced in the discovery of the other: stroking, kissing, caressing, blessing their union.

Leonard recited Yeats to her:

Had I the heavens' embroidered cloths,
Enwrought with golden and silver light,
The blue and the dim and the dark cloths
Of night and light and the half-light,
I would spread the cloths under your feet:
But I, being poor, have only my dreams;
I have spread my dreams under your feet;
Tread softly because you tread on my dreams.

They saw ribbons of light slip in through the gaps in the shutters and heard the chapel ring its hourly bell. Leonard ran his fingers over her smooth skin.

'*Set me as a seal upon your heart, as a seal upon your arm; for love is strong as death,*' whispered Leonard, as he lifted the Star of David on a chain from around his neck and hung it around Marianne's. 'That is from the Song of Songs. I am deeply happy that I have found you, Marianne. Please never leave.'

For days, the islanders had been preparing for Easter. As Marianne wheeled her son's pushchair towards Leonard's house, for the Passover meal, women white-washed their steps. Men with buckets scrubbed the quayside. Even the donkeys had new canvas bags on their flanks. Everything seemed polished: the almond blossoms and the marble sky looked cleansed, as if they, too, recognised the significance of this holy day.

And then the procession began, the papos at the front. Marianne walked at the side of the road as trails of people traipsed down the paths: little girls dressed in white with peonies crowning their hair; boys carrying sacred banners, and adults holding candles. Gifts were offered: slaughtered lambs and calves threaded on spits; loaves of bread; paper lanterns; and a trailer on wheels bearing an effigy of Christ's bleeding body through the crowded streets.

She waited for the procession to pass and watched it vanish into the hills.

On Leonard's terrace, he had set out two tables and covered them with cloths. Around them was an assortment of chairs; one from his study; a few from his kitchen; collapsible ones from the storeroom. The Silver family arrived with presents of fruit and wine and everyone hugged. Esther was in a new pale pink dress especially for Pesach and her mother had threaded gardenias on string around her head. Esther was so pleased to be with Axel Joachim and she cuddled him and his wooden giraffe on her lap. Gideon stood by the balustrade, gazing out at the view.

Seated at the table, Leonard welcomed them all. Gideon joined them, reluctantly.

'Where better to have Pesach,' he began, 'than with Mount Elijah behind us? And here is the cup of wine for Elijah should he join us at any point.'

Marianne was fascinated by the rituals. She had never been to a Passover meal before and wanted to learn.

Leonard looked more handsome than ever, his dark hair capped by a white kippah and he had a silver-tasselled shawl around his neck.

'This is called a talit,' he told Marianne, 'a prayer shawl that belonged to my father Nathan, who died when I was nine.'

'How sad,' said Frieda. 'So he missed your bar mitzvah?'

'Yes, and strangely he always had a premonition that he would not be there.'

They read from tiny books, *Haggadot*, which Leonard's mother Masha had sent him. For the Silver family, it was all familiar: the books opening from right to left, the Hebrew writing the same, and the moving back and forth between English and Hebrew, but for Marianne it was new. Leonard helped her. They read aloud around the table, Frieda worried that Gideon might not want to take his turn in front of others but he did, quietly and fluently.

'Well done, Giddy,' she said, holding his hand beneath the cloth. She was surprised when he pushed it gently away.

They learned about the Jews being slaves in Egypt under the Pharaohs and how God led them out of bondage into freedom. Although Esther could not read yet, she sang *Mah Nishtana*, the song the youngest child sings, helped by her parents when she stumbled on the words.

'And now we come to the symbols,' said Leonard, pointing for Marianne's sake to the plate at the centre of the table. 'This is the matzah, the unleavened bread, as the Jews did not have time for the yeast to rise. The hard-boiled egg represents the universe in its wholeness.'

'Why is it burned?' she asked, noticing the black smudges across its shell.

'To represent the sacrifices made at the temple. The shank bone is the Paschal lamb; the bitter herbs, and maror, which is horseradish, represents the tears shed by the Israelites when they were slaves. The parsley symbolises hope, spring. And this is called charoset: it is a mixture of nuts, apple and wine and symbolises the mortar used by the slaves when they built the Pyramids. Masha makes a wonderful one with dates as well. There are many different versions of it.'

Marianne was impressed by Leonard's ability to move between Hebrew and English, between spoken prayers and sung ones, taking command, including everyone in the evening. He thought of his father, hoped he would be proud of his son, leading the service.

'So we have here the water and the wine,' explained Leonard, 'the bare essentials of life and also the magic, the mystery.'

32

When it was time for the meal, Kyria Sophia brought out the hard-boiled eggs in salt water and then fasolatha soup, made from cannellini beans and local vegetables, fresh oregano and thyme. The main meal, roast lamb with artichokes, was delicious, the food shiny and glazed. Afterwards, they drank coffee and ate baklava and halva, and the children had sticky hands and faces. Axel Joachim fell asleep in Marianne's arms and she laid him carefully on Leonard's bed.

They sang songs, clapped and cheered, Jack's voice particularly strong and his energy never flagging while they watched the sun dunk itself into the sea.

Walking home, Frieda said to Jack, 'I think that Leonard and Marianne are lovers. Did you notice that at the end, she stayed when we left?'

'I keep telling you,' said Jack, 'this is a bohemian, free community. The bourgeois rules don't apply here.'

Frieda fell silent: why was it that they got on quite well when in the company of others but as soon as they were alone again, the old conflicts and accusations immediately resurfaced as if they had been there all along?

When Axel and Patricia went away, Marianne found a kind of peace. She loved the silence of the house and time spent with her baby, thinking about the way ahead. Increasingly, Leonard came to see her and would sing Axel Joachim lullabies and rock him to sleep.

Then they would sit on the terrace and watch the cool evening draw its glimmering screen over the harbour. The once-busy boats were still now, the velvet sky studded with stars. The night was furry, wrapping them in its softness.

'Today a man came from an American magazine and photographed me in the harbour,' she said.

'Why would he not?' said Leonard. 'You are the most beautiful woman in the world.'

Sometimes when they were sure that the baby was asleep, they would go inside and make love, their hot bodies writhing on cool sheets, and then they would share a joint and read poetry.

One evening, Leonard and Marianne were on the terrace, smoking and talking. The cow bell at the front door rang and Marianne, in her bathrobe, went to answer it.

Nick Katsikas handed her a telegram. 'For you, Marianne,' he said.

'Thank you. I'm sorry you have had to come all this way.'

He nodded, went back to his donkey, and she closed the door.

Up on the terrace she read Axel's message aloud to Leonard: 'PATRICIA IN ACCIDENT. HOSPITAL ATHENS. PLEASE COME.'

'What should I do, Leonard? He has treated me so badly but he sounds desperate.'

'If you need to go, I will stay here with Axel Joachim. He knows me now and I can give him a bottle.'

'Really? You would do that?'

'My love,' said Leonard in his gravelly voice. 'Life sends us tests all the time. This is yours. Go.'

She left the following morning. All along the journey – a donkey to the harbour, the boat to Piraeus with Mikalis and Spyros, and then the bus to Athens – Marianne was in turmoil. She still felt some fondness for her husband but also fury at the way he had treated her by taking other women, making her feel that she was not enough. She had gone from one writer to another. What was it in her, she wondered, that was drawn to trouble?

But Leonard was different. He was gentle and good. She liked the way he devoted himself to his writing, to her, to her child. He would not let her down: she was sure of that. On the last part of her journey, she peered down at the dark waters where the sun had only stroked the surface and she hoped and prayed that all would be well.

Marianne was shocked by the hospital in Athens. Steel beds side by side, with thin sheets, and the walls were bare. The only sound was of patients moaning in pain. She gasped when she found Patricia, almost completely bandaged and with Axel by her side. He jumped up when he saw Marianne and she was surprised at the state he was in: unwashed, unshaven, dark circles under his eyes.

'Oh thank you, Marianne,' he sobbed, welling with tears. 'I hoped that you would come.'

He pulled up a chair and she sat beside him. Patricia did not stir.

'What happened?' He looked into her blue eyes and felt that an angel had come to rescue him.

'There was a party at the military base. Drink, you know. Patricia said we should drive the guests home and as we were on the way back to the base, she collided with a farmer on his donkey and cart. They were on the bridge. She swerved the car to avoid them and crashed into the wall. She was thrown from the car and into the riverbed full of cement and debris chucked there from a workshop. Most of her bones are broken. She was the only one who was seriously injured.'

'Oh, that is terrible.' Marianne's heart went out to Axel and all her anger seemed to dissipate.

'The nurses were supposed to put antiseptic on to stop infection but they haven't done so and now she has gangrene. One of her thumbs has been amputated. I am without hope. I haven't slept for three nights, just sitting here watching her.'

'You need to go and wash and sleep,' said his wife.

'Will you stay with her? You have to apply antiseptic in the gaps between her bandages every hour. You'll do that?'

'Yes, Axel, I will.'

So Marianne sat there all night and the following day. She did as Axel had told her and every hour she dabbed antiseptic on any gaps that she could find. All the time, Patricia did not stir. Her eyes remained closed. The tanned colour had drained from her face and her long black hair was tucked into a nest behind her neck.

It felt strange for Marianne to tend to and touch the woman who had stolen her husband. She wept as she sat there, fuelled by jealousy and rage and compassion and confusion. She thought of when she and Axel had met at the party in Oslo and how their lives had seemed to glisten with possibilities. When they had arrived on Hydra, she thought that they had reached paradise, the island gleaming under an optimistic sky, the deep, emerald sea striped beneath a gentle sun. How could anything go wrong? And yet it had, their love crumbling and their dreams turning to ash.

She fingered the Star of David and thought of Leonard. It was a blessing that he had come into her life, but moving between two writers: how would that work? She trembled at the thought that he would leave her. She had never loved anyone the way she loved him and she wanted

35

to stay on the island with him for ever, lock the gates, build walls around the shore, drain the sea of water and boats, and focus on their love.

She thought of Momo and how she would bring a plate of crispbread and brown goat's cheese on a ceramic plate and hold her and love her, trying to replace the family that she had lost.

On Hydra, Axel Joachim woke in the night, sweaty from a bad dream. Leonard rose and went to him.

'It's alright, little one,' he said. 'Your mummy will be home soon. I am here with you.' He sang softly to the child and, soothed by his voice, Axel Joachim slipped easily back to sleep.

After several days in the hospital, sitting by Patricia while Axel rested, Marianne started the long journey home. On the bus from Athens to Piraeus and then the boat back to Hydra, she searched the depths of the water and wondered: how do we all move forward? Are there any answers? And if so, where?

It was wonderful to be back with her lover again. They woke in the gentle morning, Leonard and Marianne in her bed, the shuttered light upon the walls. Leonard had picked wild anemones and let them fall loosely in a crockery vase. The flowers' subtle scent perfumed the room. Sometimes he read her poetry, leaning on his elbow in bed, facing her, his other hand holding the book:

Of the Dark Doves

Through the laurel branches
I saw two doves of darkness.
The one was the sun,
the other one was the moon.
I said: 'Little neighbours,
where is my tombstone?'
'In my tail-feathers,' the sun said.
'In my throat,' the moon said.
And I who was out walking
with the earth wrapped round me,
saw two eagles made of white snow,
and a girl who was naked.
And the one was the other,
and the girl was neither.
I said: 'Little eagles,
where is my tombstone?'
'In my tail-feathers,' the sun said.
'In my throat,' the moon said.
Through the laurel branches
I saw two doves, both naked.
And one was the other,
and both were none.

'That's beautiful. Who is it by?'

'Lorca. A Spanish poet. It was actually written as a song and in the instrumental score, the notation is cleverly circular to represent the sun and the moon.'

'That could be us,' she said.

'Yes,' Leonard agreed. 'One was the other and both were none. You know, Lorca said he had the blood of gypsies and Jews. Like me. And he was a dreamer in a world of material preoccupations.'

'I am so happy to be back in your world,' she said and they kissed slowly, hard, as if time did not exist in that room.

'I missed you, Marianne, my Nordic turtle dove. When you were away, I struggled to write but now that you are back, my muse, I know that the words will flow again.'

'Which part of the novel are you on?'

'The relationship between Breavman and Tamara, where they rent a room in the east end of the city. I need to get the tone of their love right and you coming back from Athens has helped me.'

'I'm so pleased.'

'I don't find writing easy. I am compelled to do it, and in a sense I am the right person to do it because I feel joy and pain intensely and I can see the paradoxes of daily life. If you don't see life as a contradiction you cannot be a writer, but that doesn't mean I don't struggle, because I do.'

When she had left the Athens hospital, Marianne had felt her heart torn in every direction: towards Axel and Patricia, towards Leonard, and towards her baby boy. Now she felt more at ease.

'We have a picnic planned today on Bisti,' said Leonard. 'A welcome home for you.'

'How lovely. Who's coming?'

'Wait and see,' he said. 'If I can ever stop kissing you, we will get dressed and meet them.'

They gathered in the centre of Kala Pigadia: Leonard (his guitar strapped to his back), Marianne in a white dress which billowed about her like a cloud, and baby Axel Joachim in his pushchair. As each person joined the circle, swiping the many mosquitos away, the shape grew like a flower spreading its petals wide: Jack, Frieda, Gideon and Esther; Charmian and George and their three children; Chuck and Gordon; Norman Peterson;

Czech Magda, her Italian husband Paolo and their son Alexander. Magda had a flame of red hair that rose and crowned her handsome face; she wore large, coloured Mexican beads and chunky, silver bangles on her arms.

They embraced as they arrived, laden with baskets, rolled-up stripy rugs, towels and paniers and then made their way down the hill to the harbour. As they passed The Gardenia Dwarf's home, she waved to them. As always, dressed in black, she was tending her flowers, pinching away dead leaves with her wrinkly fingers, watering the pots. The blossoms' white faces shone brazenly in the sunlight and the waxy leaves were equally unabashed.

'*Kalimera*,' the group called as they passed.

The Gardenia Dwarf pointed to the faces of the friends and then to her flowers. She mumbled something in Greek.

'She is saying that we are the Greek gardenias,' George explained.

'But we aren't Greek and we aren't flowers.' Charmian was already arguing with him.

'Maybe that's the point,' Leonard tried to help out. 'But we think we are.'

As well as The Gardenia Dwarf, they had names for other people: Vassilis, the crippled sponge diver whose only two teeth were yellow, was nicknamed Fangs; the two island policemen, Costas and Constantinos, one fat, one thin, were referred to as Laurel and Hardy.

They named places too: the road they walked down now was Donkey Shit Lane and the crossroads, the Four Corners.

They had to take turns in Mikalis' boat as there were too many of them for one trip, but young Spyros helped them on and off, taking the hands of the women, lifting the babies into the boat, then patiently passing picnic hampers aboard. Mikalis took them along the northern side of Hydra to Bisti, from where they could see the island of Spetses, lying low.

On the beach, they laid out their rugs and towels and shared their picnics: feta, warm bread from Demi's, salami, hummus, olives, tomatoes, beer and retsina for the adults, apple juice for the children. Magda and Marianne were still breastfeeding their boys, although trying to wean them off, so they found some shelter in the cove and chatted.

'Any news from Axel?'

'He writes me long, painful letters. They've gone to America and he will stay with Patricia while she recovers. He can write there. His novel is overdue. Maybe she can help him where I could not. He seems devoted to her.'

'But you are happy with Leonard?'

'So happy that I am afraid. I love him more than anyone I have known and that scares me. When we expose ourselves to love, do we also not expose ourselves to potential pain?'

'Yes, between pain and pleasure is a very thin line.'

'Are you happy on Hydra, Magda?'

The woman tossed her red hair back over her shoulders. 'Well, I have an exciting new project.'

'You always have wonderful new ventures!'

'I am buying the old boathouse in the quay and I will make it into a club or wine bar for us all to meet in, and the locals, too. We can't spend all our evenings at Douskos'!'

'That's amazing.'

'Yes, it's great, and I have bought the two old boats to put on the roof so that we will always remember the building's origin.'

The women laughed.

'You,' said Marianne, as she moved Axel Joachim carefully from one breast to the other. 'Your energy: I love it. I wish I could work out who I was and what I am meant to be.'

'You will,' said Magda, cradling her now sleeping child, 'you will.'

Back with the others, the women laid their babies in the shade and covered them with towels. Leonard was playing his guitar and Magda sang with him, Russian Jewish songs with sad words: Babushka about her grandmother, and others about the trees casting their dark outlines against the forsaken sky.

The older children played on the beach, building sandcastles, decorating them with shells, building moats around their citadels. As the sand grew wetter, it darkened until their fortresses were black. The children told each other stories about their empires, of battles and conquests. Jason, the youngest child of Charmian and George, draped his shoulders in seaweed and declared himself the king. They shrieked with delight when they saw turtles swimming slowly, their wrinkled heads visible just above the water line and their manner slow and regal, as if they too belonged to the kingdom. They could hear cicadas clicking around them.

Martin lay on a rock, reading a book by Virgil and underlining important sentences with a pen. Shane played with Esther, showing her how to draw in the sand with a stick.

Fishermen nearby caught octopus and squid, laid them on a rock and hammered the flesh to soften it, ready for cooking. Gideon watched them do this. George gave one local some coins and brought back an octopus for them to cook on a makeshift fire. They all waited until the tentacles were roasted and then pulled them off, one leg at a time, and chewed the rubbery limbs.

Boats and time slipped past. The children played happily but after a few hours of drink and heat, some of the adults grew irritable.

'When I write, I lose all sense of who I am,' said George, swigging back beer. The drops gathered on the cool glass.

'That could explain why you never help with the housework or the children.' Charmian looked pleased at her put-down.

'Jeez, Charm, you could wring an insult out of nowhere. It's a real talent. Maybe you could take up writing insults rather than journalism. You're better at it.'

Charmian glared at him. 'I'm a very good writer, George, but you are such a male chauvinist that you believe women are put on the earth to clean and cook while the genius men focus on their art.' She clutched her chest to make it more dramatic.

'Too right, Charm.' George was enjoying their baiting. 'You've got it in one, love.'

'Well, if I'm such a bad writer, do feel free to stop pinching my bloody ideas.'

'Pinch your ideas?' George had now moved from beer to brandy, as if their quarrel warranted something stronger as fuel. 'I have enough of my own, thank you.'

'Fine. Then don't ask me to read your work in progress and comment.'
'Suits me.'

'Maybe the point about writing is that we escape when we write,' Gordon tried to move the discussion away from their toxic marriage, 'or are we more ourselves than ever?'

Leonard looked up from the guitar that he was strumming gently. 'Both,' he said. 'We cannot be detached from our work if we must appear involved but nor can we be universal if we are too focused on ourselves.'

'But are we the creators or are we merely the conduit through which the words flow?' Chuck said.

'Both,' Leonard chimed.

Gordon joined in: 'Our words must seem to be inevitable though, as Yeats said.'

Chuck nodded in agreement. Marianne thought: why do Charmian and George not see how other couples work, and learn from them? It upset her the way they always fought and spoiled the day for everyone else.

As night fell, the sky was pierced with tiny stars and the adults wrapped their children in blankets and rugs. Marianne enclosed Axel Joachim inside her coat, winding it round the two of them so that she could transfer her body heat to her baby. Leonard looked at her and smiled.

No-one wanted the day to end. They bought red mullet from a fisherman for a few drachmas and cooked it on the fire, pulling at the soft flesh until it fell away. Marianne had brought along lemons and they squeezed the juice on the fish until the skin sizzled and blistered. Gathered together around the fire, watching the tiny sparks, their faces were lit by the flames and the sun lowered itself slowly into the sea as if on string, gently released, while Leonard's guitar and his voice provided a soothing backdrop.

In the darkness, the figures melted into a single shape, as if the fire had taken away their edges and made them one. As the flames turned to ash, it was hard to make out faces. It didn't matter. For those hours, they were united, talking, laughing, listening, sharing their dreams and planning their futures.

Marianne leaned against Leonard and thought: if I could stop time, I would, and stay here on this dark beach for ever.

Anthony Kingsmill's studio was at the top of his tiny house. He greeted Marianne at the door and led her through the kitchen, up the stairs past the floor where he slept and then to the attic room. She was shocked at the bareness of his home, hardly furnished at all, but she was not wholly surprised. Stories of his drinking and gambling were rife on the island.

'So good of you to come, dear Marianne,' he whispered. 'Have you posed before?'

'Oh yes, for several photographers. And have you heard of Marcella Maltais?'

'Of course, she's a wonderful artist.'

'She painted a portrait of me with Axel Joachim.'

'Were you pleased with it?'

'Very much. She has captured my love for my son. I am holding him in the foreground and behind us the houses of Hydra climb the hill. The style is primitive.'

'But on that occasion you didn't pose naked? You are happy to do this?'

'Of course.' Marianne slipped off her sandals and lifted the lavender dress over her head, letting it fall to the floor like a pool of purple water. She wore no underwear. Anthony pointed to a cushion on the floor where she positioned herself, shifting slightly in order to be comfortable and relaxed.

Anthony held a pencil up for measurement, looking carefully at Marianne, and then moving his eyes back to his easel to start sketching her on his canvas. He found her beauty a distraction: her slim waist, her satin skin, her small breasts pert and firm, but fuelled by the desire to capture her beauty and the bottle of retsina he swigged from as he worked, he made some progress. He liked to talk to his models as he sketched.

'How is your delightful child?'

Marianne tried to ignore the bits of sand and paper that fell from the ceiling as Anthony worked.

'He is beautiful, but easily upset. I think that he will be a sensitive soul.'

'And you look after him on your own?' Anthony saw how her blonde hair curled itself around her neck. Her lips were perfect, as if they had been painted on.

'Yes. Axel is in California while his lover Patricia recovers. You heard she was involved in a car crash?'

'Yes, I did. Terrible.'

'Axel says he is looking after her but his long letters are more about his friendship with John Starr Cooke. He is an astrologer who also uses tarot cards and the Ouija board to help his friends uncover the truth.'

'I don't know him.'

'Oh, he's quite a character. Axel met him in the Sahara when John was riding a white camel. He claimed to be descended from the Pharaohs. He comes from a wealthy family in Hawaii but chose a different way of life. One day he and Axel swung a chain and wherever it landed they had to go. It was in Norway, in the north. Axel just blindly followed him.'

'Do you think he has actually helped Axel?' She could hear Anthony's pencil scratching on the canvas.

'I don't know. There are drugs that they have been taking, psychedelic drugs, and that may mess with his mind or maybe it will help him. Now he says he wants to go to Mexico to travel with John. Axel is struggling with his new novel, *Line*, but Henrik Groth thinks that it will make his name. I hope so. But I have to make my own life now with Axel Joachim.'

'And Leonard Cohen?'

Marianne's face lit up. 'He's the most amazing man. Everything he says is wise and thoughtful as if he never wants to waste a word. I love to listen to him speak and sing. And Axel Joachim loves him also.'

'Will you leave Axel and live with Leonard?' Anthony had finished the rough sketching now and was starting to paint. He mixed yellow with white to try to convey the corn-flax gold of her hair.

'I am unsure. Leonard is busy writing also, his novel *The Favourite Game*, and his poetry and songs, and I do not want to interfere with that.'

'So you are a muse to two writers?'

'I don't know that I am a muse. I don't know exactly who I am.'

The hours passed and Marianne was worrying about her baby although she knew that Maria would care for him well.

'Good,' said Anthony after a period of silence. 'I think I can continue by myself, Marianne: thank you. I wish that I could pay you but I haven't a bean in the world, my dear.'

'No need,' she said graciously. 'The pleasure is mine.'

She slipped on her lavender dress and went towards the easel.

'Not yet,' he said, shielding the painting with his hands. 'I will let you know when it is finished.'

As Marianne left his house, she saw Charmian arriving. She looked thin, red-faced and she was walking unevenly.

'Darling Marianne, have you been modelling for Anthony?'

'Yes. Are you going to sit for him, also?'

'Well,' said Charmian, her dark eyes shining, 'I will sit for him and then I'll lie for him.'

'You are wicked,' said Marianne hugging Charmian and smelling drink on her.

'A woman has needs and as my husband can't satisfy them, I have had to look elsewhere. Between Anthony and Nature Boy, I am well catered for.'

'Nature Boy?'

'You've seen him in the harbour, surely? His real name is Jean-Claude Maurice. Tanned body, earring. Sucks eggs. Paints nudes. A knotted cloth around his groin, which he will untie if you want him to. And I do. Frequently.'

'Charmian!'

'What? George knows I have lovers. He's a once a year man, and that's if I'm lucky. Nature Boy satisfies my carnal desires; Anthony is more sophisticated and genteel.'

'I hope you have a good time,' said Marianne, walking away.

Anthony always liked to draw Charmian before they made love. It was a good way to lead in: to look at her lying on the cushion still warm from Marianne and the two women one after another, one slender, blonde, small-breasted, and the other larger, dark-haired, exotic and mysterious, excited him.

As always, he liked to sketch the outline in pencil first, before committing himself to paint. As he worked, he listened to her complaining about George, the children, the housework, the maid, her writing which was often not going very well, so that this time provided them both with something: him with a chance to move himself into the mood for love; her to be allowed a safe space in which to rant.

So when the sketch was done, he left the painting to another time and lay beside Charmian. Light streamed in from the window and he felt as if he were stepping into his drawing of her: the curves and hills made of flesh, her long dark hair, her sculpted features, her wide mouth which she had painted crimson and her long legs which seemed to lure him in.

From Nature Boy she got a good fuck when she wanted it, but with Anthony they took their time. Anthony made love as he painted and spoke: carefully, elegantly, with style. Somehow he was erotic without being crude.

He stroked her skin, kissed her large mouth, placed his paint-stained hands between her legs, feeling her push against him, part resistance, part playfulness, but he persisted as he knew she wanted him to. He felt himself stiffen to a rock and she stripped him, teased him, so that he gripped the sides of the couch and could hardly control himself. He tried to wait but he wanted to enter her and reach the very heat and heart of her.

Lying naked side by side afterwards, Anthony wondered whether his art improved if he slept with his models. He knew them inside out, saw them differently to the painter standing face on. He did not want to leave the softness of Charmian's body but when he did, he would take his pencil and make a few adjustments, just slightly redraw the nose, widen the mouth, add more shading around her eyes.

It was difficult being torn between a lover and the portrait of her but when he felt her body relax and realised that she was asleep, he lifted his arm carefully from her, stood up and returned to his other passion.

Walking home across the island, Marianne felt that spring was now rooted. Earlier in the season, the flowers had emerged tentatively, as if anxious of what awaited them. But as March turned to April, they seemed more self-assured and ready to open fully. Their colours were deeper and more authentic as if they had shed their doubt and accepted that this was indeed spring. A lemon-blue light filtered through the gaps in the trees, as if determined to reach the flowers and nourish them. From a dovecote in one garden came soft white birds, in and out of the wooden holes, their feathers and tails frilly.

When Marianne looked up, she saw the hawthorns, freshly green, reaching for the sky, and the almond blossoms stamping their whiteness on the air, like transfers. The world had been affirmed today, restored without losing its authentic colours. The dark red tulips were even more so; and the white gardenias purer than ever.

The air felt fresh as if someone had lifted the dustsheets from the island and swept it clean. It smelled of sunshine, of almonds, of the sea, of love.

She hummed as she walked and she thought: I am happier than I have been for years.

Back at Leonard's house, Marianne told him about her modelling session.

'No painting can ever do justice to you,' he said. 'There is no bird in the sky or tree on the land that has what you have but I would like to see the picture and maybe buy it. Then you could be with me all the time.'

A week later, Leonard saw the artist at Katsikas' store. 'Anthony, can I come and see your painting of Marianne, please? I want to make you an offer for it.'

Anthony looked down uncomfortably at the sawdust-covered floor. 'Sorry, dear chap,' he said. 'I lost it as a bet in a poker game.'

Olivia de Haulleville and her husband, Georgos Kassipidis, lived with their children Michael and Melina in a beautiful house jutting out from the clifftop like a bird ready for flight. Their home was hung with brightly coloured rugs which Olivia had brought to Hydra from India. Tibetan paintings and ornaments brightened each room. There was always Oriental music playing and a gold statue of Buddha dominated, with offerings at his feet. Guests at their frequent parties were encouraged to bring him bowls of fruit and flowers. The house was heady with incense and a log fire, upon which Olivia tossed rosemary and sage.

Marianne and Leonard arrived later than the others. He had been singing to her and reading her his poetry and neither of them had wanted to leave, afraid to break the spell in case it would not return later. It did.

'Marianne, my Nordic troll,' Olivia greeted them at the carved wooden door. 'Come in. Oh, you have made your famous kofte meatballs? How lovely.' The women winked at each other. 'Hello Leonard, welcome.'

Olivia wore a psychedelic kaftan and a beaded headdress. She resembled an exotic bird and no matter how many colours she wore, somehow they worked. Marianne wished that she had the confidence to wear such dazzling outfits.

'Where is that blond god-child of yours?'

'Asleep, with Maria watching him. Thank you for *The Crows of Pearblossom*. He loved it. Not everyone has Aldous Huxley as an uncle to write for them.'

'Wasn't it a delight? Come and see everyone.'

The usual partygoers were there: Norman, his plate full of curry and rice, probably the first hot meal he'd had in ages. Chuck and Gordon standing, as always, side by side, and Charmian and George nearby, less harmoniously. Magda's bright-red hair and her orange dress made her look like she was on fire.

'A conflagration,' Olivia said, as she sailed by, a plate of onion bhajis in her hand. 'Darlings,' wafting around graciously in her kaftan, 'please, eat!'

There were lots of colourful characters there: Zina Rachevsky, a Russian princess who was on her way to Nepal to live as a nun; Madame Paouri, who had painted all the window frames of her house blue and given polka dot dresses as gifts to the local girls; and David Goshen from the UK, whose wife was a Scottish aristocratic sculptor who owed a spinet but had no money.

Jack and Frieda were also there, still settling in on the island and adapting to its ways. Jack had embraced it, loving the colour and the chaos, but Frieda was still doubtful: had they done the right thing in moving there?

'My dear friends,' said Olivia, introducing them to others. 'Have you met Carl?'

A tall man, short brown hair, defined, chiselled features as if he had been carved, stood before them. His eyes, though deep set, held a magic in them. 'Carl has seen the light and given up the world of corrupt law to paint,' said Olivia, and having introduced them, she floated away.

'Have you just arrived here?' Frieda asked him, blushing without knowing why.

'Two months. I'm from Toronto. And you?'

Frieda turned to include her husband. 'We've just recently arrived from Israel, although we are from South Africa originally. Jack's a writer. I'm a painter, too.'

'Really? What do you paint?'

'Darlings,' called Olivia, 'gather around. We have a surprise for you.'

They all obeyed and stood round a mosaic table on which there was a parcel.

'It's come from India,' announced Georgos. 'Our friend has sent it as a gift.'

Everyone stared and gasped as Olivia and Georgos opened the package. Bits of brown paper and string flew to the floor. Gradually a toy mule emerged.

'Darling, we love you,' said Olivia blowing the mule kisses.

Georgos released a tag on the underbelly of the colourful mule and there, sealed in wax, was a lump of hashish. He shred a few pieces off it, put it in a pipe, lit it and passed it round the circle. Jack saw that Frieda's eyes were shining and thought: maybe on this island she will finally discover who she is.

As the pipe was passed around, the room filled with sweet and spicy smells: the incense smoking in pottery holders, the almost flat bowls with purple stock and wisteria blooms draped seductively in them, heady with their perfume.

All over the house, Olivia had placed large cushions and poufs covered in mirrored sequins and tie-dyed, which she had collected in Nepal. Guests were invited to lie down, close their eyes and relax. Marianne and Leonard did so, feeling like they were floating over the island, all thoughts of Axel and money and fame dissolving in the sky.

Jack and Frieda took turns to go back hourly to check on Gideon and Esther, Evgeniya being unable to babysit that night. When it was Jack's turn, Carl saw him leave and took the opportunity to talk again to Frieda.

'Tell me about your painting,' he said, leading her out onto the terrace, below which the harbour of Hydra sparkled like a feast.

'Not much to tell.' Frieda felt shy with this good-looking man, his short hair and glasses making him seem earnest. 'I paint what I see: landscapes, seascapes, the fishermen with their nets, the monasteries on the hill, nuns, goats.'

'Have you ever thought of painting what you do not see?' He brought them each a glass of retsina.

'How can I paint it if I can't see it?'

'You can feel it,' he said quietly. 'I never reproduce what is in front of me. What's the point? It's already there. Yes, in a sense, the colours and the light might come from memory but everything I try to capture can't be put into words and I try to convey those feelings and emotions to the viewer.'

Frieda felt her world open. She smiled when she thought back to her provincial high school and how her mother had fought successfully with the headmaster to provide a few art lessons. And here she was, years later, on a terrace overlooking Hydra harbour with a man she found alluring, talking about art, her head spinning with the effects of hash and wine and attraction.

'As Olivia said, I am a lawyer, but I have taken a year out to come to Hydra to paint.'

'How has that gone down with the family?' Frieda felt her cheeks burn. She was talking to Carl as if he were an old friend. She felt disloyal to Jack. They didn't speak like this any more.

Carl laughed. 'Not well. But I was an easy child and I think my parents have accepted this as my mid-thirties rebellion. They hope that I will get it out of my system and then return to normal life.'

'It occurs to me that many of the artists and writers here come from quite conventional families.'

'I agree. Lawyers, businessmen. I think we are people who are searching for something else. We don't feel satisfied by the restrictions of everyday life and want something more creative, more imaginative than that daily office grind. We are all dreamers, maybe.'

Frieda nodded.

'What are you dreaming of, Frieda?' he asked.

She looked out to where the candlelight in houses and stars in the sky had joined forces to illuminate the island.

She thought carefully about how to answer. After all, Carl was a stranger. She looked at his deep-set eyes, his forehead which jutted out slightly, his warm smile. It felt good to be listened to, as if her views counted. He waited for her to answer but there was no awkwardness in the silence, as if he would wait years, if necessary.

As she looked back into the room, she saw that Jack had returned from checking on the children. He raised his hand to signal to her that all was well and then he joined a group that included Charmian and George, the latter offering him a drink and slapping him warmly on the back.

'What I would like,' Frieda said to Carl, 'is to paint but also to be loved, to give my love to someone and to be happy.' She blushed at her own confession. She had never admitted to herself what she wanted, what she lacked.

'That is exactly what I want, too,' said Carl.

They stood in silence as if holding that moment.

'Where do you paint?' she asked.

'In my home. I deliberately found one with a light, airy space. The studio is bigger than the rest of the house put together. And you?'

'I rent a studio behind Demi's bakery. I love it there, its big windows looking out onto the quayside. The light is wonderful.'

'It sounds perfect. Maybe I can come and visit you there sometime? I would love to see your paintings.'

Frieda blushed again. 'I would like that, Carl.'

51

'Come on, darlings,' said Olivia, clapping her hands as if rounding up sheep. 'Dinner is served.'

The dining-room table was covered in an exotic cloth and many plates of food. It was mostly Indian: curries, bhajis and bowls of steaming rice, and there was lamb tandoori and spicy vegetables. Olivia had taught her maid, Ellina, to cook Indian dishes and there was something incongruous about this Greek woman carrying in bowls of what must have seemed alien food to her. It reminded Frieda of how the Jewish women in South Africa taught their black maids to be wonderfully adept at making gefilte fish, chopped liver and chicken soup with kneidlach. They sometimes ended up being better cooks than the women who trained them.

The guests moved in a slow square around the table, helping themselves and gasping at the delicious spread. Frieda and Jack ended up beside each other.

'Here,' said Frieda to her husband, 'try some of this,' and she scooped chutney onto the edge of his plate. I feel guilty, she thought, when I have done nothing wrong. Can one be culpable, she wondered, just for your feelings alone?

Carl was in her head. She could not think of anyone or anything else. She saw that he was talking now to John Dragoumis but she avoided his gaze. She knew, and so did Carl, that their lives had been changed for ever.

The friends enjoyed the evening and mingled freely. For dessert, Olivia had made her speciality, chocolate mousse spiked with marijuana. The wine and coffee flowed.

After they had eaten, Leonard played the guitar and Magda sang Russian songs.

Frieda went back this time to check on the children. The sight of their still bodies, so unaware of life's complexities, brought tears to her eyes.

Later, walking back to Olivia's house, the sky dizzy with stars, she thought about Carl. She knew that to embark on a relationship with him would be dangerous, but she also wondered whether she deserved to be happy.

Outside Olivia's house, white and stark against the magical sky, Carl was standing in the doorway. His angular features were half-lit by the candles inside. Frieda was surprised to see him.

'I've been to check on our children,' she said.

He stepped forward and held her face in his hands and then he kissed her. It was long and soft and tender, and Frieda responded warmly to him. Then he held her in his arms as if he had come to save her and she wept.

She knew that it was too late now to turn back.

It was not difficult for Frieda and Carl to find time together.

She walked down each morning to her studio where she had hours and space to herself. Carl's narrow cottage was nearby.

At first the affair began tentatively: coffee, talking, learning about each other through their painting, feeling their way, cautiously, as if wanting to avoid mistakes.

Frieda's small canvases depicted boats and fishermen, trailing their nets of silver fish. She could see them from her studio, bringing their coloured vessels in, fat-bellied, bearded men, talking, laughing, slapping each other warmly on their backs, pleased with their catch and sharing retsina afterwards.

Or she painted the donkeys, their furry skin, their slow reluctance as they trudged over the hilly island in the searing sun, the young boys at their sides, hitting their flanks irritably with sticks when they needed to move more quickly.

She also painted the whitewashed houses with the women in black scrubbing the doorsteps, stray cats lurking near the taverna, searching for scraps, the goats on the rocky terrain, or the monasteries on the hill, built as close to God as possible.

Carl's paintings could not have been more different: huge swirling canvases, alive with movement but with no figures, neither human nor animal, in sight. There was a suggestion of water and boats and light and trees in the blocks of colour used and the atmosphere conveyed but he wanted them to be as abstract as possible, 'In order that the viewer can make his or her own images,' he explained, 'and therefore the painter is in collaboration with the spectator: working together to make sense of what we see.'

Gently, carefully, he encouraged Frieda to be less photographic in her work, blurring edges, hinting at reality rather than depicting it. The more she was with him and he praised her use of colour and brush stroke, the more she wanted to paint. She felt as if she had been opened up, as if Carl had prised apart the bars of her prison and set her free, or unlocked the oyster shell in which she had been trapped and released the pearl. For the first time since she was a teenager, she started writing poetry and he helped her with vision, with words and with passion. She could not stop painting, writing poetry, falling in love with Carl. She slipped poems in envelopes under his front door:

With you, I can drink the juice of lemons
And think it sweet.
You have opened my eyes to the sea
And its endless possibilities.
I am every cypress tree,
Each fantail dove, each pomegranate.
It is you who has helped me,
Who has lifted me to the clouds
And enabled me to be
Whatever it is that I need to be.

The more she slept with Carl, the more adventurous her paintings became.

The more she painted, the more adventurous her sex with Carl became.

So her canvases began to use colour that was deeper, brighter. She no longer felt the need to make her landscapes realistic and her figures so lifelike, but more abstract, hazy, as if she was willing to run the risk of people not knowing exactly what it was she was depicting. She transferred more responsibility onto the viewer and less onto her and this freed her, gave her the courage to paint the way she had always wanted to. Even her movements as she painted changed. She lifted her arms wide, more expansive, more expressive.

Hydra had liberated her in other ways, too. She knew that her children were safe and were being looked after: Gideon, quiet and guarded but doing well academically at school, Esther happy with Evgeniya. Jack was immersed in his own work: she had accepted now that their marriage was dead and that any hope of reviving it was unrealistic. She saw that. They had married too young, on the kibbutz, mistaking their shared idealism and Zionism for compatibility. Both virgins, they had hoped that sexually they would be in harmony but had discovered that they were not,

55

and lacked the language to air their problems so that they tended to argue rather than explore.

At the start of her relationship with Carl, they had taken it slowly, tenderly, as if there was no hurry. They did not talk of the future or how long they would be on the island. More sexually experienced than Frieda, Carl led the way, being careful not to rush or put pressure on her. As well as pleasing himself, he was concerned with helping her to discover what she liked. She had not said much about her sex life with Jack (she felt bad enough about her disloyalty to him without humiliating him further) but she implied that he charged at it hungrily without due consideration for her needs.

Carl felt himself blessed. He had come to the island not knowing anyone, escaping the pressure to stay at the law firm in Toronto and take it over when his father retired. All his life, Carl had done as he was told to. An only child, able at school, exams had not been a problem, and at law school he had continued to sail through. The issue was that none of this excited him.

Bored by law, he kept life interesting by painting his huge canvases and sleeping with as many people as possible when the day's work was over. It was easy to find women to have sex with, but it did not satisfy him. He sensed his life shrinking, felt suffocated. Complying with his father by day and his mother by night, being introduced to nice, dull girls whom she considered eligible at her frequent stiff dinner parties, he could hardly breathe.

After ten years like this, he rebelled. There was a terrible argument during which he told his mother that he did not want children and probably did not want to get married either. He told his father that he had always found commercial law stifling and tedious, a pretence at doing good while lining one's own pockets, that he had felt pressurised into studying it when he really hadn't wanted to, and that he wished to focus on his painting. It did not go down well. His mother wept for days and his father's face drained of colour. How Carl wished he had a conventional sister living near their parents, who had five children, so that they would be guaranteed the grandchildren they so desperately wanted.

In one of his arty magazines, Carl had read about an Aegean island called Hydra where people went to escape the trappings of capitalism and focus on their art. He had saved enough money from his work and could afford to live and paint for a while. Arriving on Hydra had been so effortless. Locals such as Douskos knew where the rented houses were, and Carl found one easily. It was wonderful to live simply, swap suits and ties for shorts and cotton shirts, and paint whenever he wanted. He loved the island, its simplicity, its beauty, the light which enveloped the whole place in a golden haze and slipped itself onto the canvas.

And then, best of all, at Olivia's party he had met Frieda. A few years younger than him, she was beautiful, talented, kind, and as passionate about art as he was. She was clearly unhappily married, so he had no qualms about their affair, and she was not demanding of him, so it was perfect.

At first their love-making was gentle, Carl conscious of not pushing himself onto her and scaring her away, but as their work and relationship became stronger, and they were more certain of themselves and each other, they moved the boundaries, opened the possibilities out. They learned more about each other and about themselves, what they really desired from life and from their affair. Freed from expectations of marriage and children, which so many women wanted to push him into, Carl relaxed. Without discussing it, they consented to keep their relationship a secret and avoid hurting others. In the letters he wrote to his parents, trying to heal their rift, Carl described the island and his work but said nothing of his relationship. Neither he nor Frieda expected love and maybe that is why, unexpectedly, it came so naturally to them.

In her shuttered studio, they liked to make love against the wall, Frieda naked and her one leg bent, her foot pressed against the cool bricks so that she could offer herself to Carl like a book, open wide at its centre. He would suck her breasts and then her mouth and she became bolder and more demonstrative, much less passive as time went on, and more an active participant, raking her fingers through his hair, directing his mouth, holding his hardness, and begging him to enter her when they could not wait a moment longer.

Or they would lie on the blue settee and she would take him in her mouth while he kissed and licked her, and they would be beyond ecstasy as if they were both there and beyond there, present and elsewhere. Time meant nothing then as if, sulky at being ignored, it had slipped through the shutters and dissolved itself in the sea.

57

When they emerged hours later, their faces and bodies hot, Demi would wave from his bakery. They never knew how much he had guessed, but diplomatically he made no comment when Frieda went in later to collect her daily bread.

Back home, family life was busy. They liked to eat on the terrace and Evgeniya had always prepared them something delicious: a lamb stew or a roast chicken in a big pan, surrounded by potatoes, chickpeas, onions and beans. It reminded Frieda of cholent, which her mother had taught her nanny to make, and sometimes it made her homesick for South Africa, although she knew she could not have stayed there. She remembered seeing benches labelled *whites only* and how sick it had made her feel. How could it be that Nanny was to be trusted with childcare and preparing their food but could not share a seat with them? When Frieda saw the bond between Esther and Evgeniya, it reminded her of the comfort she had felt in her nanny's arms, and hearing her sing her Afrikaans songs: *Jan Piriwitz*, her favourite.

Evenings passed quickly: meal, reading, playing games, bath-time, and then, when the children were in bed, more work or evenings at Douskos' Taverna. It was easy to hide their broken marriage from others. It was when darkness fell, and the stars gave little light, that Jack and Frieda were left alone, faced with the stark reality which they could not escape.

One night they spoke in hushed whispers on the balcony while the children slept.

'We are barely even husband and wife,' said Jack sadly. 'We never speak to each other and I can't remember the last time we had sex.'

Since she was sleeping with Carl, Frieda could not bring herself to be intimate with Jack, as if that would take the betrayal too far.

'I'm sorry,' said Frieda looking out to the dark hillside for answers and finding none, 'but we have just grown apart. Maybe all those years of you teasing me about my background and not taking my painting seriously have taken their toll.'

'You've done the same to me, Frieda: all those barbed comments about my parents' wholesale business and my failure to become a successful writer.'

'We thought that Hydra would heal us.'

'We were naive. How can an island do that?'

'Maybe nothing can. I suggested we went for counselling, but you wouldn't go.'

'I think we've gone beyond that, don't you? I'll sleep on the sofa tonight – again.'

And with that they each went to their separate places to sleep, rooms and worlds apart.

'Leonard! Leonard! Can you open the door?'

He came down from his study, hair ruffled, his mind still in his writing, to find Marianne on the doorstep. She held a letter in her hand.

Sophia Kyria brought them coffee in tiny cups and they sat on the terrace. The early morning summer sun was warm, coating the island in amber.

'I've had a letter from Axel. Another long one. He's got malaria and now he's decided that he wants to come back and live in our house on Hydra again. He says he needs the sun. What am I going to do? I can't live with him any longer. It will affect Axel Joachim badly.'

Leonard smiled warmly. 'It's simple. You both come and live with me.'

'Really? You are so kind. But is that a good idea? Axel will be so jealous.'

'Then let him be. He's the one who betrayed you. Is he with Patricia still?'

'No, I get the impression that it's over. I think he's returning alone.'

'There's no problem. I have so much space here. The thought of waking with you every day and going to bed with you every evening fills me with such joy. It will be like bedding the sunlight. And I love your little boy so much. You know that sometimes I can get him to sleep more easily than you can! Think about it.'

Marianne drained her cup and stroked Leonard's hand. 'Thank you,' she said. 'I will try to work out what to do.'

Marianne kissed Leonard and thought: I love every hair, fingernail and pore of this man but I do not want to disturb him or stop the flow of his writing. I would hate to do that.

She left his house, full of angst and indecision. Her dreams had been troubling lately and she had been trying to interpret them and understand herself.

Although Austin Delaney had only lived on Hydra for a while, everyone was aware of him and all spoke well of him. Olivia said he had trained in psychoanalysis at the Jung Institute in Switzerland and practised in India. As Marianne walked along the dusty path from Leonard's home to Austin's, she wondered: how do we know how to live? Which decisions should we take? She had tried the *I Ching*, and meditation and yoga, inspired and encouraged by Olivia and Magda. She had read Freud and attempted to interpret her dreams, but she had found no easy answers.

When she had met Axel in Oslo, she had thought that their lives would be simple and uncomplicated, yet here they were separated with a young child, her in love with Leonard, Axel restless and ill, and the future seemed uncertain.

She hurried past The Gardenia Dwarf's house, past the two wells where chickens roamed, hoping for a few drops of water spilled from the bucket of a careless visitor.

Austin's house was in a shaded spot, guarded by pine trees, and there was a goat's bell at the door. Tentatively, Marianne rang it.

'Hello Austin,' she said nervously, when he appeared. 'We met the other evening at Douskos' Taverna. I'm Marianne. Is this a convenient time?'

'Come in, my dear,' he replied warmly.

In the living room, she saw book-lined walls and sculptures from India, of couples loving each other, of women and children embracing. There were ceramic pots and African masks.

'You look distressed, my dear,' he said, gesturing for Marianne to sit on the sofa, an orange Indian cloth draped over it.

'I am. My husband Axel and I live in a house here together and we have a son, but Axel and I have separated. He has been living in America but now he wants to come back and I cannot live with him. Leonard, my lover, a Canadian writer, has invited my son and me to stay with him but I am undecided. And my dreams are so confused at the moment. I don't know what to do.'

'I see, my dear, that you are very troubled. Tell me what your dreams are like.'

'Last night I had one where I was standing in a field, in a deep, you know...' She gestured with her hands.

'...Furrow?'

'Yes. I recognised the field. It was one in Larkollen in Norway, near my grandmother's house, where I worked one summer, picking cucumbers. I was wearing an orange shirt, but it was Leonard's, not mine. Then suddenly, my penis fell to the ground. It was so strange.'

'I see.' He smiled kindly as if nothing could ever shock him.

Austin placed a sandbox on the table between them.

'You see this, Marianne?' Around the box lay dolls, tin soldiers, matchboxes and other toys and artefacts. 'You can play here however you like. Take your time. Do what you like but let me observe you.'

Marianne paused for a moment and then she made a little altar out of the sand. She took the wedding ring that Axel had given her and buried it there. Then she lit a candle with the match and waited.

'Interesting,' said Austin. 'You need to come and see me every day for five days, at the same time. Ten o'clock. You will have to write down each day what happens and then you will be able to reach a decision. Will you do that?'

She agreed.

The following day she arrived at his house, and he led her in.

'Yesterday,' she confessed, 'what I wanted to do was to pee in the sandbox.'

'Yes,' said Austin. 'I know. Now our work begins. You are ready to be truthful. It is time to live your life as you want to.'

Over the next few days, Marianne found that she could be increasingly open with Austin. They discussed her dreams, she read from her notes and he again used toys and soldiers to enable her to reveal her feelings. She realised that she was opening up more and more each time. He said little but watched with his kind eyes and egged her on, like a parent running behind the child on a bike, not touching but being near.

On the fifth day, Austin said, 'I am going to Zurich for a while, but I think you have you found your answer now, my dear, and you know what you need to do.'

She did, and a short while later, she and Axel Joachim moved into Leonard's house. She brought with her some furniture: the brown writing desk that Francisco had carved for Axel; a fishing board washed up on shore; Axel Joachim's old carved cradle; his trainset; and the black table with woven-backed chairs that she loved. She arranged Momo's white shells in a circle on the bedroom table. Some had serrated edges; others frilly. Some spiralled into themselves in cornets as if trying to return to the sea; others fanned themselves wide, stiff and boned as corsets.

She was careful not to invade Leonard's house, but he was happy for her to soften the edges of his spartan home and add her pretty touches: a mirror in the hall; a rocking chair in the living room; gardenia plants on the balcony. Each morning she cut a single bloom and put it in a glass by Leonard's typewriter, hoping that the freshness would help him start each day.

Later they also grew marijuana on their terrace.

Leonard continued his routine, rising at seven and working at his typewriter, being quiet, compelled, he told Marianne to create, whether the work was good or not. She admired him, respected him, listened to the tapping of his keys and sensed part of the joy that she imagined he was feeling. In a small way, she felt that she contributed to his work by being in his life, making him happy, being present but also absent, an enhancement to his writing without being a distraction from it.

She and Kyria Sophia were careful not to disturb him when he wrote. Some mornings, while the maid swept the house and cooked, Marianne would take Axel Joachim in his pushchair down to Katsikas to stock up on fruit and vegetables and to collect their mail. Leonard sometimes received cheques from his publisher for his work and she from her grandfather's inheritance fund. Axel's publisher even sent her small cheques from time to time. They lived simply, Marianne making their clothes, Axel Joachim wearing hand-me-downs from Charmian and George's children, and their food was frugal. Kyria Sophia was adept at using simple ingredients, often foraged in the hills and turned into something delicious.

In the afternoons, after lunch and a siesta when Axel Joachim slept and Marianne and Leonard made love in their cool bedroom, the three of them would go down to the beach or walk along the harbour and then, in the evening, after dinner when the light faded, Leonard would write again or sometimes they would go to Douskos' Taverna and join their friends.

But the mornings were their favourite time. They woke early, the shutters failing to block out completely the eager, bright and early sun, which wanted them to open the windows. Sometimes they made love but, at other times, they lay naked on the white bed and just looked at each other and the possibilities they saw there. Leonard liked to stare at Marianne while she slept and could not believe her beauty, the way her eyelids caught the light and shielded her from it while also allowing it in.

One time, Leonard fingered the scar on Marianne's stomach.

'What's this?' First thing, his voice was even more gravelly than usual.

'When Axel and I were in Athens, I had appendicitis and had to have an emergency operation.'

'What was that like?'

'Primitive. The hospital was very basic and they hung up sheets so that I couldn't see what was going on. Axel sat by my bedside and typed on little pieces of paper. The first time I was able to go to the bathroom on my own, there were small sheets hanging up to be used as toilet paper. They were Axel's writing: the nurses had not realised the significance of his masterpiece.'

They both laughed.

'So, I'm sorry, Leonard, but I am not perfect or unblemished.'

Leonard ran his fingers gently across her scar and blinked in the sun. 'It is only when there are imperfections that we see the real beauty,' he said.

Some mornings he awoke really early to work on his novel and would leave Marianne sleeping. She would awake, turn to look at the dent in the bed where he had lain, and stroke that space with her hand. Sometimes he left her signs of love: a poem entitled 'Breaking the Wish-Bone' and underneath a drawing of a chicken wishbone snapped in half and the words *Poem for Marianne*. Another time, he wrote her a cheque, a real one, and the recipient was Marianne Ihlen and the signature was Leonard Cohen but where the sum of money should have been there was a drawn heart. One another occasion, a silver mirror and a note, reminding her to look at her reflection as often as she could. He also gave her a tortoiseshell comb, mottled, its teeth sharp.

No-one had ever treated her with such love and kindness and her eyes filled with tears at his affection. She could hear him, tapping away at his typewriter, and was pleased that he had the fresh gardenia to spur him on.

She would not disturb him when he wrote but waited until later to thank him for his kind gestures.

'You are everything I desire,' he would whisper. 'I wish for nothing more.'

Sometimes Leonard and Marianne would look at themselves in the mirror that hung in the hall – her, blonde, small-breasted, and him dark-haired, slender – and think: how could anyone be that lucky in love?

But when the light faded and darkness fell, they searched for their reflections in the flat, black surface and could not find them.

News spread faster across the island than the wildfires that sometimes caught on the dead grasses and licked the dry earth with their orange tongues. The main spreaders of gossip were the maids who, in spite of their long working hours, always managed to find time to talk. Unlike the artistic expats, they didn't have the luxury of long, candlelit discussions at Douskos' Taverna or leisurely picnics on the beaches. But they found other places to meet.

One such location was at the twin wells where the maids went to fetch water, only a few houses having their own supply in their courtyards. Also, there was the huge communal oven at Demi's bakery where, for a few drachmas, the maids would take raw food that needed cooking, often lamb kleftiko or goat stew, which demanded more space than the tiny cookers in their employers' houses. In the ovens, as well as twigs and leaves, there were juniper berries so that all the food came back infused with that extra scent. Demi labelled each dish so that every family took the correct meal home. Bread could be collected from Demi's at the same time, vegetables, fruit and oil bought from Katsikas, and maids looking after the children would often coordinate their visits so that whilst the youngsters played, the women would talk, their fast, babbling Greek guaranteeing that what they said remained a secret from the foreigners.

So Kyria Sophia (Leonard's maid) would tell Evgeniya (Frieda and Jack's maid), and she would tell Maria (Axel and Marianne's maid) who would tell Sevasty (Charmian and George's maid) who would tell Agape (Magda's maid) who would tell Ellina (Olivia and Georgos' maid), so no-one needed to buy a newspaper. Speech carried so much faster than print (most of them could not read anyway) and it was free.

Between them, they had already spotted Frieda and Carl's affair; they knew that Marianne had moved in with Leonard; that Charmian was sleeping with Anthony Kingsmill and Nature Boy; that Axel, who had now broken up with Patricia and had contracted malaria, was back in his old house. And that was how Marianne discovered that he had returned. Kyria Sophia told her.

Leonard and Axel Joachim had grown close (the little boy always calling him 'Cone') and so Marianne, on hearing news of Axel's return, left them home together while she went to visit him. She took with her warm bread and a basketful of goods: fruit, bottled water, cold meats.

Axel looked pale and tired, black rings under his eyes, and Marianne noticed that he was sweating and shivering although it was a warm day.

'How are you, Axel?' she asked. All the anger and resentment had vanished and she now felt pity for him. He looked so unwell.

'The vomiting and nausea have gone, and the doctor says that the malaria is fading but I still feel rough.'

'You have Maria to look after you.'

'Why would I have Maria when I could have Marianne?'

He held out his hand to touch hers. She squeezed his back in a platonic way so as not to encourage him and then quickly removed it.

'That is over now, Axel, but we can be friends.'

'I do not want to be your friend, Marianne. I love you. You are the only woman that I have ever loved. Leave that new man of yours. Come back to me. Bring little Axel Joachim. We can be a proper family again.'

She poured Axel a glass of water and passed it to him. 'No, Axel. You had your chance. Do you not remember how you treated me? All the women you slept with when you said you loved only me?'

'That was just sex. It means nothing, Marianne.'

'Not to me. I think sex is something you share with someone you care for or love. Not just something you hand out like sweets to anyone who passes by.'

'Leave him. What do you see in him? Some dark-haired Canadian dwarf, who writes poetry to depress everyone? Come back to me.'

'You have Maria to take care of you and I will come from time to time to run errands, but you need to understand, Axel, I am with Leonard now. You can see your son, but I will never, ever live with you again.'

Axel's face twisted in scorn and anger. He held his glass high like a weapon and smashed it against the wall. It shattered into many pieces, splinters all over the stone floor and the water darkened the white paint. Marianne tried to stay calm. She had seen him lose his temper many times.

'Axel,' she said, 'you are behaving like a child. Stop it.'

'Come back to me, Marianne, or I will smash all the glasses in this house,' and he began to cry.

'That is stupid. You can destroy whatever you want but I am never coming back to you. Do you understand? I loved you and you betrayed me and it is over.'

She took her basket and left. As she walked to the front door, she could hear him wailing and the sounds of more glasses exploding against the wall.

All the way back to her house, her empty basket swinging in her hand, her heart raced. She remembered what Momo had said: at least you are breathing. Concentrate on that and be calm.

By the time she reached Leonard's house, Marianne was sobbing. Axel Joachim was on the floor playing with his tin soldiers and Leonard held his lover tenderly, felt her cries throb through her body, let his linen shirt moisten with her tears.

'I wish he would move away from Hydra and leave us in peace,' she sobbed.

'I know, my love, but you have Axel Joachim and me.'

He lifted the baby from the floor and held them together so that the three of them made a tight circle. Leonard kissed Marianne on her cheek and Axel Joachim on his soft white head.

'Now this will amuse you. Do you know what we boys have been doing while you were out?' Marianne shook her head and dried her eyes. 'We tried to do an experiment. We had a bath and put the typewriter in to see if it would work underwater.'

'What? Why?'

'Just as an experiment.'

'And did it?'

'Not well but we had fun trying.' He ruffled the boy's hair.

'Your lovely green typewriter. Is it ruined?'

'No. It is very wet, but it will dry.'

'Silly you,' and they laughed again.

That evening they ate the meal that Kyria Sophia had made them, on the terrace with Hydra below offered to them like a gift. As usual, on Shabbat, Leonard lit the candles, and recited blessings on them, the bread and the wine. '*Baruch atah adonai, elohenu melech ha aolum...*'

'Why do you still do the Jewish blessings?' she asked, 'as you read so much about Buddhism?'

'Other philosophies and religions don't make me turn against my Judaism. In fact, they make me turn to it more. It reminds me of the difference between grace and guilt. Traditional Judaism never suited me but after my father died, I felt that I had to be the man of the home, looking after my mother and sister. My mother wanted me to take his place and for a while, I was comfortable with it. But here on Hydra, I feel free to be the kind of Jew that I want to be.'

'Does this island set us free?'

'To some extent. It is the contradictions that I love. We live on an island called Hydra where it hardly ever rains. We are both free from society and yet enchained to it.'

'Yes, I agree. I thought I would find happiness and love here and I have, with you, but Axel is nearby reminding me always of reality and pain.'

'Rather than blot out his darkness, you have to edge closer to it.'

'What do you mean, Leonard?'

'Accept what you wish to reject and take it in. Learn from it, lean into it, as you would the night.'

Over the next few weeks, Marianne tried to heed Leonard's advice. She still went to see Axel regularly and took him shopping but she refused to engage in his fights or arguments even though he seemed to want her to. She lifted herself above them, let him rant if he wanted to, and shielded herself from it.

'I did everything I could for Patricia,' he said one day, 'and what thanks did I get for it? I sat there for days on end at the hospital, by her side' (Marianne did not say: so did I) 'and then I helped her get treatment in America and still she rejected me. Life is a struggle, every day and month of it. Every minute, even. Writing is the same. I toil and slave away at it and try to form perfect sentences, the best I can, and even then I am not appreciated.'

Marianne listened but did not respond. She remembered Leonard's advice, to edge towards it but not be swallowed by it. Axel did not like to be patronised or told that it would get better soon. She avoided contentious subjects, such as when he was going to see his son again, or pay any maintenance for him. These topics made him angry. She watched him erupt and let him do so.

After she left his house, she would feel relieved to be away from his toxic anger and back in the fresh summer air. Yellow flowers beaded the gorse bushes; wild gladioli dotted the island with their colourful blooms and the eucalyptus leaves caught the sun. One day she was walking back when she saw an osprey land on a nearby wall. She paused for a moment and observed its hooked beak, its green, glassy eyes and the marbled feathering on its back and wings. Stunned by its beauty and its willingness to let itself be seen, Marianne found herself smiling. There might be pain on this island but there was undoubtedly beauty, too.

She felt great comfort knowing that when she returned to Leonard's house, he would be there with her son. She loved their daily life: the meals they shared; the walks they had in the harbour, showing Axel Joachim the boats and the cormorants that stood still as iron on the boulders; the picnic lunches carried in Marianne's deep baskets and drawn out like secrets. She felt they made a family, the three of them, hands held, facing each other.

And in the evenings, when Axel Joachim slept and Kyria Sophia had gone home, she and Leonard made love with tenderness and passion. The more sex they had, the more they wanted. She liked to receive him in her mouth and between her legs, anywhere she could feel his hardness within her, and they took their time, as if they hoped that the night would never end. Her breasts were small but he liked to take her nipples in his mouth and then find her lips and kiss her, as if he would never stop. Sometimes they had sex two or three times in a row, pausing only for a few moments in between, desperate for more of what they had already had: more and more of it.

One night as they lay in the darkness, satisfied, he said: 'By the way, my mother, Masha, wants to come and visit me here.'

'That's good,' said Marianne.

'Is it really?' he answered. 'Wait and see.'

'My love,' said Marianne, placing her hand gently on Leonard's shoulder. 'You have been working so hard. Won't you come and rest?'

'No,' he said. 'I have to finish this. The publisher is waiting for it. I'm focusing on the characters of Shell and Gordon and I have to get them right.'

'I understand, Leonard. I will leave you in peace. Kyria Sophia has taken Axel Joachim to Katsikas to get groceries and collect the mail. I'm going to visit Axel.'

'Why do you still bother with him? He doesn't deserve your care.'

'I know, but he's ill and lonely and still the father of my child.'

She kissed the back of Leonard's neck and as her lips brushed his feathery nape, she noticed how the sun had warmed it. On the wall in front of him she saw that he had written in gold paint: *I am change / I am the same.* He wrote on paper, the walls, tables: any surface receptive to his words.

Her basket filled with food, and the marked manuscript of Axel's novel, *Line*, she set out on the walk to her old house. Today, the summer brought with it the Meltemi wind from the north, which blew harshly from a marble and granite sky. Marianne wrapped her headscarf tightly around her head to protect her from the blast and clasped it close to her throat with one hand. In Norway, this wind would have created rain and cold, but how like Hydra for the wind to be hot as if it were delivering bad news but in a sweet coating.

Along the side of the path she saw purple stocks growing haphazardly from any patch of ground they could find, sometimes a single stem, sometimes in clumps. Wild roses clambered the walls and filled the air with their scent. A goat looked up nonchalantly when he saw Marianne appear and then bent down to his clump of weeds again. It made her smile: Kyria Sophia often boiled nettles for them to eat, money always being tight, and the wild greens, herbs and garlic made a nourishing broth, a swirl of olive oil over the top. You and us, mumbled Marianne to the goat: sharing the same meal, making do with whatever we can find, and enjoying it.

71

Arriving at Axel's home, Marianne saw that Maria had cleaned for him although she was nowhere in sight. The kitchen tiles were gleaming; the stone floor still slightly damp. Marianne put the food in the kitchen and went to see Axel, writing in his study. Moving between one novelist on a green Olivetti typewriter and another novelist on a Remington black typewriter, she sometimes wondered who she was. She had the sense of not quite being anyone, as if her identity was shifting, dependent on and determined by others. She thought: maybe I am destined to be a daughter, mother, wife, lover and muse to other creators, while my own creative self never seems to evolve.

There were times when she felt the role to be a privileged one: both men needed her. But there were other days when she felt like nothing, a ghost of who she might have been, an invisible shape wafting between the two houses, less effective than the Meltemi wind.

'Have you eaten today, Axel?' she asked, speaking to the back of his head. She remembered kissing Leonard's nape and thought: I haven't even seen either of these men's faces today.

'No time. Groth is waiting for the final draft to be finished. Have you brought the marked copy?'

'Yes. I've put red dots in the margins where I feel there needs to be more work or embellishment.' She handed him the edited manuscript, disappointed that he had not even thanked her or looked up.

In the kitchen, she mashed some avocado into a paste, added chickpeas, olive oil and lemon juice and warmed pitta in the oven. She thought back to the manuscript, the novel about Jacob, a young seaman, whose parents both have psychiatric issues. He goes back to Norway and falls in love with Line, to the disapproval of everyone. She did not say to Axel that Line reminded her of herself and that the novel seemed to be a thinly disguised account of their relationship. He needed to stay focused and she did not want to rile him when the novel was due. He was talented, of that she had no doubt, and she was not going to block that.

She carried the food through to him, insisting: 'Please take a small break to eat and then you can carry on.'

He half-turned towards her and obeyed, ripping bread and shovelling it in the paste, like a digger through cement.

'How is it going?'

'Better now that I know Groth likes it. I hadn't heard from him in ages, you know how long the post takes to come from Piraeus, but he has now written to say it's good. With your suggestions and one redraft, I may finish it this week.'

Marianne smiled. Axel and Groth, his publisher, had had their difficulties. Although Groth had declared Axel a genius, the two men had often argued, for example, over the title of the novel. Axel had favoured Linedansen – *The Line Dancer* – punning on the character's name but Groth disagreed. *Line* was the compromise they had grumpily reached. That was just one of many quarrels they had had.

'Good. You are feeling better?'

'Yes. No more sweating or nausea. I have lost a lot of weight though.'

He ate the food hungrily. It looked to Marianne as if he had been so absorbed in his writing that he had not eaten for days. The plate soon empty, he turned back to his typewriter.

'I will bring you a pot of coffee,' she said, 'so that you can have it by you before I leave.'

She removed the soiled plate.

When she brought the silver pot and cup through, he seized her hand and said: 'Don't leave me, Marianne. You are the only woman I have ever truly loved.'

She withdrew her hand but tried to do so graciously. She did not say: remember, you were the one who betrayed me. He needed to be calm in order to write.

Walking back, Marianne felt tears stream down her face. Maybe it was the summer wind, she thought, but maybe it was also the endless strain of trying to understand life and knowing how best to live.

At Leonard's house, he seemed even more absorbed on *The Favourite Game* than Axel did on *Line*. Now she prepared food for him: an array of salami, olives, tomatoes and dolmades. She arranged them prettily on a plate and made him a carafe of coffee, too.

'Leonard,' she whispered, her hand pressed gently on his back, 'here is some food and drink. You need nourishment to keep you going.'

His hair was messy as if he had been rifling his fingers through it and he was sweaty, damp patches spreading under his arms and staining his cotton shirt.

'Thank you, my love,' he growled, 'but I can't stop. I have to keep writing. I must finish this novel if it kills me. Please leave me alone.'

She went through to Kyria Sophia who was doing the ironing.

'As Axel Joachim is having his nap,' she told her, 'I am going for a walk.'

These were days when Marianne felt angry and restless. Walking down the hill to the harbour, the wind had died down a little and she saw the donkeys standing irritably in the heat, twitching their ears to rid them of the midges that encircled them in a hazy cloud. The houses piled haphazardly along the bay, and the boats were now resting after their busy morning.

Suddenly she heard her name being called: 'Marianne, over here!'

She turned and was delighted to see Sam, an old friend. She and Axel had worked for him on his schooner, her cooking, Axel sailing. She had never told Axel of her affair with Sam and they all became friends, Sam, Eileen, his wife, and their young son, James.

They embraced and he seemed so pleased to see her again. 'You look amazing, Marianne, as beautiful as ever. So, you're still here on Hydra? How's Axel?'

'There's so much to tell you,' she said shyly, noticing how tanned, blond and beautiful Sam was. 'Do you have time for a drink?'

They sat behind Katsikas' store where, at those same tables and chairs, she had first met Leonard. The light made the place seem more pleasant than it really was: old sacks of flour and rice stacked in the corners; the ubiquitous stray cats, moody, sulky, on the lookout for scraps.

'Where do I begin?' she asked once they were seated and they had clinked their glasses of lemonade. 'After we had our beautiful boy, Axel Joachim, we separated.'

'No? What happened?'

'He found someone else. An American painter named Patricia.'

'What an idiot. Are they still together?'

'No, but Axel lives in our old house, alone. He has not been well.'

'And where do you live?' Marianne noticed Sam's muscular physique. She had forgotten how attractive he was.

'I am with Leonard. He is a writer, singer, composer. Very talented. He is wonderful.'

74

'Axel is stupid, a loser. He was never good enough for you. I do not know Leonard. Live with me, Marianne. Marry me. We were so good together. We can sail the seas and move between Oslo and Hydra. I could make you happy. You know it could work.'

Part of Marianne thought: I have two men on Hydra who do not appreciate me. Maybe I should go with Sam? He was always so attentive to me. But she shook her head.

'Thank you, Sam. We have always been friends. But it is Leonard I love. He makes me happy. Anyway, what happened to Eileen?'

'It didn't work out either. She found a new lover.'

'And James?'

'He remembers you warmly, the way you told him stories. He is fine, growing up fast.'

They paused and Sam looked at her fondly.

'I would like you to have this, Marianne,' said Sam, digging in his duffel bag. He drew out an old captain's watch. It was silver and elegant, the numbers Roman. She threaded it through the chain so that it hung next to the Star of David that Leonard had given her, and which she wore each day. 'Think about what I've said. Contact me. You could have a good life with me.'

'Thank you, Sam. Thank you for the watch. Tell me about you,' she said, moving the conversation away from the past.

'I am well, but I have never stopped thinking of you.'

Later while Marianne made her way up the hill back to Kala Pigadia, she fingered the watch from Sam and the star from Leonard in the same hand, at the same time. The sun and wind grazed her face as she walked. Decisions, choices, all the time.

When she arrived home, Leonard greeted her.

'I am sorry, Marianne,' he said. 'To choose between writing and the woman I love is torture to me. I want you both all the time. I cannot have one without the other.'

He embraced her and she let her head lean against his chest.

'What's this?' he asked, fingering the watch.

'Oh, I bumped into an old friend in the harbour. Axel and I worked for him on his yacht one year and he gave it to me.'

Leonard's eyes filled with tears. 'If you leave me, Marianne, the world will shrivel up and die. Life will be lightless without you.'

'Of course I will not leave you,' she said and they kissed long, slowly, to tell him what she felt.

They made love that night, carefully, gently, as if in fear of losing each other. When Leonard kissed her, she felt that they were capable of anything and that nothing would ever destroy their love. With his mouth upon hers with his body in hers, with his words whispered in the depths of her ear, she knew that she always wanted him within her, as deeply and often as possible.

Leaving her to sleep, he took one glance at her: her curved body and closed legs like a beautiful sea-creature washed up on the bed, her skin translucent even in the dark, her hair soft and white like sand, then he returned to his other lover, the one with keys, which pulled him to it with such force that he could not resist. He felt like a man in a storm, wondering which door was better to go through and wanting to enter both.

The next day, Marianne wrote to Sam, asking him to be Axel Joachim's godfather but returning the watch with the words: *Thank you, but I cannot love anyone but Leonard.*

The amphitheatre at Epidavros lay in a bowl at the bottom of a hill. It looked as if a giant had come along in 400 BC, scooped out a huge chunk of earth with his hand, and walked away. The tiered arena could hold fifteen thousand people in its honey-coloured stone.

The party – Marianne and Leonard; George and Charmian; Gordon and Chuck, and Magda – arrived after a long journey. Mikalis and Spyros took them in their boat to a blue and white cäique; then a trip to Napflio, followed by a taxi ride to the amphitheatre. The heat had been stifling and Marianne's cheeks were burning.

Walking from the taxi to the theatre, Charmian whispered to Marianne: 'I'm deeply involved with Anthony now. George's problems mean that he can't manage it any more.'

Marianne couldn't help feeling sorry for George who ambled slowly behind them, his coughing always audible. He walked with Leonard and the two men talked about their writing.

'I've finished my novel,' said George, 'but I'm struggling to find a title.'

'What's it about?' asked Leonard.

'My brother Jack.'

'There you are,' he laughed. 'You have it!'

The group shared salad and meats that Marianne had prepared, while waiting for the performance to begin. Magda had brought along black grapes and figs, which struggled to contain their juice within their bulging skins.

'Did you leave the children their meal, Charm?' George asked.

'No, Sevasty's fucking doing it,' hissed Charmian. 'Did you think I would let the children be hungry? And besides, it's a bit late now to be asking when we're miles away, isn't it?'

'Jeez, steady on, love. You angry again?'

'It's always me who has to do everything. Why don't you prepare the dinner for once and take your fair share of the housework and cooking? Why is it always down to me?'

'You're a moody little bitch, aren't you?' said George, taking a swig from a bottle of ouzo and coughing so harshly that some of his blood entered the bottle.

'And you're living in the past, when women were expected to do everything and men just sat around looking important.'

'Sounds great to me.'

'I'm as good a writer as you are, and don't you forget it,' she hissed.

'Oh, I'm sorry, I forgot: you've written nine novels in ten years, have you?'

'Quality, George, not quantity.'

'Sorry, are you talking about writing or sex, Charm?'

Yet again, Charmian and George's arguing was ruining the evening for everyone.

Marianne turned the attention to Gordon. 'I hear your novel's doing well?'

'Yes, there have been some good reviews, but Chuck is now writing as well. He has left the world of dance to concentrate on the written word,' and the two men smiled warmly at each other.

Before coming to Hydra, Marianne had never known a gay couple but she found them delightful and wished that Charmian and George would learn from them. How wonderful Hydra was, receptive to different kinds of love. She turned to Leonard who was quiet and looked drawn.

As the evening fell, the stage was lit by candles. Marianne sat close to Leonard, enjoying the warmth of his body as they watched the play. Hecuba, the Queen of Troy, was dressed regally in white edged with gold braid, and she commanded the space with her many children. Marianne was so absorbed by the drama that she forgot that she was sitting on bare stone. When Hecuba avenged the murder of her youngest son by stabbing out the eyes of the King of Thrace and killing his sons, the audience gasped. The applause at the end was deafening.

And then they had to make their way back: the taxi ride to Napflio, the cäique and then Mikalis and Spyros' smaller boat. The sky was black now and the stars merely pricks of light studding its velvety cloth.

Floating along in the boat in the still night, they shared retsina, passing the bottles between them, delighting in its sweetness. Someone else had a few joints and they smoked and drank and spoke in soft voices, respectful of the night. The sound of the water lapping when it could not be seen was calming. Leonard was subdued. Having just finished *The Favourite Game*, Marianne had hoped that he would recover and spend some time with her and Axel Joachim, swimming, taking picnics, but he was already planning his next novel, *Beautiful Losers*.

Leonard had told Marianne how he used to lay flowers at the statue of the seventeenth-century saint Kateri Tekakwitha, also known as Lily of the Mohawks, in St Patrick's Cathedral, New York. When she died aged 24, her skin turned white. He had been thinking a lot about this fascinating figure and wanted to write about her, but in a new way. As the boat sailed along the supportive sea and the rest of the group chatted, Leonard was thinking about the plot. This novel would have to be carefully structured. It would centre around a love-triangle and there would be three books, each with a different narrator: *Book One, The History of Them All; Book Two, a Letter from F, the friend who may or may not exist, to the narrator; and Book Three, Beautiful Losers: An Epilogue in the Third Person*. The book would be shocking, full of wonderful symbolism and imagery. What was the point of replicating something already written? He had to unearth new ground.

By the time they reached Hydra, it was the early hours of the morning. They felt as if the night was wrapping them in its black shawl, enveloping them in its cashmere softness, shielding them from too much reality. The island was still and dormant.

'Leonard,' Marianne called and woke him from his reverie. 'We're here. Back in Hydra.'

The passengers left the boat and thanked Mikalis and Spyros. As they were gathering their belongings, Leonard said, 'Marianne, I need to walk alone for a while and think something through.'

She was disappointed but hugged him. As they embraced she felt his bones through his shirt. She strolled home alone.

Back in the house she woke and thanked Kyria Sophia, who had fallen asleep on the settee, and went to check on her son. Beneath the mosquito net, he lay like an angel, his blond hair soft, his head turned to one side, his thumb in his mouth and his breathing gentle and shallow. She could feel the warmth coming from his cot.

Undoing the buttons on her dress, she walked through to Leonard's study and saw, by his typewriter, pages and pages of typed words. As she read, tears sprang to her eyes. Beneath the sheets were packets of pills, amphetamines. She had decided early on that in this relationship she did not want the discord that she had had with Axel. But did that mean that she should say nothing, ever?

That night she had a dream. She was walking along a windy harbour and had several pieces of coloured ribbon, which she was trying to hold onto. At the end of each ribbon were the men in her life: her father, her brother, Axel, Leonard, Sam, Axel Joachim. One by one, they could not withstand the wind and had to let go so that, in the end, she was holding empty leads. Marianne woke in a sweat and thought: is that my destiny? To try to hold on to others while they abandon me? She turned to Leonard's side of the bed. He was still not home.

She was not the only one unable to sleep that night. Not far away, Frieda lay in her bed, thinking about Carl. On the living room sofa, a humped shape in the dark snored softly. Jack was a good man. They argued but he loved her and the children; and she had betrayed him. Over and over. She did not want an unhappy family life for Gideon and Esther. It wasn't fair on them. She would have to keep Carl as her secret.

And in a sense, although she felt guilty about deceiving Jack, it made it all the more special, like a stash of chocolate truffles hidden away. Each day, she started work early; Carl rose later and could drop by whenever he wanted to. She loved the thrill of it, that in the middle of her painting, he would suddenly appear. It was good of Demi to make no reference to it when Frieda went in to get their bread. Like all the locals, he tolerated the artists' bohemian behaviour and was even entertained by it. It provided them with work and trade and gave them something to gossip about.

When Carl did arrive, they would close the shutters on the large windows and undress in the striped light. By now, they had made love all around the studio, even in the corners of the room, so that it was covered with their scent, like cats marking their territory.

Carl did not often make references to his many former lovers, but he used what he had learned to guide Frieda slowly. Until she had met Carl, sex had been a disappointment to her and she found herself making excuses to avoid sleeping with Jack, saying she was on her period when she wasn't or pretending to be asleep when he came to bed. Carl helped her as a tutor helps a student: tenderly, patiently and without making the learner afraid.

Afterwards, they liked to lie naked on the chaise longue and Carl would stroke her hair, now unpinned and free. He said that he loved her, and she found herself, after a while, being able to say the same back. When he felt ready to tackle his own canvases back in his studio, he left, and Frieda chose not to wash in the nearby bathroom but kept herself moist and aroused by the smell of him, hoping to transfer that energy to her work.

It wasn't just the sex that opened to her a world of pleasure that she had not known existed, but it was Carl's focus, those deep eyes on her. Whether it was her canvases or her body, he looked without staring as if, for that stretch of time, there was nothing and no-one else. She started to see herself and her work as beautiful and that self-confidence benefitted her work.

When Magda came to her studio one day to buy a painting of a goatherd with her flock, she remarked on how Frieda's work had improved dramatically since she had arrived on Hydra, the colours bolder, the outlines more defined, the whole painting more confident.

'It must be the sunlight,' Magda said.

The morning after the trip to the amphitheatre, Marianne awoke and saw that Leonard was still not in their bed. She wrapped her silk gown around her and went to his study. There was the typewriter, yesterday's gardenia limp in its glass vase, the typed sheets on the table, strips of amphetamines half-hidden beneath them.

In the kitchen, Kyria Sophia was giving Alex Joachim his warm milk and bread and Marianne bent to cuddle her son. 'Hello, my little chicken.'

Leonard did not come back until mid-morning when he stumbled in, looking tired, black bags under his eyes, stubble on his face.

'Where have you been? I was worried about you.'

'You don't need to be. I was just thinking.'

'Really? Who with? What's her name?'

'Don't be silly, Marianne. I need to wash and write,' and he left for his study.

She made him coffee and stirred honey into yoghurt, his favourite, and put them by the typewriter. She removed yesterday's dead gardenia and put a fresh bloom in the vase. As the weight of the flowers left her hand, she felt excluded.

He said nothing, mildly irritated by her intrusion, wondered why she hadn't replaced it earlier rather than disturb him now. He knew that, if he spoke to her this time, it could become a habit. The dark fringe of his hair seemed to her like a curtain, hiding him behind it, leaving her on the outside. She felt hurt by this treatment, as if she was good enough to bring him flowers but not bright enough to understand his ideas.

When he did emerge hours later, he tried to be loving but she was not receptive. She still felt resentful of his earlier treatment of her, she wanted to recover but could not.

Instead, having dressed Axel Joachim in blue shorts and a white T-shirt, she said, 'We are going to see your daddy now.'

Axel had complained the last few times Marianne had been to visit him that he never saw his son. It was a difficult issue: in theory, Marianne agreed that he had a right to have access to him, but in practice Axel could be moody and volatile and she wanted, more than anything, to make Axel Joachim's life stable and happy. But today, angry with Leonard, she put the child in his pushchair and wheeled him over to her old house. The gorse bushes were covered in gold blooms and wild white orchids appeared erratically, at the side of the road, their random presence part of their charm.

She felt full of trepidation. When she was a child, all she had dreamed of was a stable, happy family unlike the fragmented one she'd had; and yet here she was, her ex-husband difficult, and her lover not very different. No, that was unfair: much of the time, Leonard was warm and loving to her but recently he had been obsessive about his writing and been so distant, so cold, shutting her and her son out.

Apprehensively, she knocked on the door. Maria opened it and led her onto the terrace where Axel greeted them more warmly than usual.

'How is my gorgeous boy?' he asked, holding his arms out to Axel Joachim. The child stared at him as if at a stranger and turned to cuddle his mummy.

'What about you, Axel? You look brighter.'

'I am. I think the malaria tablets are working at last and I do feel better.'

'I'm pleased.' Marianne was amazed.

Axel smiled, looking so much happier and she wondered what could have affected such a dramatic transition when the door to the terrace opened again. A blonde young woman in a wraparound gown stepped out.

'Marianne, this is Sonja,' said Axel.

Back at Leonard's home he was still tapping away at his typewriter. He had not touched his yoghurt and his coffee was cold, a dark rim staining the cup. The strip of amphetamines was emptier than earlier.

'Leonard,' she said softly, 'you have not eaten or had anything to drink.'

'I cannot,' he said, not looking up at her. 'The angels have told me that I must get on.'

'Did you remember, Leonard? It's Norman's exhibition today?'

But he brushed her away with his hand as if she were a moth.

'Leave me, Marianne. I have to write.'

Olivia and her husband had given over a large room in their home to Norman for his first ever show: *Objets Trouvés*. That was the kindness of Olivia: she did what she could to encourage artists.

Norman stood awkwardly in the corner of the room, trapped between excitement and modesty like a fly between two panes of glass. When anyone complimented him on his work or even bought a piece, he blushed and thanked them but could not look them in the eye.

The room was full of his creations: structures made of paper, metal, sticks, tin cans, anything he could find. There was a kind of beauty in his work as if he were making a statement: what you think is just rubbish and only fit to discard, look again. There may be more to waste than you think. Maybe we are the ones at fault in seeing anything as useless.

With a glass of white wine in one hand, and the other steering the pushchair, Marianne walked around the pieces, thinking: maybe it applies to humans, too. We see others as limited, with nothing to offer, but maybe they do. Her life flashed before her: her father, mother, brother, Momo, Sam, Axel, Leonard.

She was gazing at one structure, which looked like a precarious column of paper, metal and cigarette packets, when Magda came over to greet her. Unusually, she was wearing black, but she had so many silver bangles and chunky necklaces on, that the dress became a backdrop to showcase her finery, as if she were a velvet cloth in a jewellery window on which the products were displayed.

'Isn't Norman's work amazing? I so admire him,' said Magda.

'Me too. I hope he has some success.'

'He is so poor that he has a tree trunk in his hovel which he lights when he needs fuel.'

'Poor man. And he's so talented. I didn't know that ugly objects could be made to be so beautiful.'

'Let's hope you think the same of my new wine bar. I have restored the old boathouse and it should be open soon.'

'How lovely.'

'You look sad today, Marianne. How are you?'

'Struggling at the moment, Magda. Leonard is very down, obsessed with his new novel, and he hardly has time for Axel Joachim and me.'

'That must be hard. I read some reviews in the *Athens Post* of his first novel. They were very favourable.'

'Yes, it was well received but he wants to do more, be more, than that. And Axel has been very ill and I have tried to help him but now he has a new woman and so I just feel that he uses me and discards me when he likes. A bit like this rubbish,' and she pointed to the structures on display.

'Men, they're impossible. I think Paolo is having another affair. He is going all the time to Athens and staying in the Hilton. He says he has business meetings, but I am not convinced. You give these men your heart and soul, your life, and they destroy it.'

'Maybe we should leave them, Magda, and go and join the nuns in the monastery on the hill?'

'The peace and quiet would be good!'

The women laughed and hugged each other. Marianne was so pleased to have Magda as her friend, the older sister she had never had.

That evening in Douskos' Taverna, the usual conversations were flying around. Leonard hadn't come, wanting to stay at home and write. Axel wasn't there either, obsessed by his new love. Marianne wasn't enjoying the evening. She missed the strumming of Leonard's guitar beneath their words; she usually enjoyed the conversation but tonight it felt flat.

'Jeez, Charm, you say you want to write. Just darn well do it. Stop complaining about it.'

'Me? Complaining? It's you who is always moaning about your writing.'

'Moaning? Me?'

She turned to talk to Norman but she found him uninspiring; his passion was in his work, not his words. It seemed as if the exhibition had worn him out.

Jack was talking to Gordon and Chuck about Buber (Frieda having an evening at home, he said), John asking Olivia about Buddhism; Magda singing to herself, her voice thin without the guitar chords to support it.

'I'm rather tired tonight,' said Marianne. 'Excuse me,' and she left early.

Walking along the harbour, she saw that the lights in Frieda's shuttered studio were on. That's unusual, thought Marianne, and made her way slowly home.

Frieda and Carl usually only saw each other in the day, but they had decided to meet that evening. They were resentful that only parts of the day's cycle belonged to them. It felt different being together at night, the room cosy, shutting the darkness out and keeping their light inside. Carl had brought a bottle of white wine and two glasses and a candle in a jar.

Frieda had written Carl another poem and he listened carefully as she read it aloud:

We shared a peach and it was good,
The juices running down our loving arms.
You asked me if I wanted to fly away
And I said I did
If it was with you.

So we laced fingers
And mounted the sky
And looked down on the earth and on the sea
And the land we had left behind.

Now, high above the world,
We laugh and love
And eat our juicy peaches
And see how the juice runs down our arms.

'That is so beautiful, Frieda,' said Carl, and they sipped their wine. 'I see a real change in you of late. Your poetry, your painting, your loving. And even your skin is glowing.'

'It is because of you, Carl,' she whispered. 'You have given me such self-confidence. I never thought of myself as talented. The focus was always on Jack: so clever and charismatic. I thought I was ordinary, but you have made me feel that I do have a gift for painting and that I am worth something.'

'There is nothing ordinary about you, Frieda. You are very special. It is sad that no-one has ever made you aware of that before. I sensed it that very first evening that we met. It was obvious how wonderful you were, but it was hidden, like a flower under leaves which just needs someone to uncover it.'

They kissed and drank wine and for a few hours, Frieda allowed herself to believe that they were living together and that they were in their home. They were having an evening together, that's all, sharing some wine and doing what couples do. It was only when the bottle was empty that they needed to leave.

They locked up the studio and Carl walked her a little way up the hill. Then they kissed goodbye and she continued, light-headed, back to her house.

The children were fast asleep. Jack returned late from the taverna, and settled for the night on the sofa.

In her bed, Frieda closed her eyes and felt dizzy with love, sick with deceit.

As soon as Marianne heard the jingle of the goat bell, her heart sank. 'She's here,' she called to Leonard. 'You're going to have to make an effort.'

She smoothed her hair as she ran down the stairs and opened the door. In front of her was a small woman, dressed in layers, a cardigan draped over her shoulders like wings, in spite of the oppressive heat. Marianne could immediately see the features that she and Leonard shared: dark hair, high cheekbones, beautiful eyes.

'That ride was the most uncomfortable experience of my life,' she said, struggling through the front door with so many suitcases that Marianne worried for the donkey's welfare. 'I'm Masha, Leonard's mother.'

'How do you do? I'm Marianne.'

The mule boy tapped the animal and led it sulkily away.

For a few moments the women stared at each other and tried to take the other in, like acclimatising to a different country: a slender, blonde woman and a dark-haired short one; a Norwegian accent and a Russian-Canadian one; his lover and his mother.

Leonard came down the stairs. He was still gaunt, but he had shaved and washed for his mother's sake. Marianne wondered why he couldn't do the same for her. The last few weeks had been hell with Leonard fasting, addicted to his amphetamines, working obsessively day and night, sweating, hallucinating, neglecting her and Axel Joachim, which had puzzled the boy and made him tearful, confused as Leonard had changed from a friend to a stranger.

'Hello, Mother.' Leonard kissed her politely on the cheek and carried her cases miserably upstairs.

'Ach! The heat! I'm telling you, it's gonna kill me!'

Don't give me cause for hope, thought Leonard but he smiled and said, 'Let's get you inside, Mother, and cool you down.'

They led her into the living room, the shutters keeping the sun out. Books lined the walls, and the only furniture was a sofa, chair and a small table. Leonard liked to live simply, fearing that too much clutter would impede his ability to write. Masha looked round disapprovingly. It made a monastery look lavish.

Marianne gave her a cold drink, and Masha had a chance to see her son clearly. 'Leonard,' she began, shaking her head. 'You look terrible. You're wasting away. I can see you aren't eating properly.' She turned to Marianne. 'When he was a child, he loved to eat, and I fed him chicken soup, kneidlach, lokshen pudding, doughnuts. I'd spend half the night cooking for him. That's what you do when you love someone.'

'Leave it, Mother. I've been busy with my novel.'

'Novel shnovel! You should have taken over the clothing business when your father died. That would have been better for you, not writing these terrible, depressing books that make people lose the will to live. What's the point of it? You're too sensitive, Leonard, I've always told you that, haven't I?'

Leonard covered his face with his hands and it seemed to Marianne that Masha had, within minutes, transformed him from a brooding, sexy man into an agonised adolescent.

Masha turned to Marianne. 'You know what happened when he lost Tinkie?'

'Tinkie?'

'For God's sake, Mother.'

'Leonard, don't blaspheme.'

She turned again to Marianne. 'His Scottish terrier. Ach, did he adore him! And then Tinkie died, was lost in a snowstorm, and the following spring he was found, dead, under the neighbour's porch. Oy, was Leonard broken-hearted? I'll tell you something, that boy was devastated, cried for days. Isn't that right, Leonard?'

'Mother, I'm sure that Marianne doesn't want to...'

'What? Are you embarrassed that you cried for your dog?'

They heard Axel Joachim wake from his sleep. 'I'll just go and fetch my son,' said Marianne, feeling quite worried about Masha's stay.

Once she was out of the room, Masha leant forward to her son: 'Are you and that woman...'

'Marianne.'

'Yes, Marianne. Are you with her?'

'Yes, I am, Mother.'

89

'So that's what it's come to, Leonard, a blonde shiksa with a baby living on a Greek island with drug addicts and painters who can't earn a decent living?'

'That's what I've chosen. Yes.'

'But why, Leonard, why? I can't understand it. You could have stayed with Freda Gutman, a lovely girl, and joined your uncles in the business. You could have lived in Westmount and been company for me, Leonard. Since Harry and I separated, it's been lonely for me with Esther now married to Victor and busy with their own lives and I miss you so much and...'

Into the room came Marianne carrying Axel Joachim. He had just woken from his nap, his cheeks pink and soft, rubbing his sleepy eyes, his blonde hair ruffled.

'Oh hello, sweetie,' said Masha, jumping up to see the baby. 'What a beauty.'

To the surprise of Leonard and Marianne, Axel Joachim let Masha hold him and she fell in love with the baby at once.

'Ach, is this baby a doll or what? I'll tell you something. I've never seen such a beautiful child in my whole life.'

Axel Joachim leant his head against Masha's chest and fingered the beads around her neck.

'You are something else,' she said cooing. 'What a little angel,' and she held him tightly.

Over the next week, Marianne took Masha around the island, leaving Leonard at home to write. Axel Joachim continued to woo Masha and she fell more and more in love with him. One day, they took a picnic in Kamini where the water was so clear that they could see the rocks and coral on the seabed, as if they had been preserved beneath glass.

Another time, Mikalis and Spyros took them on a beautiful boat trip around the coastline, pointing out the dolphins and turtles gracing the emerald sea. As they sat on the boat, Masha's eyes filled with tears.

'I have really enjoyed today. Thank you. Let me tell you, Marianne, I am very lonely,' she sobbed.

Marianne put her hand gently on the older woman's arm.

'For many years, I was on my own but then I married again. Harry, a pharmacist. He got MS, sadly – I think he knew he was developing it when we got married – and I nursed him, that was my training after all, but we weren't happy and we decided to go our own way. He moved to Florida, better for his condition. Your children grow up, your friends are busy and the next thing you know, you are totally alone.' The tears fell softly down her face. 'I do read and go to concerts, but I miss Leonard so badly. After his father died, he was the man of the house, doing the Brachot, helping me. He is very special.'

'I know,' said Marianne kindly. 'You can come and see us whenever you like, Masha.'

They embraced while Masha sobbed. 'Thank you, Marianne. You have a very kind heart.'

Marianne showed Masha their special landmarks, letting her wheel Axel Joachim in his pushchair. They went to Demi's bakery where Masha bought bread for the baby to suck and Marianne showed her the communal ovens. She introduced Masha to some friends on Hydra who she thought she would like: Olivia, always warm and gregarious, and Gordon and Chuck, without explaining the nature of their bond. When they saw Axel and Sonja, in the distance, Marianne waved without telling Masha that it was her husband and his lover. She wasn't lying, she told herself, just holding back certain pieces of information that might shock her.

One day, they were in Katsikas' store, buying chickens for Masha to cook for their Shabbat meal. Masha was rather horrified when Katsikas brought out two, their drooping heads and clawed feet still attached. Marianne made a chopping signal to Katsikas and he understood, carrying them out like limp puppets and bringing them back a few minutes later, amputees.

'Hi, Marianne,' said Magda, her bright red hair matched by a crimson dress and orange beaded necklace so that she looked like she had been set alight.

Marianne embraced Magda. 'This is Masha, Leonard's mother.'

'Oh, how lovely to meet you, Mrs Cohen,' said Magda. 'I see where Leonard gets his good looks from.'

'Oh, why thank you.' Masha put her hands coyly to her face.

'I'm so pleased I bumped into you. It's the opening of my new wine bar, Lagoudera, tomorrow. You are all invited.' She turned to Masha. 'You too, of course. I have bought the old boathouse and renovated it. It's amazing. I'm so pleased with it. Please come.'

Back at the house, Leonard prepared the Shabbat candles, wine and bread from Demi's (no challah, but a sweet white loaf) and Masha worked side by side with the maid in the kitchen. The arrangement didn't work out well, Kyria Sophia annoyed at having her space invaded and Masha restricted by what she could prepare on the two-ringed cooker. Leonard and Marianne spoke in hushed voices in the living room.

'Thank you, Marianne,' he said. 'I am very grateful to you for looking after my mother so well and giving me time to write.'

'That's okay. Axel Joachim has helped so much, Leonard. She adores him. But when she goes, you need to pay more attention to us. We are your family here.'

'I know. I will. Has my mother said when she's leaving?'

'I don't know. She says she has an open ticket, but I don't think she's in any hurry to go.'

'Shit.'

'When we were in Katsikas, we saw Magda and she invited us all to go to the opening of her new wine bar Lagoudera tomorrow. Even your mother.'

'Shit again.'

'Exactly. What are we going to do?'

'I will talk to her.'

Masha was so happy to be with her son on Shabbat, the first time in years. He lit the candles, sang the blessings and she beamed with happiness. Marianne's heart went out to her. She knew how lonely she had felt with Axel before she had met Leonard: isolation could eat you away. She felt a pang of guilt but then she consoled herself: even if Leonard were not living with her, he would not be living with his mother.

Masha proudly brought out the pot of chicken soup. It was a hot meal to eat in the July weather, but it tasted good.

'Lovely,' said Leonard. 'It's got a lovely flavour.'

'Well, I found some herbs on the terrace, oregano, I think, and I added a few leaves in.'

Marianne and Leonard looked at each other in horror: the marijuana plants.

'Mother,' said Leonard tentatively and Marianne noted that he seemed afraid of her. 'I don't think you would enjoy going to Magda's wine bar opening tomorrow. It's not really your thing.'

'Don't tell me what my thing is, Leonard. If I want to go, I'll go. Anyway, Magda's invited me.'

Lagoudera was lit by candles and kerosene lamps so that from the outside it looked like it had been overtaken by pyromaniacs, albeit romantic ones. On the roof, two dinghies had been positioned to acknowledge its sailing history. Friends had worked for days to help Magda prepare: little tables and chairs; more comfortable seating areas in the corners with sequinned cushions; rugs and fishermen's nets hanging on the walls; a bar made of rough wood from discarded boats; and jars of burning incense.

Masha hardly knew where to rest her eyes. It was a world away from her home in Montreal which was large and light and spacious. Rooms were divided by frosted glass and she had subtly lit display cabinets with Judaica, silver artefacts, and photos of her family.

'Let me get you a drink, Mother,' said Leonard, sounding grumpy and resentful. She had been with them for a fortnight now and he had felt himself struggling to breathe. Marianne would not sleep with him in case his mother heard them.

'I think she might have guessed that we are together now, Marianne,' Leonard remonstrated, but she would not bend.

'It's not respectful,' she said.

Leonard thought: we are so alike. We both carry the bourgeois conventions of our childhood like a cloak and have not, in spite of trying, shrugged them off.

They knew most of the guests at Lagoudera: Norman Peterson, happy after his exhibition but still thin and malnourished; Gordon and Chuck who she had met before ('Are they brothers?' asked Masha); Charmian and George; Jack and Frieda, and Olivia; John Dragoumis, his long white beard and squashed pudding hat fascinating to Masha. Everyone was friendly to her and soon she was dancing in the centre of a circle with the group clapping around her and the music blaring from a radio.

Dazed and excited by her newfound popularity, Masha twirled and spun, her short figure dressed more for synagogue than a wine bar. They passed her drinks and she swigged, then danced, then smoked a joint, then danced again.

Leonard pulled Marianne aside. 'Tell me I'm having one of my hallucinations, Marianne,' he whispered, 'or is my mother really dancing in the middle of Lagoudera with everyone watching?'

'Calm down, Leonard. She's having a great time.'

'Yes, but I'm not.'

Leonard went over to his mother who seemed to be spinning in a kind of frenzy now, a whirling dervish. 'Mother,' he pulled at her sleeve, 'I think we need to get you home now. It's late.'

'Leave me alone, Leonard.' She shrugged him away. 'You know what? I'm enjoying myself for the first time in years and I am not going.'

Suddenly, to Leonard's horror, many hands lifted her into the air, where she spread her limbs out like a starfish and allowed herself to be twirled.

When Masha was returned to the floor again, she lost her balance and collapsed and Leonard and Marianne had to put her, slumped, onto a donkey and walk it slowly up the dark velvety hills of Hydra, one of them at each side.

The following morning, nearer lunchtime than breakfast, Masha awoke with a terrible headache. Her face was drained of colour. She summoned Leonard and Marianne.

'Thank you for having me to stay,' she said carefully, 'but I think it's time for me to go back home. Let me tell you something. Your friends are very nice but it's not quite my scene.'

A few weeks later, a parcel arrived at the post office and Marianne brought it back to the house. Inside were gifts from Masha: a toy panda for Axel Joachim, rubber gloves for Kyria Sophia, Leonard's father's old Kiddush cup for Shabbat wine, and a floral headscarf for Marianne.

'How kind of her,' said Marianne. 'I grew very fond of your mother.'

'Really?' said Leonard. 'Why?'

'Because she is a good soul and she has suffered.'

After Masha's departure, Leonard had taken a short break from his writing and Marianne felt that he had, at least temporarily, returned to her and Axel Joachim; but now he was deep in his writing and fasting again. He may have complained about his mother but at least she had returned him to the fold.

Marianne missed his company, their conversations, their long meals on the terrace, being a unit of three, and the feel and smell of him.

'You know, Leonard, do you ever wonder how Axel Joachim and I feel?' Marianne placed his daily gardenia on his desk. He did not look up but stopped typing for a moment.

'What do you mean?'

'Sometimes you are involved with us, loving and giving, and then suddenly you are absent as if you are not even here. It is very difficult. We miss you so much.'

Leonard turned and buried his head in her chest. The smell of her, the warmth of her, the way her body curved – he longed for her.

'I am truly sorry,' he said, 'but I have to write, Marianne. I cannot explain it to you. I have no choice. My novel is a corpse and I have to work on it with my scalpel.'

She ran her fingers through his dark hair and bent to kiss him full on the mouth. It tasted strange and she wondered what he had been taking.

'This morning, Axel is coming to see his son and then later, after he has gone, the three of us are going out together as a family.'

She went out of the room, closing the door behind her. She heard him typing again.

When Axel arrived, Marianne led him onto the shaded part of the terrace where Axel Joachim was playing on a rug. He had his wooden giraffe and tin soldiers to play with. The harbour shimmered in the morning sun. Citronella candles burned in tins, to deter the circling mosquitoes.

'Why have you not brought him to our house lately?' he asked, looking at the boy as if at a stranger.

'It is too confusing for him with all your various women: first Patricia, now Sonja, and who knows how long she'll last? The child needs consistency.'

Axel looked sullen.

Kyria Sophia brought them coffee, and apple juice for the baby. Marianne saw how disapproving she looked as she left: this crazy family.

'If you would come back to me, Marianne, we could be a family unit again.'

'You mean until you grew tired of us and found a new woman?'

'What do you see in Leonard? He is not good enough for you.'

'I hear that *Line* caused some controversy?'

'Yeah. That's good, isn't it? I don't want my work to be bland.'

'How's your new novel going, Axel?'

His eyes lit up. 'My fourth. Actually, it's called *Joacim*,' he pointed to his son, 'but before you worry, it's not about us. Or our son. Joacim is in advertising and is married to Cecilie but he is searching for meaning in his life and wants to be an artist. He takes his family to a Greek island…'

'That sounds familiar.'

'…and he falls in love with a Danish student. He is torn between his duty to his family and his desire for his art and his lover.'

'Don't tell me: I am Cecilie, the abandoned wife?'

'No, you are not. True, the novel is set in Oslo and Greece and I write in the first person so readers might assume that it is autobiographical, but I have to draw on my experience. Where is my material supposed to come from? Believe me, Cecilie does not do you justice, Marianne. No-one could be as beautiful as you.'

'It is easy to say that now, Axel. You did not always appreciate me.'

'I hold myself largely responsible for what happened to us, Marianne. I want you to know that.'

'Really? You've never said that before.'

'Well, I am saying it today.'

96

'Have you heard from John Starr Cooke?'

'Yes. I write letters to him and the nurse replies for him. You know he is paralysed since the insect bite?'

'You told me. It's so sad. More coffee, Axel?'

He stayed for two hours and by the time he had left, Marianne realised that he had not asked her a single question about herself or shown any interest in his son.

Marianne gave Axel Joachim his lunch, he had a nap and she read some of *The Tibetan Book of the Dead* which Magda had lent her; then she went to see Leonard in his study. He had not eaten the food that she had left him and he looked tired and wan. Prickly stubble darkened his chin.

'Leonard,' she whispered, 'you promised that you would come out with us just to get some fresh air and then you can write again.' To her amazement he obeyed.

They walked for half an hour across Kala Pigadia. The sun was intense and Marianne had put a hat on Axel Joachim and cream on his arms to protect him from burning. She wheeled the pushchair, Leonard by her side.

They went to Demosthenes, the barber, to have their hair cut. Inside it was plain: stone walls, two chairs, a mirror in front of each, and a crucifix on the wall. There were no basins at all: if he needed to moisten your hair, he poured water from a bottle into his large hands and sprinkled your head, so the islanders joked that you could get your hair cut and be baptised in one go. Demosthenes was bald, which did not inspire confidence in his haircutting skill, but everyone went to him. Leonard reluctantly sat in the chair first. The black locks fell to the stone floor as the barber chatted in a language they didn't understand, as if the words were his rhythm, his music, spurring him on. Leonard rubbed his hands over his shorn head.

Marianne liked to wear her hair short in the heat and Demosthenes trimmed it now, adding her blonde curls on top of Leonard's.

Axel Joachim cried when it was his turn so he had to sit on Marianne's lap. The soft locks of his hair fell like snow. They paid Demosthenes and Marianne saw, before she left his shop, how their hair had combined in one heap on the floor and it brought tears to her eyes, how connected they were – or rather they would be temporarily – until Demosthenes took his brush and swept them away.

The island was bright with colour and light, as if someone had been up early and painted it as gaudily as they could. Camellias caught the sun like mirrors in their bleached blooms and blood-red hibiscus seemed a warning of danger.

The Gardenia Dwarf was out in the garden, pinching dead leaves with her pincer-fingers. Donkeys walked slowly by, loads of fruit and vegetables on their backs, the mule boys snapping at their sides.

Men were installing electric wires across the island so that phones could be used.

They stopped at Katsikas' and sat at the back where they drank cool lemonade from curved bottles. Marianne remembered her first meeting with Leonard all those months before. Little had she known then what awaited them, what challenges they would face. Axel Joachim had fallen asleep and Marianne parked the pushchair under the shady pine tree.

'There are some wires by my study window now,' said Leonard. 'This morning, I looked up briefly to gaze at the almond blossom as I wrote, and the men were there, placing these dark lines across my vision. It was as if the modern world was impinging on the mystical one. Time upon timelessness. A stain on perfection. Man's destruction of nature. The birds perching there looked like notes on a stave.'

'You could write a great song about that.'

'I have started one.'

'It might be good for us to have a phone, though?'

'Don't tell my mother! She'll ring every day.'

'I like Masha.'

'I know you do.' He smiled gratefully at her. 'I do, too.'

For the second time that day, Marianne heard of the dilemma of responsibility versus desire. 'Actually, I have been writing the lyrics for a song, *Bird on a Wire*. It just came to me and I was thinking of you. I wrote that if I was unkind to you, I didn't mean it but that I was torn. Between my writing and you. Between the familiar and the new, between stability and risk.'

Marianne smiled, and the sun caught her hair.

'I don't know where my writing comes from. I don't even know if it is any good, but I feel that I am beholden to it. I am not the master. I am the servant. It controls me. It comes and demands to be written.'

That afternoon, Leonard went back to work and Marianne took Axel Joachim to play with Charmian's son, Jason, on their terrace. Jason had brought out some books for the boy and was reading to him. The sight of the older blonde boy with the younger blonde boy moved her.

Charmian knocked back a glass of whisky in one go and dragged on a cigarette. 'You know, Marianne,' she said, 'that man drives me crazy.'

Marianne smiled politely. Sometimes she tired of the Johnstons' quarrels, wished that they would sort themselves out rather than airing it all in front of friends, and more importantly, their children. Charmian did not care that Jason was within earshot. There was no attempt to protect him from adult issues.

'He only thinks about himself and his writing. Nothing else matters to him. Not me. Not the children. He is the centre of his own little world. He doesn't rate anyone else's work. The arrogance of the man. He thinks that he is the only person on the planet who can write.'

'I suppose writers and artists have to believe their work matters or else why bother?'

'But why are writers special? Maybe doctors and teachers take their work seriously, but they don't then look down on others in the same field, do they? Are they competitive in the same way?'

'Creativity is hard. I try to write and draw but I get nowhere. I have ideas but I can never see them through.'

'It's because you are not conceited enough. You don't have a strong enough sense of your own importance. You are more interested in bending to the needs of others than satisfying your own.'

Walking back home, Marianne remembered what Charmian had said. She probably meant it kindly but it made her feel as if she were nothing: less substantial than the summer poppies which only lasted a few days before shedding their paper-thin petals on the ground.

That evening, when the baby was asleep, Marianne and Leonard made love more intensely than ever. It had been weeks since they had really connected and it was as if they had stored their passion up for that occasion. They loved and kissed each other with energy and a desire to be as close to each other as they could be. Even when Leonard had entered Marianne, he felt that he wanted to be more inside her, more connected to her, more with her and to never be apart from her again. They cried and moaned and licked the tears from each other's faces.

Marianne slept well that night but when she awoke in the early morning, the other side of the bed was empty.

Leonard was typing again.

The intense summer heat made the island more fertile. Citrus groves bulged with orange and yellow globes which hung like coloured lightbulbs among the shiny leaves. Fig trees heavy with fruit lowered their branches to the ground like boats allowing their passengers safely to disembark. The black spheres burst open like overfull sacks of grain, releasing their sticky seeds in a gluey syrup, much to the delight of wasps. Peaches and plums swelled with their own juicy importance and grew fat.

In this time of growth, death was the last thing on their minds.

Kyria Sophia was the first to bring the news. She came rushing into the house one morning, her face blotchy with tears. She mimed strangling to Marianne, her hands around her own throat.

'What is it, my dear? What's happened?'

'Spyros,' the maid wailed. 'Spyros,' and she ran from the room, weeping.

Not long after, Magda came by Marianne's house, her usually rosy face ashen. She was carrying her dark-haired son Alexander, who she put on the floor beside Axel Joachim. The boys stared at each other and then played with their own toys.

'Oh, it's so awful, have you heard, Marianne?'

'What? Kyria Sophia was trying to tell me something.'

'Spyros, the son of Mikalis, the boatman, he got caught in his rope when he was mooring and has died.'

'Oh my god. Poor boy. He was so lovely and young. And poor Mikalis.'

'Yes, he is already a widower. Spyros was his life. Will you come with me this evening to view the body, in the church? The Greeks always have their funerals soon after death.'

'Of course, Magda,' she said.

Later, the two women walked up the hill together leaving Kyria Sophia to mind the boys. Most people were wearing black and the body lay in an open casket in the church hall. Mikalis wept, tears running down the grooves in his leathery face. The papos was there in his black cloak and high headdress, a large wooden cross on his chest, muttering prayers and

101

incantations. They filed past in an orderly line, forming a square of mourners around the coffin. When Marianne looked inside, she saw a young boy taken away in his prime. His dark hair and handsome face seemed unsuited to death. Tears filled her eyes and Magda held her hand. That night the bell in the waterfront tower rang solemnly, as it did whenever there was a death on the island.

There were no spare seats in the little stone church the following day and many people had to stand. It occurred to Marianne that there were not many times on Hydra when they all came together as a community. There were fishermen and sailors comforting Mikalis; maids such as Evgeniya, Maria, Agape, Sevasty and Kyria Sophia; Demi the baker; Douskos from the taverna with his wife Polixenes and her mother, The Gardenia Dwarf; Demosthenes, the barber; Vassilis, the crippled sponge diver, and Francisco, the carpenter, as well as Tzimmi, the log deliverer. Many of the expat artists attended, too: Magda, toned down in black with no adornments; George and Charmian; Frieda and Jack; Norman, who had made an effort by trimming his beard and wearing a clean (but crumpled) shirt; Olivia and Georgos; and trembling John Dragoumis in a black hat.

The coffin was once again open and the congregation stood when the papos entered. The building was heavy with incense and smoke from the fat white candles. The foreigners did not understand the words of the priest, nor did they recognise the prayers or hymns, but they stood quietly, respectfully, and felt part of the event even without the language.

The weeping of Mikalis needed no translation.

After the service, they all moved to the graveyard on the hillside behind the church. Spyros' coffin was buried deep in the ground, a cross on its lid moulded from soil, and people threw single roses on top. The papos chanted in pain as if it were his own son who had died.

The following evening, people gathered at Mikalis' humble home for the wake, or makaria. There was not enough room for everyone so some mourners stood on the cobbles outside and the windows were open to the night. Friends brought food: bread, cakes, pots of stew, fruit, and people ate modestly and quietly, talking in low voices. Mikalis' face was red as if he had not stopped crying.

After that, he gave up his job. His brother Alexis took over and Mikalis turned his attention from the boat to the bottle. Anyone passing his cottage at night could hear him sing songs of the sea and dirges in a wailing, mournful voice.

Frieda would walk a different way down to the harbour to avoid hearing his moans if Esther was with her. The little girl had a tendency to get upset, and Mikalis' laconic singing could pierce the heart.

'Why are we going this way, Mummy?'

'I thought it would make a nice change, sweetie.'

Marianne was upset for days after the funeral. Although Leonard was still writing crazily, not eating and being very distant, he did come out from his study when he heard her crying.

'You know, my love,' he said, holding her close to him, 'that the ash we become is the testimony to our lives, that the more fully we live, the more fully we die.'

'But you and I are hardly living together any more,' she sobbed. 'We were so close. You write all the time and I understand your need to do that but I feel that we are growing apart, Leonard. Being at the funeral yesterday has just reminded me that life is so short, that it will soon be over. We only have a little while. Please spend some time with me.'

'It's the writing, Marianne. It isn't a question of you coming first, or it coming first, but I want and need you both.'

'We've been invited onto Onassis' yacht this afternoon. Will you come with us or must I be a widow again?'

'I'm sorry, Marianne. I absolutely have to write.'

'Magda will come with me then. Do you think I am wrong going on a yacht when Spyros has just died?'

'Marianne,' said Leonard, looking her directly in her eyes. 'It is life and death and shit and orchids. There is no division here. It is all connected. Just go.'

They had met Aristotle Onassis at one of Olivia's many parties and he had immediately found Marianne attractive. With her blonde hair, fair skin and blue eyes, she stood out from the swarthy Greeks around her.

Onassis, grey hair swept back, a tanned, sculpted face, and wearing a blazer and cravat, sharp linen trousers and suede loafers, oozed money and sophistication.

'Where are you from, my dear?' he had asked, intrigued.

'Norway.'

'Oh, I have been salmon fishing there. It is so beautiful. And what are you doing on Hydra?'

'My husband is a writer and so is my lover.' She blushed at her own candour.

'Splendid.' He smiled warmly. 'Well, you must come on my yacht sometime, with either one of your men, or both, or preferably neither.' He smirked at his own flirtatiousness.

In the end, she had gone with Magda who, having been on the yacht before, dressed in white with silver necklaces and earrings. Marianne had worried about what to wear, settling in the end for a buttercup-yellow dress which matched her hair. She felt her leather sandals were too casual but they were all she had.

Christina O was a huge yacht, moored close to the harbour. As Magda and Marianne embarked, they were greeted by stewards in white uniforms who offered them champagne. The women stared at all around them: a helipad and an outdoor pool with a minotaur-themed mosaic floor, flanked by carved dolphins from whose mouths more champagne spurted.

'The floor of the pool becomes a dance floor,' said Magda, 'at the push of a button. There is a master suite and eighteen staterooms, and in the drinking area, known as Ari's bar, the barstools are covered in material made from the foreskins of whales.'

Marianne shifted nervously: she felt horribly out of place and wished she was back in her simple house with Leonard and her baby.

'Hello, you found us,' said a voice and they turned to see Onassis coming towards them. Once again, he was dressed like a naval officer and his grey hair was swept back. 'I am so happy to see you.' He kissed each woman on both cheeks. 'Please follow me.' They saw the gold rings on his fingers catch the light.

He led them down a spiral staircase that resembled the polished inside of a shell to a dining room, laid with white linen tablecloths and napkins. Young pretty women in diamonds flirted with older, pot-bellied men at tables, and Onassis directed Magda and Marianne to one of those. Introductions were made but Marianne was so overwhelmed that she could not take in the names.

'Look over there,' Magda whispered, pointing to Onassis' head table. 'His ex-lover Maria Callas, and Richard Burton and Elizabeth Taylor. Aren't they handsome?'

The meal included caviar, salmon and crab shaped into little towers, followed by lobster and oysters on beds of crushed ice with lemon wedges at their sides. The room was full of laughter and chatter.

Afterwards they were served toppling mounds of chocolate profiteroles and lemon mousse which melted on the tongue; then they went up on the deck and sat by the pool, dipping their toes in the water, drinking coffee from tiny cups.

'You know,' said Magda, conspiratorially, 'they say that Onassis is seeing Jackie Kennedy. What a scandal – with her husband having been assassinated only two years ago and him being involved with her sister, Lee. So exciting! I love it!'

When it was time for the dream to end, the women thanked Onassis. He bowed graciously. 'The pleasure has been all mine. Please come and see us again, here, or on Skorpios, my island.'

Walking back from the harbour to their homes, the women held hands and giggled.

'How do we reciprocate?' asked Marianne. 'Do you think he would like to have beans and cold meats with my baby and me on the terrace?'

'Probably,' said Magda, 'he would love it.'

And they laughed.

That evening, she tried to describe it all to Leonard. They were on the terrace on a warm summer's evening, with a welcome breeze blowing in from the harbour.

'Sometimes I find life so confusing.'

'Why?' He felt guilty for ignoring her for so long and so tried to focus on her words, even though his mind was still obsessed with the song he had been working on. Maybe he would leave out the last verse?

'Because I can't make sense of it. On the one hand, there is Mikalis weeping for his dead son. And then there is Onassis and his yacht and crab and lobsters.'

'I think your mistake is seeing it all as different or as two contrasting events.'

'Aren't they?'

'No. They are all part of the same. Life and death are not opposites to each other. They are the same as each other. It is all there: the darkness and light; death and birth; love and hate. They are one. The rose and the thorn tree grow from the same earth. The lion and the mouse are of the same matter. If you embrace the light, you also embrace the darkness.'

Marianne listened, amazed. She could not totally accept what he meant.

But when he took her hand, circled her palm with his thumb and then bent forward to kiss her, she thought: now I understand.

Leonard did not really like the cables that sliced dark lines across the view from his study windows – and through his beloved almond blossom tree, as if dissecting it – but the new telephones connected the Hydra community to the world. True, Masha rang too often for his liking, as did his sister, but it also meant that publishers and editors could be more in touch. His work was being appreciated overseas, especially in America, and he was frequently phoned for interviews and comments. His novels were well received but didn't make much money and he felt sure that the songs and poems were the way ahead.

One day, Marianne came back from Katsikas' post office with a package for Leonard. He opened it and was thrilled to see the first edition of his new collection of poetry, *Flowers for Hitler*.

'Look, my love,' he said excitedly, showing her the title page. To her delight she saw the dedication: *For Marianne*. He turned to page 52 and the poem he had written for her. Marianne's eyes filled with tears as she read the words about her and about Hydra.

'Leonard,' she said, 'I am so proud of you.'

'I don't know if this compensates for the misery I have brought you but maybe you realise that I have not been totally wasting my time.'

She held the book close to her chest and knew that she would treasure it. She had a mother of pearl box full of his gifts: the Yves San Laurent tortoiseshell mirror he had given her; a pair of tiny scissors shaped like a bird with the blades as its beak, opening and shutting; a collection of poems by Lorca; and an anemone flower that he had picked on a lovely walk and then pressed between books.

Usually when the phone rang it was for Leonard: his publisher, his agent, a radio presenter asking for an interview, but Marianne's mother sometimes also called from Norway. One morning it rang and it was Magda.

'Marianne, it's me.'

'Magda? You sound upset. What's wrong?'

'Just my idiot husband again. He's run off with an Egyptian princess he fell in love with. He met her at the Hilton Hotel in Athens. I knew he was seeing other women.'

'Oh god.'

'That's not the worst of it. He got in trouble with the police but they can't find him, so I took the blame, was arrested and covered for him.'

'What? Why?'

'Because I'm crazy, I suppose. I'm in Athens now and I have a court case looming.'

'That is terrible. Do you want me to come, Magda?'

'No, you've got the baby and Leonard to cope with. I'll let you know what happens. Please tell everyone that Lagoudera is shut in the meantime.'

'What will happen to little Alexander?'

'Charmian and George have him at the moment: he loves their three children so he will be happy there, but we will have to see what happens. Pray for me, Marianne.'

She heard Magda's voice crack. Marianne didn't believe the Johnston household was the best place for a child, but she said nothing. Poor Alexander. Poor Magda.

'Bye, Magda, my love. Be strong.'

Magda was special to her, warm and protective, and to think of her suffering when she had done nothing wrong made Marianne's face burn.

Each time she dressed Axel Joachim and brushed his hair, she thought of Magda and what she must be enduring, and about that poor little child who had lost both his parents. Marianne prayed that the judge would see that she was innocent and release her.

All the way to Axel, steering the pushchair along the sandy track, Marianne thought: life, it is so unpredictable. Today had started with a dedication but had turned to bad news.

She never knew what mood Axel would be in, sometimes angry and moody, other times calm. She wondered why she took the little boy to see him when Axel showed little interest in his son, but she was still hankering after a perfect family unit, although she knew that she was deluded.

A happy, smiling Axel opened the door.

'Come in,' he said and ruffled his son's hair.

On the terrace, Maria brought out white wine, and juice for the baby.

'You look happy,' said Marianne, bemused. She lifted her glass. 'What are we celebrating?'

'*Line* is going to be made into a film.'

'That is amazing, Axel. Congratulations. When?'

'They are casting it now and searching for the best actors.'

'I have a suggestion,' said Marianne coyly. 'Maybe I could play Line?'

'You?' Axel downed his drink and laughed. 'You are not an actress.'

'I have not acted, that is true, but do you remember in Oslo when I worked on the film *Tonny*?'

'That was production work, not acting, Marianne.'

'I know but the director, Sver Gran, said that I had a real feeling for film. Also, remember I have done a lot of modelling for painters and magazines.'

'Modelling is not the same as acting, Marianne. They are thinking of casting Margarete Robsahm as Line and Toralv Maurstad as Jacob.'

'I see.' Marianne put down her glass. One could not argue with Axel. All that proofreading she had done, and the fact that Line was so clearly based on her, obviously meant nothing to him.

She stayed a while longer. Axel hardly bothered with his son but talked about the film, his next novel which was going well, and his blossoming career.

On the walk home, Axel Joachim slept. Usually Marianne looked at the poppies and anemones growing randomly along the path but today she did not see them. Her heart was racing. It was flattering to have books dedicated to her and to be seen as a muse, but it made her wonder who she was. Was she there merely to inspire and help others or did she have any value of her own? Was she substantial, or merely a floating spirit entering the minds of talented writers while they slept?

As she walked distractedly back to the house, she saw Charmian in a long white kaftan, the bottom dirty as if she had been traipsing through mud, and a wide straw hat. She looked ashen and there were black lines beneath her eyes.

'Darling.' It was obvious that she had been drinking heavily even though it was only mid-afternoon. 'Good news. My *Mermaid Singing* has had great reviews in America and Britain. One paper even said that I had changed the face of travel writing!'

'That's lovely, Charmian.'

'Yes. Now I'm writing *Peel Me a Lotus*, moving the focus from Kalymnos to Hydra.'

'Wonderful.'

'But you look unhappy, Marianne. What is it?'

'Oh, you know, Leonard, Axel, Magda. Isn't it awful?'

'Yes, it's terrible. The poor woman has done nothing wrong. Fucking men. That's all they're good for and my poor husband can't even manage that these days!'

'How is George?'

'Not great. Dr Benedictus says it is either tuberculosis or lung disease and he wants to refer him to the hospital in Athens, but George won't go. He's not in a good way. It would help if he could stop smoking or drinking but he won't listen.'

'That's frustrating.'

'It is. He's lost so much weight, he looks scrawny, but he's mad about his writing. He's onto the next book in the trilogy and he's obsessed with it. Thank heavens I have Anthony to satisfy my needs.'

By the time Charmian had staggered home, she could hardly see straight. In her house the noise was overwhelming. She could hear the children in the living room, screaming and laughing, but she was seeing double.

'Hey everyone,' she called.

'Hi, Mum,' called Shane. 'You pissed again?'

'Not at all,' said Charmian. 'How's the baby?'

On Shane's knee was little Alexander, overwhelmed, and on the verge of tears.

'We've been trying to play with him and tell him stories,' said Jason, 'but he keeps crying.'

'He's missing his mummy.' Charmian belched. 'Pardon me.'

Shane looked up, parting her blonde hair: 'Mummy, Martin's come first in Classical and Modern Greek at school.'

'Have you, darling? I'm not surprised. You are a genius. Maybe now the teacher will stop saying that the English are beasts and bloody butchers.'

'Well, we're not English,' Martin corrected her. 'We're Australian.'

'No, we're not.' Shane thumped him. 'We're British.'

'No, we're not, stupid. We're Greek,' said Jason bouncing the baby on his knee. Alexander started bawling.

'We are not Greek,' shouted Martin. 'Imbecile!' and the children started hitting each other.

Sevasty stormed into the room, picked up the baby, muttered something and took him to a quieter room.

Charmian walked out, tripped over a stray cat that had installed itself in the hallway and burst into George's smoky study. She saw the ashtray full of fag ends, an empty bottle of gin on the table and piles of typed pages. 'You just do your fucking writing, that's it, and leave the house in chaos and the kids punching each other and the poor baby crying its eyes out. You just carry on.'

George leapt from his chair and shook her. 'You've been drinking again, and you're wasted, so don't go making out that you're the mother of the year.'

'How dare you speak to me like that? I'm a brilliant mother to all my children.'

'What? Including Jennifer who you only kept for two weeks before you gave her away?'

'Don't you drag her into this. There's not a day goes by when I don't think about her. You're a hypocrite. What about Gae? You were happy to leave Elsie to bring her up on her own, weren't you?'

'Yes, I left her for you. Biggest bloody mistake of my life!'

'Oh, I thought Melbourne was too provincial for you? All those trams and grey skies and suburbia. What do you call it: antirrhinums?

'Leaving Melbourne was the best thing I ever did. Marrying you was the worst.'

And she lunged at him, punching him in the face, trying to grab at his hair; he tried to stop her, her breath foul from drink, his stale with nicotine, and he shouted and coughed at the same time: 'Control yourself, Charmian, you're out of your head,' but she wouldn't stop. She bit at his cheek; he slapped her so hard that her face instantly burned and stung, but she laughed and tried to grab his genitals, shouting mockingly, 'Is it working yet? Can you get it up or do I need someone else to fuck me?'

'You're a little shit, did you know that, Charm? I don't know what I ever saw in you, but you are hard and cruel.'

George swiped her so hard that she fell instantly to the floor. She was crying and wailing, he was coughing and shouting when Martin ran in.

'Mum, Dad, what the hell are you doing? We've got the baby distressed in the other room. What is wrong with you both?'

Shane started crying when she saw her mother on the floor with a swollen face and screaming. Jason came in too, his lovely blue eyes welling up in dismay.

'Stop it!' shouted Martin. 'Stop it, both of you. You're upsetting us all. It's not fair. We are children. Why should we have to deal with this over and over again? You should be looking after us. We should not be caring for you,' and he dragged the two younger ones away, both sobbing.

Sevasty walked in, fuming, picked Charmian up, took her away from George, and bathed her swollen face with warm water and cream. Then she led her to the bedroom where Charmian could rest. George closed the door of the study and wasn't seen again that day.

In the living room, Martin looked after his younger siblings. He wiped Shane and Jason's eyes – the latter held the now-calmer Alexander, with a cup of milk, on his lap – and sat between them on the sofa. On his lap was a copy of Homer's *Odyssey*.

'Now where did we get up to?' he asked the younger ones, trying to quell the quiver in his voice and hide the fact that all he could see in his mind was his mother lying bleeding on the floor.

'Oh yes. We're going to read the ending tonight. Here we go:

'On this, pale fear seized everyone; they were so frightened that their arms dropped from their hands and fell upon the ground at the sound of the goddess's voice, and they fled back to the city for their lives. But Ulysses gave a great cry, and gathering himself together swooped down like a soaring eagle. Then the son of Saturn sent a thunderbolt of fire that fell just in front of Minerva, so she said to Ulysses, "Ulysses, noble son of Laertes, stop this warful strife, or Jove will be angry with you."

'Thus spoke Minerva, and Ulysses obeyed her gladly. Then Minerva assumed the form and voice of Mentor, and presently made a covenant of peace between the two contending parties.'

Autumn brought the terrible Sirocco wind, carrying dust from the Sahara, which crept in everywhere: through the windows, under the door, between the slats of the shutters and any gap it could find. The walls in Leonard's white house turned pink and everything was covered in a film of dust. Marianne had to sweep her step each day like she'd seen the Greek women do.

Having finished *Beautiful Losers* and posted it to his publishers, Leonard was in a state of total exhaustion. For several weeks he stayed in bed, sweating, calling out when his dreams disturbed him. He refused to see Dr Benedictus or let his publisher know how ill he was, so when the telephone rang, Marianne had to carry it to him and listen while he feigned a strong voice. She didn't like it when magazine editors, interviewers and publishers called. Then she would prop Leonard up on pillows, pass him the phone and leave the room.

'Yes, that is true to some extent but that was meant more symbolically than literally. The whole point about language is that...'

The greens and herbs that Kyria Sophia picked made Leonard warming soup, which was all that he would eat. As well as looking after Axel Joachim, Marianne tended to Leonard, holding a wet flannel on his head when he had a fever, warming the room when he was cold. When it rained, Marianne closed the shutters and tried to keep the bad weather at bay, but the old house and its hole-filled walls did not withstand the fierce winds well.

Kyria Sophia showed her how to heap hot coals on silver trays to keep the rooms warm and Marianne borrowed a gas heater from Charmian. It had wheels and was covered in chicken wire, but it provided some warmth. The friends were good at sharing and giving. Some of the children's clothes were passed down: from Jason to Gideon, to Esther to Axel Joachim, anyone spotting a hole, happily darning it along the way.

Leonard stayed in bed a long time. Marianne fed him as if he were a baby bird, spooning tiny helpings of Kyria Sophia's broth into his dry mouth. Much of the time his eyes were closed and he moved seamlessly between sleep and wakefulness, calling out in his dreams. When he was able to, he told Marianne some of his hallucinations:

'There were swans with great beaks and in each one there was a watch with a silver chain. I had to gather as many watches as I could, but it was impossible as the beaks wouldn't release them and besides there were guards nearby...'

'Ssh, Leonard,' said Marianne, stroking his forehead. 'Sleep some more, my love.'

Although his prose was praised, it was becoming clear that it was his poetry and songs that touched people's hearts. *Bird on a Wire* was now often played on radio: listeners identified with its longing for purity and rebellion in an ugly world.

'I must be mad but I think I could make a living from poetry and songs. Just don't tell my mother,' he croaked.

It seemed ironic to Marianne that while his body was ailing, like a beautiful exotic bird recovering from a bullet wound, his work was taking flight. Sometimes she worried about how long their love would last. He would become famous and in demand – and he deserved to be – but their relationship would turn to ash. In a sense, when he was there in bed with her seated beside him, she could keep their love going just that bit longer. At least she knew where he was.

Although these weeks were a struggle and the weather was bad, it brought some surprise benefits. With Kyria Sophia and Marianne in charge of Leonard's diet, he was eating better than he had done for months. Also, they hid the amphetamines and only gave them to him when he made a fuss. Too weak to type, he was compelled to lie in bed and the rest was helping him. They brought him paper and a pen when he demanded it. Sometimes he slept for twelve hours in a row and they let him. Marianne kept Axel Joachim away even when the child called out through the closed door for his absent friend, 'Cone! Cone!'

Gradually, Leonard's health improved. The colour returned to his cheeks and his eyes shone again. Even his hair was sleeker, his body a little fleshier although he was never fat. Marianne kept the shutters closed against the rain which they could hear battering the windows. With the help of Kyria Sophia, who had been like a mother to her, she nursed Leonard back to health again.

'I hardly know how to thank you,' he said, holding her hand. 'My heart is plump with your love.'

Once he grew stronger, Marianne carried his typewriter to his bed, where, supported by pillows, he could work. She heard the familiar tapping, albeit muffled by the bedding. Marianne felt that she could leave him for a few days in charge of her son and go to visit Magda in the prison in Athens.

Once again, she made the arduous journey: the boat to Piraeus with Alexis; a bus to the prison. It was a huge concrete building which looked as if an architect had been told to design something as hideous as possible, as if that were part of the punishment. After the beauty of the sea, it was a shock to see iron railings, barbed wire and concrete slabs.

At the gates to the women's wing, Marianne had to show her identity card and visitor's pass and was then led through to a hall where guards stood menacingly at the side and prisoners could briefly meet friends and family.

Marianne was told to sit down at one of the tables. She waited for a few minutes and then a woman dressed in a grey uniform, her chalky hair tied back in a rubber band and her face ashen, sat in front of her.

'Marianne,' she said softly. 'It is so good of you to come all this way.'

'Magda?' asked Marianne, trying to adjust to the altered face. 'How are you?'

'I am surviving. The conditions here are very basic and the cell is horrible, but I can get through this. I try to fill my head with poetry and visions of nature and delicious food, and my lovely Alexander.'

Marianne felt tears fill her eyes and wiped them away. 'Why did you agree to take the punishment for that awful husband of yours? You have done nothing wrong.'

'I can't talk about that now, Marianne.' The guard behind her shifted, checking his watch irritably. 'How is Leonard?'

'He has been in a bad way. A kind of breakdown. He was working too hard and not eating properly, taking pills he shouldn't, and he ended up in bed for weeks. But I feel that he is slowly getting better. Kyria Sophia has been wonderful, feeding us, helping in any way she can. Axel Joachim has found it hard as they had grown so close and how can you explain to a baby that his friend is ill?'

'Leonard is a genius and the world will recognise that at some stage.'

'It's starting to happen, especially in America, but no-one knows the pain behind the glory, do they?'

'No, Marianne. He is lucky to have you. You are his Nordic pixie, and mine. I miss you so much.'

'How is Alexander?'

'He has gone back to Czechoslovakia to be with my mother.' Marianne thought of Momo and how she had saved her when the family was fragmenting.

'There is a large family there with my sister and cousins. He will be well looked after.'

Marianne noticed that not only was Magda's hair and uniform grey, but her eyes had lost their sheen, as if all shine had been removed on entry, along with her possessions.

'Is there anything you need, Magda, anything that I can send you?'

'We are not allowed luxuries.'

'What about books? I can post you Leonard's novel when it comes out.'

'I don't know. We will have to find out. Do not worry about me, Marianne. I have not lost hope. I know that eventually I will leave here and come back to Hydra and my friends and I know that I am loved.'

'Always.'

A guard shouted, the prisoners stood up, scraping their chairs on the concrete floors and Magda was ushered out. As she left, she smiled at Marianne through the bars and disappeared.

On the long journey home, Marianne could not stop thinking about her friend. How could someone's appearance and personality alter so quickly? What remained when you took away a person's home, clothes, belongings and freedom?

On the boat home to Hydra with Alexis, Marianne searched the deep velvet water and could find no answers. The pinpricked stars reflected in the sea, so that some areas were jewelled with hope, but then there would be large parts where the stars were swallowed up by the slate darkness.

Marianne could not dispel the image of the wan Magda from her mind. She thought of her friend alone in her cell and of Leonard's imprisonment in his bed. She could not understand why the good suffered and the bad prospered. There seemed to be no logic to it.

116

On the bumpy night-time donkey ride back to their house, the mule boy was grumpier than ever, hitting the animal with a stick even when it paused for a second to shit or shake the fleas from its ears.

Back at home, Marianne opened the door. The baby would be asleep, Kyria Sophia would be in her own home looking after her family and Leonard would probably still be in bed. She entered quietly so as not to disturb anyone but to her delight Leonard was reading in the living room. The shutters closed against the hostile night, candle flames danced in glass jars and a pile of coals glistened on a silver tray.

'Leonard,' she cried, 'you're up! How are you?'

'I thought I'd surprise you.' He smiled warmly, his skin still sallow but his eyes regaining some of their previous radiance. 'I still feel weak but I am on the mend, thanks to you. How was Magda?'

'Amazingly strong, given the horrendous prison she is in. You would not put a dog in there. It is squalid.'

'Come and sit by me.' She did so and he poured her a glass of retsina. 'What would we all do without you, my angel? I have had a phone call from my publisher in New York. He wants me to do a tour, performances, interviews.'

'Do you think you are well enough? I don't.'

'I do feel much stronger but I will tell you more about it tomorrow. For now, let us spend time together: *Lay your sleeping head, my love / Human on my faithless arm*.'

'When you say a tour,' said Marianne, the following day, 'when do you have to leave?'

'I'm not sure exactly. It won't be for a few weeks.'

'A few weeks! Oh no. Do you think you are able to travel?'

'I am feeling much better, due to your wonderful care. I have some more time to rest still but I do need to go. I'm sorry, Marianne.' He held her hand in his, rubbed his fingers over her soft skin. 'We need the money. Hydra is idyllic, but idylls don't pay the bills. The novels won't make me anything. I need to build a reputation as a poet and singer-songwriter.'

'I know. I understand. But I do not want you to go.'

Tread softly because you tread on my dreams.

Marianne noticed that he did not invite her to go with him and it stung.

'The thought of being here without you is so painful.'

'I am always with you, my love, even when we are apart. I carry you in my heart day and night.'

'I will have to find something to do.'

'Your modelling and posing for paintings has gone so well. Why don't you go to Paris?'

'Paris? Who do I know there?'

'My friend Madeleine. She has a lot of contacts in the modelling world and her boyfriend Derek May knows people in films. I can write to them if you like. We are old friends; they live in the Latin Quarter.'

'And where would Axel Joachim go?'

'To Axel and Sonja?'

'Absolutely not. They wouldn't care for him properly. Axel hasn't even seen him for weeks, he is so wrapped up in himself.'

'Then what?'

'I will have to think.'

Over the next few weeks, plans were finalised for Leonard to go to the USA and Marianne to Paris. Her mother had agreed to meet her there and take Axel Joachim back to Oslo. She missed him badly and it would be a chance for her to be a grandmother.

As the day of departure approached, Marianne and Leonard felt closer than they had ever been before.

'I am scared,' she confessed one evening as they sat on the terrace and watched the sun bleed across a granite sky, 'that we will never meet again and that this is the end.'

Leonard turned to face her.

'No, Marianne. Our separation is only the affirmation of our love.'

Paris in autumn had a particular glow and elegance, as if the trees chose which leaves to wear and, rather than be covered in bushy mounds, they simply selected a few of ochre and russet to adorn themselves with. As she looked out through Madeleine's large windows over the grey ribbon of the Seine, Marianne thought: a plate with little on it is so much more graceful than a heap of meat stew.

Leonard had, as promised, arranged it all. Marianne stayed with Madeleine. She did not worry about Axel Joachim: he would be well looked after by her mother.

It began well. The dark-haired Madeleine and the blonde-haired Marianne became friends and soon Marianne had photo shoots arranged.

One day, Marianne wore a tight black dress, lined in red, with a zip running up the whole back, like a narrow road. The photographer, Pierre, placed her on a checked black and white backdrop so that she looked as if she were reclining on a huge chess board. Marianne did not mind posing: she had become used to it and she found herself stretching, bending, curling like a cat. Pierre gave strong instructions and clear orders. The day went well but at the end, Pierre came so close to her that she could see each hair on his beard.

'You would like to come to bed with me?' he whispered. 'I would enjoy that very much.'

'No, thank you,' said Marianne. 'I have a partner.'

And how she missed Leonard and Axel Joachim.

More photo shoots, more assignments, and to each of them, Marianne wore a ring made from a yellow-orange gem. The stone had belonged to her paternal grandmother. On one shoot, the ring bothered her and she took it off.

Later that day her mother told her that her granny had died.

Marianne went back to Oslo and was reunited with Axel Joachim, stayed for the funeral and did not return to Paris. All she had to show for the trip was a strip of black and white photos, given to her by Pierre. She could not help but feel disappointed. Another possible opening had led nowhere.

Being back in Norway was a mixed experience. With her mother and Axel Joachim, they went to the house at Larkollen and Marianne showed him where she had learned to feed the birds. She saw the garage where the old car was kept, which Momo had said was really a horse. She remembered her grandmother's stories of princes and faraway lands and her beautiful singing voice.

She recalled meeting Axel and thinking how clever he was. He had taken her to The Theatre Café where young writers aired their views. She'd hung on every word he said. And he'd taken her drinking at Doverehallen, a student bar where people with shiny eyes and new ideas discussed the world. It had given her a break from her parents' home where she would hide under the table and wait for their quarrels to end.

She wondered if maybe she was too easily led, too impressed, by others, especially men. As a child, she had fantasised about Genghis Khan, imagining herself on horseback with him, galloping through vast, tented deserts, her bright scarves trailing in the wind.

Now, in the evenings, she sat with her mother when Axel Joachim was in bed. They were cautious with each other, avoiding contentious subjects.

Marianne did not say: my childhood was difficult, even before my brother and her father were both ill. She remembered her father having to give up his law practice as tuberculosis took hold of him and visiting him in the Mesnali sanatorium, staring at the pale man with closed eyes and thinking: is this man really my father? She did not accuse her mother: did you protect me enough?

Her mother did not say: you could have married any man you liked, Marianne, and you chose Axel, a man from a broken home, a university drop-out who was never going to hold down a proper job. You were blown away by his writing and his charm and the books he lent you – Jung, Nietzsche – and the jazz records he played you: Duke Ellington, Charlie

Parker. Now you are a single woman with a child and a new lover, with no permanent home.

Instead they chose their words carefully and listened to each other. From her mother, Marianne had learned stoicism. When her parents used to argue, her mother was strong, answering back, retaining her dignity through it all.

Marianne remembered how erratic Axel was, even in those early days. He would suddenly be impulsive, angry, wild. There was that dramatic time when, at a party in Bygdoy, he was so drunk that he put his hand on the kitchen table and drove a knife through it. Other times he was crazy, losing his temper for no reason, shouting.

And that is how Marianne and her mother survived those few weeks, with caution, as if they knew they had too much to lose and might need each other in the future. They edged around each other, in the kitchen, with the baby, with their movements.

Marianne was aware that her mother, living alone, had her own set routines. Her mother had an expression: if you have to break a glass, make sure it is a mustard glass and not the crystal. Marianne often wondered what she meant by this and thought, maybe what she was saying was, always value what is precious in your life and make do with the everyday pain that life brings: enjoy the wine but also learn to love water.

Leonard was staying at the Chelsea Hotel in New York: the rooms were bright and large as if sending him a message of hope. The foyer gleamed with marble and mirrors, the silver and the white trying to outshine each other. He was sleeping well, had put on some weight and was feeling healthy. He was pleased that his work, at last, was being recognised.

He wrote to Marianne:

My dear Marianne,

I am so sorry to hear about your grandmother. As we say in Judaism, I wish you long life.

And it is a life that I wish to share with you. I miss you so.

A peach eaten without you lacks flavour.. A rainbow seen without you is grey. A sea dipped in without you is dry.

You would love the Chelsea Hotel. The family who own it are the Bard family. Originally Jewish refugees. How can I not write with that name here? I hope someday that you will see it. Twelve storeys high, red brick, with black railings, it has something Gothic about it, like something out of Edgar Allan Poe. There is a staircase which rises all the way to the top. To be here is humbling as I am so aware of all the great people who have stayed here before: Janis Joplin, Andy Warhol, Arthur Miller are just some. Dylan Thomas even drank himself to death here.

The tour is going well. I have met Bob Dylan and Joan Baez and they are helpful. I played some songs to Judy Collins and she said that she would back me. While we have been living on that Greek rock, music has exploded. People seem to like the poetry and the songs. I have been booked for some festivals. All of this makes me want to write more. I am torn constantly between paper and the guitar.

Send my love to that sweet boy of yours. I am sure that Kyria Sophia will keep our house warm.

I dream of being with you in our Aegean shuttered home and making love day and night with you. That is what sustains me.

Your loving, Leonard.

His letters became increasingly full of longing for Hydra and for Marianne.

My dear Marianne,

I cannot bear another day without you.

It is going well here. Flowers for Hitler and Beautiful Losers *are selling and I have been asked to sing in concerts and do interviews. This means more money too, hopefully, so that I can support you and that dear little boy who I love as if he were my own.

I count the days, hours and minutes till I can hold you in my arms again.

What is the point of life if I can't share it with you?

Your loving, Leonard

The letters from Leonard comforted Marianne hugely. She stared at her strip of black and white photos from Paris and was sad that she had no further modelling deals. She had hoped that the shoot would have led to more work, but no. She wondered sometimes if she were enough for

Leonard. Here he was, a sparkling star, and who was she? A pretty Norwegian girl without a career.

She wondered whether Leonard was sleeping with other women when he was away. She wouldn't ask him, for fear of arguments, for fear of ruining what they had. Self-doubt flooded her, but then Leonard's letters arrived and she was reassured that he did love her. The last one she received was just one line:

I have my guitar and my notebook, my songs and my poems: now all I need now is you.
Leonard

Marianne and Axel Joachim were the first to return to Hydra. The little boy had been tearful when he left Oslo and his granny to begin the long journey home. Marianne held him close and read him stories and also spoke to him of his friends, especially Alexander and Jason, Melina and Esther – whom he would see again soon. She thought: all this change and upheaval is not good for him. Like the wallflowers around Hydra, which search for a patch of soil and flourish there, he needs roots.

The island was more beautiful than Marianne had remembered. Although cold, the sun was bright and brazen, coating the land and sea in a glorious varnish. Campanulas held their beauty modestly in white bells. The sky was wide and expansive, and everything seemed fresher, crisper, than when she was last there.

It was wonderful to be home again and have her own space without fear of upsetting her mother. Kyria Sophia had kept the house clean and shielded against the winter. There again were the familiar sights: silver plates heaped with hot coals and the green soup simmering. When Marianne hugged the elderly maid, she felt that she had really returned, that the woman was a second mother to her, without the emotional history that shadows families.

On the day that Leonard was expected to return, Marianne lit candles in tiny glasses and placed them on the cobbled courtyard outside their house and in a line leading him towards their shared haven.

When he arrived back, after a tiring, lengthy journey, he was delighted to see the lights dancing and flickering, and even though it was the early hours of the morning, Marianne had waited up for him.

He slipped off her gold kimono, untying the wide sash at the waist and letting it fall to the floor so that she stood in a pool of light.

They went to the bedroom and made love, his illness and their absence from each other only fuelling their desire. Their sleeping together was not only physical – to feel, again, that skin and softness and hardness and touch – but also an unspoken reminder that their love had not diminished over time but had only strengthened.

'Every leaf, every cloud, every paving stone reminded me of you,' said Leonard as she lay on his chest afterwards and he stroked her boyish blonde hair, her soft neck and her smooth skin.

'I missed you so badly, Leonard, my love.'

They could not believe how lucky they were to have rediscovered each other like finding treasure thought lost. The dream was clearly not yet over.

Walking around the island the following day felt like finding beauty again, as if they had been hibernating and had awoken. Hydra seemed more delightful than it had before: the sea lifting its waves up high before flattening them out again; the earth wet and heavy as if preparing itself for spring; the firs and evergreens holding defiantly onto their foliage.

In the evening they walked down to the harbour, avoiding the sight of Lagoudera, dark and locked up. At Douskos' Taverna, the friends sat talking under the pine tree as if they had never left. Everyone was happy to see them and they slotted back into the previous conversations.

'So you knew Buber well?' Chuck asked Jack.

'Oh yes. Very. I first went to him because my sister was ill and I thought that he could help me. I rang him from a phone box and asked if I could make an appointment with him and explained why I needed his help. He spoke to me softly and quietly as he always did and said that I could see him that day. "I know that you are standing in my street," he said. A few minutes later, I was sitting in his book-lined study, opening my heart to him.'

'How did he know that you were close by?' Charmian took the carafe and poured herself more retsina. George raised his eyebrows at her but then did the same.

'I don't know.' Jack looked around him as he spoke, excited by the interest. 'That was just the way he was. Intuitive and wise. I was twenty-five and he was seventy-five but that didn't matter. He taught me to search inside myself, to make sure that all my relationships were I-Thou, not I-It.' He looked away from Frieda as he spoke. 'We need to listen to every word that is spoken, be alert to everything we see, make connections, build bridges.'

'It reminds me of the Buddhist distinction between the eye-mind and the eye-heart. We need to get to what is essential, to what really matters,' Gordon observed.

'There is some fucking bullshit in the world,' said George.

'So true,' said Charmian, glaring at him. 'Closer by than we realise.'

'I suppose that is why we have all come to Hydra, to get away from what is irrelevant and focus on the real, the significant.' John Dragoumis stroked his beard to steady his shaking hand as he spoke.

'I have left behind the rubbish of the world to collect the rubbish on Hydra,' said Norman. He did not speak often but when he did it was always wry and thought-provoking.

'As long as you don't think you're living amongst rubbish, mate,' said George and everyone laughed.

'I wish that Buber could be here to see all of us,' said Jack, his eyes glassy with tears. 'We are living out his ideas about responsibility, truth and the existential test. Living on Hydra is our test.'

'Cheers to that.' Charmian raised her glass.

'L'Chaim! To life!' said Leonard.

'What are you working on now, Jack?' Gordon was always interested in other people.

'I've been given a grant by the Institute of World Affairs in New York to write a book about the ongoing conflict between the Arabs and the Israelis, a situation that breaks my heart. I open it with a story I read from the Antilles Islands. Two neighbours live on either side of a wall. One side is painted black, the other white. Then one neighbour calls out, "The wall is black!" "No," shouts the other neighbour. "The wall is white." A fight breaks out and both men are killed but neither of them thought of ever looking at the other side of the wall.'

'You are extraordinary,' said Chuck. 'Full of ideas and stories and anecdotes. What a brilliant mind!'

Two hours later, back at their house, Frieda echoed the words bitterly, 'What a brilliant mind!'

'Well,' said Jack, undressing, 'I am pleased that someone appreciates me and recognises the work I do.'

'It must be lovely,' said Frieda. 'I wish people acknowledged the work that I do and asked me questions and shone the light over me for once.'

'I've told you before, Frieda. You just have to join in. No-one invites you to speak. It is not a tea party.'

'But they do ask you. They always do. Whether we are in the kibbutz or Hydra or wherever we are, people are always interested in you and your writing. No-one ever asks me about my painting. Why is that?'

Apart from Carl, she thought. He was the one person she knew who took her seriously as an artist, one who had ideas, an original style and talent. How she wished that he would come to Douskos' Taverna, stand on a chair and shout out: 'This woman is an incredible painter. Ask her about it! Focus on her!' but they had agreed that he should stay away from their soirées. One glance between them and their secret would be out.

'I do care,' said Jack, coming over to Frieda and trying to kiss her. She turned her head away. She simply could not bear to touch him. That morning, she and Carl had made love in her white studio, the grey light banished and their skin and mouths wet with each other.

'I've told you,' said Jack. 'You need help with your lack of self-esteem. I think it's linked to your frigidity, your aversion to sex. It's all to do with your childhood, I'm sure, but that doesn't help us. You need to get professional help, Frieda. It's gone on too long. It's not fair to me. Men do have needs, you know.'

So do women, thought Frieda, and mine, luckily, are being met.

He carried his bedclothes to the living room where yet again he would be spending the night.

Frieda felt a pang of guilt and sadness for him. He was not a bad man, but she felt that they were two islands that the sea was pushing further apart.

Not very far away, beneath the same blank sky, it had taken a while to settle Axel Joachim into his cot again, but he was now asleep. In their bedroom, Marianne and Leonard closed the shutters to make the room dark. Sometimes they felt that the whole world had disappeared and it was just the two of them, this moment, everything reduced to this as if everything they had been through had been leading them to this time.

They took it slowly: he slipped one sleeve of her dress from her shoulder; kissed her grooves and dents, loving every part of her. From there to her mouth was a short distance and he found it open. They kissed, deeply, smoothly, each receiving the tongue, lips, skin of the other with delight. She felt the dark stubble on his chin and he touched the golden silk of her hair and he moved his mouth to her neck which was long and white and like that of a swan.

He lifted her dress completely off, to reveal her satin skin beneath. Even when he saw her at the shop or the taverna he was always conscious that beneath the cotton dress was the treasure. Sometimes he felt that he could not bear to know what was there and yet not have it, so he would have to distract himself by holding the guitar to cover his stiffness whilst he sang.

Marianne lay on the bed now and he moved his mouth onto her breasts which lay pert and expectant and he found her nipples, dark and hard to the touch. He took them in his mouth while she stroked his hair and shoulder blades and legs. Then he moved down to the centre of her and his mouth was on her until she cried out.

She pushed him away and rolled him over so that she was on top and she hung above him like an angel from heaven, a golden-haired angel with white skin, and she rolled herself over him until they could bear it no longer and they called out for each other and they kissed hard and then lay together in the darkness, silent.

She liked to lean her head on his chest and listen to his heart beat. It made her feel that she was part of him, almost within him as he had just been in her. They could not be close enough.

There was no need to say anything.

They lay there happy, full of love and the smell of each other.

'I love it,' said Leonard, lighting the candles on his menorah, 'when Christmas and Chanukah coincide.'

'They don't every year?'

'Oh no, not at all. Christmas is fixed; Chanukah is changing, according to the moon. But when they are at the same time, it means that everyone has something to celebrate, something to light.'

He said the bracha over the candles and sang *Ma'oz Tzur* in his gravelly voice which Marianne loved. Axel Joachim's little face was lit by the glow and the excitement shone in his eyes.

'Look, darling,' said his mother. 'All the pretty candles.'

They ate gold chocolate coins which Masha had sent them and they flattened the foil covers into discs.

There was a knock at the door and there, in warm clothing, were children singing carols, or *kalanda*, in the street. Some played drums and triangles. A girl at the front carried a golden model ship full of nuts. Marianne gave them dried fruit to eat and thanked them for coming.

Then, wrapped up warmly, Leonard and Marianne wheeled Axel Joachim in his pushchair across the island and saw how the pine trees were shrouded in mist and the leaves were like plastic, shiny with rain. As they walked past houses, they saw Christmas trees in some windows and in others, the traditional basil in wooden bowls, a cross at its centre, to keep the kallikantzaroi (evil spirits) away.

Olivia's house was, as ever, warm and welcoming, the shrine to Buddha with offerings of gold and fruit at his feet. She also had a Christmas tree, decorated with oranges and ribbon, juniper berries and cinnamon sticks so that the room smelled and looked delicious. There was a Chanukkiah there too. 'For you, Leonard, darling,' she said, 'and for Esther, Gideon and their family.'

'You make everyone welcome,' said Marianne, embracing her and thinking: please let us stay here in this warmth for ever. Let our lives stop here, today.

So many lovely people there already and the door kept opening as more guests arrived and the house became full of dear friends: Charmian, George and their children; Norman, looking thinner than ever; Anthony Kingsmill, slightly the worse for wear; John Dragoumis, with such a long white beard that some of the younger children thought he was Father Christmas; Gordon and Chuck; Jack, Frieda, Gideon and Esther; and, on this occasion, Carl. He usually stayed away from events so as not to arouse suspicion and although he would like to have shouted his affair with Frieda from the hilltops, he respected their decision to keep it secret. She did not want to hurt Jack and, even more so, the children.

But Olivia always invited Carl to her house (he and Georgos got on well) and as he told Frieda, to refuse the invitation would have seemed strange. Where else would he be on Christmas Day? So he and Frieda made sure that they kept out of each other's way all evening and dared not look at each other.

In a side room, games had been organised for the children and some of the older ones went there. Axel Joachim, clingy since they had returned from Oslo, stuck to Marianne and wouldn't leave her even although his friends Melina and Jason tried to tempt him.

In the dining room, the table was laid with delicious food: legs of lamb, roasted and crispy, adorned with spiky rosemary; roast quail and partridge in terracotta pots; spinach and cheese pastries; fried pastry; rabbit stew and a goat and lentil casserole; whitebait encrusted in batter. Aubergines shone velvet, while baked tomatoes failed to keep their skins falling off and roast artichokes lay on a large platter.

There was also baklava smug in its own syrup, kataifi, sweetened with nuts and cinnamon and melomakarono, rectangular biscuits rolled in honey and chopped walnuts.

In the centre of the table was a Christopsomo, or Christmas bread, sweetly flavoured with oranges and cloves, a cross carved into its crust. There was white and red wine in carafes with beaded covers and when the drinks were poured, the friends clinked glasses and wished each other '*Kala Christougena*' or 'Happy Christmas', or '*Chag sameach*' as Leonard said to the Silver family.

And yes, Charmian drank too much and got into an argument about Vietnam with Georgos; and yes, George coughed and smoked at the same time; and yes, Norman gobbled the food as if he had not eaten for weeks;

and yes, John Dragoumis' hands were shaking more than ever, but Leonard looked around the room and thought: these are my dear, dear friends and I would miss them so much, each one of them, if they – or I – were not here.

As the evening wore on, Leonard brought out his guitar and sang Christmas songs, Israeli songs and those of his that people requested such as *Bird on a Wire*, *Winter Lady* and *Suzanne*, inspired by a friend ('No, I never slept with her,' he reassured Marianne later that evening) in Montreal.

'Love it, Len,' said George after the song was finished. 'Jeez, you're one hell of a creative guy.'

'What about you?' Leonard smiled teasingly. He knew that George wanted to deflect the glory back onto himself. 'Not exactly unproductive yourself, are you, George?'

'Yeah, well. I must say, I'm in a good run at the moment. *The Sponge Divers* is coming out soon, although they've renamed it *The Sea and the Stone*, and *Cosmopolitan* have bought my knife story.'

'That's great.'

'Jeez, thanks, Len. I must say, there is something about Hydra which makes everyone creative. It's sort of constructive.'

'In some ways. Destructive in others?'

'Not sure about that.' He had a coughing fit and, to Leonard's horror, spluttered blood into a hanky and lit another cigarette. 'It's been fucking good to me. *The Cyprian Woman* is still in print and I have just sold stories to several magazines. Jeez, I'm not complaining!' But in the middle of his boasting, he started coughing so badly that blood spurted again from his mouth. Suddenly, he fell to the floor with a thud and Charmian fell to her husband's side, anguish flooding her.

'George! George! Can you hear me?'

Some of the guests had gone to midnight mass in the chapel and so there weren't many people left. The children had all gone home to bed.

Leonard said, 'Charmian, can I help you?'

'What can we do?' asked Marianne, worried that the scene would upset Axel Joachim.

'Please leave us for a moment,' said Charmian. 'I will call you if I need to.'

Everyone obeyed.

131

'George, my love,' she panted. 'Can you hear me? Are you alright?'

He mumbled a reply but his eyes were closed. His face was white but the blood that dribbled from his mouth drew a crimson line from his lips to his chin and a little pool formed a circle on the floor.

'George,' she whispered, 'let me call Dr Benedictus.'

He shook his head defiantly.

'You're more stubborn than the mules that walk the island. You are very ill.'

She removed the shawl from her shoulders and rolled it into a ball to place under his head. That seemed to ease the coughing and the bleeding.

'There,' she said tenderly, and he reached out his hand to hold hers.

'George,' she whispered, tears flowing uncontrollably down her face. 'You know I love you, don't you?' He nodded. 'We quarrel about such silly things and we fight and shout and it's madness because we both know that we were made for each other and that no-one else can even come close. I am the Charmian to your Cleopatra. We are Scott and Zelda. Remember, George?'

She moved his head onto her lap now and was cradling him. In the last two days she had screwed Nature Boy in a cove down by the harbour, him releasing his loincloth with a single hand, his dick, it seemed, permanently hard and always ready. And then there was Anthony who had drawn her as many times as he had made love to her, a delicious pattern they had established in the early afternoons when the light twisted and spiralled through the large windows and onto them, coating them in its sweet syrup.

It was wrong, she saw that now. She should have devoted herself to her ill and gifted husband.

'You know what, darling George?' She kept talking as if she believed that he would not die mid-conversation. 'We will stop our petty spats. They damage us and upset our children. Let's be sure to have only harmony from now on.'

She looked him up and down and was shocked at how skeletal his body was. She thought: I know Nature Boy's and Anthony's bodies better than his. George's white shirt was stained with drops of blood and his trousers hung about his legs like a scarecrow's. His skin was sallow and his face gaunt, his cheekbones hollow as if scooped out with a spoon. She could see the veins in his eyelids, purple and transparent as if they could easily tear. They reminded her of butterfly wings that you could almost see through.

George's hands were clasped on his tummy so that he looked like a marble figure carved and frozen on a tomb. The smell coming from him was of booze and fags and the metallic stench of blood. She thought back over their life together: to when they had first met as they both worked on the *Argus* and he had seemed so clever, eleven years older, more worldly-wise than her, already married, a father, and he was so handsome and smart, always dressed in a hessian suit and shiny tie, looking every bit the journalist and novelist, always ready with words flowing from his typewriter, his pen or his mouth.

Charmian remembered how he had seemed so sophisticated, so knowledgeable. He knew everything about America and Asia. He had met Gandhi and had contacts in Washington and New York. And he had clearly fallen for Charmian with her jet-black hair pulled sleekly back over her head, her high cheekbones and her lips always scarlet and wide.

She recalled their flat in North Bondi with its Japanese prints and the mural of a ship, which George had painted. She had made curtains from candy-striped pyjamas and cleaned the flat until it gleamed. How they had partied in that apartment, even after Martin was born, and friends had shared bowls of spaghetti and bottles of red while talking about everything from the power struggle in Berlin to their individual dreams. Their lives had seemed shiny with possibility then and yet here they were, crouched on the floor, by a pool of blood.

George opened his eyes but they looked watery and grey, devoid of any glow. He looked at her, a half-smile forming, and he nodded as if to say, I am alright.

Olivia came into the room, carrying dirty bowls, tidying up. 'George!' she exclaimed.

'He's okay,' said Charmian. 'He's had a bit of a nasty turn but I am going to get him home. Can you stand up, George?'

He nodded and the women lifted him, like hoisting a flag; although he was a bit wobbly, he was able to stay upright.

'Do you want Georgos to walk him home?'

'No, Olivia, thank you. We will manage, the two of us. Sorry about the blood.'

Olivia waved her hand; it didn't matter.

For the rest of their marriage, Charmian never forgot that slow trek home. It was dark and tranquil, the trees and bushes black on black, the air crisp and cold. The chapel at St Constantine was lit for midnight mass and they could smell the salty sea although they could not see it.

The island was mostly still for the night. Walking carefully, George's arm around Charmian's shoulder and their spare hands clasped together at the front, they formed a united shape, facing the darkness, taking it on with their combined strength.

The cold air bit their cheeks and made their eyes water.

And then the bells of the chapel rang as they reached their front door and it was as if they were ringing for them, signifying their future, their starting again.

'No more fighting, only loving,' said Charmian as they arrived home and the bells filled the air with their frilly pealing and George mumbled, 'Amen.'

The cruel winter did nothing to improve George's health. The cold spells and his coughing bouts grew longer as if one was fuelling the other; he frequently coughed up blood but still he refused to seek medical help. His self-made routine was rigidly adhered to: drink, smoke and write. Day after day, no matter how rough the night before, he and Charmian sat in adjacent studies and worked, the sounds from the two typewriters creating their own percussion, egging each other on. There were times when they read each other's prose and commented. She always encouraged him 'to write something significant'.

On Charmian's desk, there were three paperweights: a pebble, a goat bell and a door bolt.

Above George's desk were three signs: one read *Fuck Virginia Woolf!* the second *And Rilke too!* and the third, *A time to write and a time to puke!* If ever he had blank spots, and he rarely did, looking at those signs and soaking up their defiance spurred him on.

If he felt tired, he thought of Old Babba Yannis who, at 87, still worked a twelve-hour day, and would do any errand on the island for some cash. Once, he shifted a vast quantity of cement across Hydra on his mules although he was rarely sober and only had one eye. His face was scarred from constantly falling over when drunk.

George had two mottos. One was *'If Old Babba Yannis can do it...'* and the other was *'Nothing important is further off than a donkey ride'* – a saying which lent itself to various interpretations.

The couple's routine rarely altered: hard work in the morning, sometimes taking a break to play darts on the terrace, getting pissed at lunchtime usually at home or sometimes in Katsikas' store, seeing their kids briefly in the evening, listening to records on the old player (Haydn's Horn Concerto was a favourite or sometimes Bob Dylan) and then a good discussion – or fight – in Douskos' Taverna.

The worse George's health was, the better was his writing, as if the deterioration of one led to the success of the other. He sometimes imagined a weighing scale where he traded his bad health for success – and it seemed worth it.

'Hey Charm!' he called out one day in between bouts of coughing, 'Guess what? Bill Collins is sending me an advance for *My Brother Jack* and enough copies for our friends. He loves the Sid Nolan cover. Jeez, that man is a genius. *Closer to the Sun* and *High Valley* are doing well and he likes the outline for the sequel *Clean Straw for Nothing*. He thinks it has overtones of *Madame Bovary*. Maybe our days of goat stew are over and triumph is on its way!'

A few days later a huge cheque arrived at the post office along with books from Sidney Nolan with money stuck in between the pages as a gift.

'Jeez,' said George, 'this is my lucky day. Nick,' he called to Katsikas, 'how much do I owe you, my friend?'

The man brought over the piece of paper with George's debts on it. He had not cleared them for over two years and it amounted to the equivalent of £900. George paid it off at once.

In the store, he treated all his family. He bought Charmian chocolate, caviar, Holland sprats and a bottle of Metaxas brandy. He purchased sweeties for Jason, perfume for Shane (she was now dating Nick Katsikas' nephew, Baptiste) and packets of paper and ink for Martin who was writing poetry and producing an island newspaper with an overtly political stance, especially anti-Vietnam. One of his pieces on Greek mountain fighters had actually been printed in the English version of the *Athens News*, making his parents proud. 'The next generation of writers is born,' Charmian liked to say. 'And so the tradition continues.'

How wonderful it felt for George to go back home and give all his family gifts. There was an air of excitement as he handed them out, even giving Sevasty some wine.

'And tonight at Douskos,' he announced proudly, 'the drinks are on me!'

True to his word, George arrived that evening at the taverna, scrubbed, in a clean suit with a gardenia in his buttonhole and his hair washed. He had even shaved. The night before, he and Charmian had had mediocre sex; he had called her his praying mantis and he was feeling great.

'Friends,' he stood up at the table when everyone was seated, 'the bill is being paid by me tonight. Tomorrow is New Year's Day – or St Vasilis

Day as our Greek friends say – and the year has started well. Have whatever you want. Len, Mari, Norm – all of you. Drink and be happy!'

And that is what they did. The wine and retsina flowed. Charmian had her favourite: champagne, peach juice and brandy.

George looked around at him and felt fantastic. Here, under their beloved pine tree, they were with their friends. Here the fire and candles were ablaze, his books were selling well, there was money coming in and life was good.

He called Douskos over and asked him to bring them food and soon bowls of brightly coloured pastes with warm pitta to dip arrived. There were olives and dolmades and kofte meatballs, and when the plates were empty George ordered more. It was not only food that he was consuming, but wine and plenty of it. As the evening progressed, his face became redder, his coughing worse, until he was slurring his words and shouting out. 'I love you, my friends, I fucking love you.'

'Take it easy, George,' his wife tried to quieten him.

'Fuck off, Charm, in the nicest possible way. Jeez, can't a man celebrate when life is good?'

Costas and Constantinos walked past the taverna and George beckoned them in.

'Hey, Laurel and Hardy,' he called. 'Come and have a drink.'

The policemen looked at each other. They did sometimes join the expats in the taverna. George drew up two chairs and they sat, clinking glasses with the artists, joking with those who spoke better Greek.

'Thingis,' said George, one word running into another, 'I think the only noble thing to do in life is to create.'

'I agree.' Jack raised his glass in solidarity. 'If you aren't going to leave a legacy of your creative work when you die, what is the point of your life?'

'So, doctors, nurses, teachers – all wasting their time?' Gordon asked.

'Not wasting their time exactly,' answered George, 'but they are not contributing to the body of culture that defines society. Mozart, Beethoven, Picasso, Rembrandt, Shakespeare: these are the shapers of our lives.'

'And George Johnston!' Charmian's voice was sarcastic.

'Well, I'm on my ninth novel, Charm. Jeez, I think that's a fair level of productivity.'

'Yes, but I always tell you, it's quality, not quantity.'

'So, you're saying that my novels are shit, are you?'

'I didn't say that. Your words, not mine.'

'What about people who make it possible for creative people to do their work?' said Chuck. 'Maids, cleaners, cooks, drivers, log deliverers. If it weren't for them, we couldn't write, but they get no credit.'

'True,' agreed Gordon. 'Maybe they are the unacknowledged legislators of the world?'

'Jeez, so you want me to dedicate my books to Old Babba Yannis and Tzimmi?'

'No,' Gordon tried to keep him calm. 'Not dedicate your books to them but recognise that we are free to create because our domestic chores are carried out by others.'

'Fair point.' John stroked his beard as if it might help him to articulate his views.

'Jeez, you're all crazy. You're attributing all our dedication and talent to the cleaners and cooks.'

'You're a fucking idiot, George,' Charmian's patience was fraying. 'No-one says attributing; they say acknowledging.'

'Probably most achievements are due to others helping out of sight: plays, shows, music, let alone muses,' Leonard smiled at Marianne, 'and the lovers who stay at home and do the dirty work while the genius creates.'

Marianne smiled, grateful for this recognition.

'Call me a snob,' shouted George.

'Snob,' said Charmian.

'Fuck off,' said George. 'But those menial jobs can be done by anybody. Anyone can cook and clean. Very few people have the ability to create. As Ionesco said, writers must be original at all cost.'

'I agree,' said Jack.

You would, thought Frieda, but she didn't say it. She found these noisy interchanges very difficult as she was never given space to air her opinions. Charmian just shouted out whenever she wanted to and Marianne and Magda would speak, if they had something of value to say. She envied them their confidence, their ability to chip in.

Leonard bowed his head to play his guitar again. Costas and Constantinos were observing cheerfully but when George ranted, they looked a little uneasy.

'The nineteenth-century romantic view of the great artist, on a cliff edge, like a Caspar David Friedrich painting surveying the landscape below, is a very dangerous portrayal of artists,' said John.

'Dangerous? Why?' George's face was angry, red, lined, blood and wine staining his mouth.

'Because the artist is looking down from his lofty heights onto society rather than being part of it, which links back to what we were saying about getting others to do our domestic work so that we can create and then be superior, but claim to be of the people.'

'At least I collect my own garbage,' said Norman gently.

'Jeez, that's fine then.' George looked ready for a fight. 'I'll let Yannis and Tzimmi do the writing for me from now on and I'll fetch the logs.'

'You can't,' laughed Charmian. 'You're not up to it.'

'Okay Charm,' he turned angrily on her, wiping the spit from his lips, his face fiery. 'You've been goading me all evening, and I have just about had enough of it.'

'Goad, goad,' she chuckled, but her laughter stopped abruptly when George leapt up from his seat, toppling it to the floor, and lunged at her. The glasses and bottles went flying, bowls were upturned. Everyone jumped up and Gordon and Chuck tried to stop George but he wriggled free. He chucked a glass of retsina in Charmian's face. The liquid soaked her hair and cheeks and she began to cry. Then George, with a massive kick, knocked the table on its side and everything broke in disarray. Shards of glass and crockery lay fragmented on the floor.

Costas and Constantinos leapt to their feet, blew their whistles and each grabbed George by an arm. He kicked and shouted but they held him tightly and escorted him off the premises.

The rest of the friends stood, shocked. They put the table back on its legs and Douskos and Polixenes started to sweep up the debris. They shrugged as if to say: we have seen it before and we will see it again.

'As we were saying earlier,' noted John. 'It is the ordinary workers who have to clean up after artists.'

The celebration had come to an ugly end.

Costas and Constantinos dragged George, still screaming and swearing, to the police station which consisted of an office and one cell. It was near the harbour and like Dr Benedictus' surgery, it seemed too attractive for its purpose. Built of white stone, it looked out to the sea so that even the cell's barred windows shared the idyllic view. They locked George up for the night to sleep off his drink and anger.

Although the cell's single bed was a metal frame with a thin mattress, he slept soundly, a pool of saliva, vomit and blood leaking from his open mouth onto the concrete floor as he did so.

In the office, Costas and Constantinos shared a bottle of retsina and played cards, unperturbed by George's intermittent coughing and snoring in the background.

There were times when Hydra felt like a fragmented community; each tolerant of the other but at a safe distance.

But 6th January, or Epiphany, was a day when everyone came together. For the locals, the day marked Jesus' baptism as a man and they called it the Blessing of the Waters. Down in the harbour, men were diving bravely into the cold water – Nature Boy, who didn't have to change his outfit as he always wore the same, whether on land or sea, day or night; the Katsikas brothers, who had shut their shop for an hour; Douskos, whose taverna was closed in the mornings anyway; Demosthenes, the barber, his stomach like a buoy, always visible above sea level; Francisco, the carpenter; Demi, the baker; Vassilis with his yellow teeth, who in spite of his disabilities could swim quite well; and Old Babba Yannis, who at 87 had never missed an Epiphany yet and wasn't going to start now.

There were whoops of delight and horror as their bodies hit the icy water, each determined to get his cross blessed by the priest first as that would guarantee good luck. A crowd had gathered on the quayside, including the expats: Norman, Jack, Frieda and Esther (Gideon had decided to stay at home and clean his stones); Olivia and Georgos with their children; Gordon and Chuck; Charmian with Jason. Shane was with Baptiste, and Martin had stayed behind to work on his writing. Leonard was playing the guitar with the other musicians, one on accordion and another on trumpet. Polixenes tapped the tambourine and rattled its bells with a sense of duty and little enthusiasm. Magda and George were both still in prison.

Some local women had dressed in black and red and they danced on the cobbles, their wide shirts billowing out into stiff bells and their headdresses adorned with flowers. The crowd, dressed in coats and hats, clapped in time and cheered and whistled. The dancers didn't seem to feel the cold: their movement or the sheer excitement of the day seemed to warm them.

A group of maids had gathered in a circle and Frieda noticed that Evgeniya had a black eye again. When Frieda had enquired about it before, the woman had waved a hand in the air: it was nothing and she did not want to discuss it.

'When is George being released from jail?' Marianne asked Charmian.

'Later today if he can control himself, bloody fool. What about Magda?'

'Soon, I hope.'

'How is she?'

'We write letters to each other, but you know how slow the post is. She misses us all, especially Alexander. Her mother is caring for him but of course he wants his mother with him and can be very tearful. She is counting down the days.'

'We'll have a great party when she returns.'

'Oh yes. Definitely.'

The papas arrived in his long black cloak and high headdress, wooden cross on his chest, and the crowd followed him down to the boats, which had been decorated with wild flowers. He made some incantations in Greek, somewhere between singing and speaking, but everyone understood that the sea-vessels were being blessed. He raised his arms and drew a cross in the sky and the gulls added their raucous shrieks to his prayers like a hoarse Amen.

Then the food came: golden-crusted pastries made with feta and spinach, and meatballs and pitta, baklava and halva, and plenty to drink, too.

Frieda held hands with Esther and gazed out to sea. Jack was talking to Gordon and Chuck about Buddhism and Anthony was drawing sketches of people and trying to sell them to passers-by to make back money he had lost on drink and gambling.

'Why is the priest speaking to the boats, Ima?' asked Esther.

'He is blessing them so that they can travel safely,' said her mother.

Frieda wished at times that Carl could be with them. She felt increasingly that they were living a double life. She felt guilty at deceiving Jack yet bad that she was neglecting Carl, and she wondered how long it was tenable. Carl had made it clear that this was not in any sense a fling, that he loved her, that he wanted to be with her for life. How and when would it all work out?

She worried, too, about her Giddy. Always a quiet child, he had seemed more and more reclusive since they had arrived on Hydra. He was a high achiever at school but had not forged any new friendships and was becoming increasingly preoccupied with his rocks and fossils. Although she and Jack tried to present a united front when with the children, did Gideon somehow detect that their marriage was a sham?

The dancing had begun again and with more vigour, now that the boats had been blessed and the food and wine were flowing. Chubby, dark-haired women were still twirling on the cobbles, their heels clicking, one hand holding the skirt out wide, the other arched in the air above their heads.

Charmian was furious with George. What an idiot to get drunk, assault her and be arrested by the policemen and put in jail – and all because he had had good news that day. They had been getting on so well but now she was just irritated by him. The world might see him as a literary genius but to her he was just a prat.

She was concerned also about Shane and Baptiste: they were becoming intense. She had tried to confront Shane about the relationship, but her daughter would not speak about it, just flicked her blonde hair and crossed her arms in defiance. She insisted that they loved each other. Charmian urged her to go and see Dr Benedictus if she needed any help but she left it at that. She did not want her daughter to endure what she had had when she fell pregnant with Jennifer, but nor did she want to hear her daughter say that her mother was hardly the person to give relationship advice. Besides, they probably weren't sleeping together yet, Charmian thought – Shane would certainly tell her when there was something to say.

The previous night, when her parents were at the taverna, Baptiste had led Shane into a wooded area behind the monastery and they had made love for the first time, Baptiste clearly more experienced than her. He had been gentle and kind, lowering the girl onto his coat, spread upon the hard ground. The way he kissed her, the way he reached inside her dress and caressed her breasts, the way he prised apart her legs to discover her warm and furry there like a mouse, was all done slowly and with delicacy, determined not to scare her away. Even his kissing was light, brushing her lips like butterfly wings and suppressing his usual cries when he came for fear of scaring her. It only made her love him more. Compared to her volatile parents, here was tenderness indeed. Shane thought: my parents think they are above the Katsikas family, but it is Baptiste who is thoughtful and gentle.

Charmian worried also about Martin becoming reclusive and his tendency to turn inwards. He often had trouble with his eyesight. Maybe she should take him to Athens and have it seen to. She fretted too about Jason. Her only child to be born on the island (she remembered the Hydriot women spitting on him three times for luck in order to ward off the evil eye), he seemed more settled in Greece than any of them, although all her children had picked up Greek more easily than their parents. They all knew that the idyll would come to an end eventually. How would Jason cope?

As the music became louder, faster, more frantic, Marianne looked across to where Leonard was sitting with his guitar and was surprised to see him surrounded by a group of girls. As she wheeled Axel Joachim's pushchair nearer, she saw that, in between songs, he was signing autographs and the admirers were taking photos with him and giggling.

So it had begun. Marianne had dreaded this day, when he would be well known and the fans, especially the female ones, would start to surround him, stalk him, find him. He would never be hers again and she would have to share him with the rest of the world, be pushed aside.

Sometimes he disappeared overnight. It had happened several times and was always unexpected.

The previous evening, they had been so happy together. There had been no quarrel. One of his songs was being played on the radio and he had beckoned Marianne to his study so that they could listen to *Bird on a Wire* and watch, through his window, an actual bird on the wire. It had made them laugh, the serendipity of it, as if the crow were in the pay of the radio station.

After the gathering at the taverna and its dramatic ending with George being hauled away, they had come home, gone out on the balcony, dressed warmly, and watched the sun stain the purple and lemon sky. They had smoked their favourite roll-ups with hash in the centre and then gone inside to make love.

That night, Marianne dreamed that she was outside a huge fortress with impenetrable brick walls, slits for windows and a moat around it. She looked up and saw Leonard at the window. The drawbridge was up and she called out to him. He laughed and would not lower the bridge. But when pretty young girls arrived and asked to enter, he let them in. She cried, she begged, but he refused and eventually she walked away.

Marianne woke with a start, her heart thudding. She turned to Leonard for comfort but he was not there. Slipping on her dressing-gown she went to his study. Not there either. It was four a.m. He had disappeared again.

Marianne tried to get back to sleep but could not. Just after seven, Axel Joachim cried out for her and his warm milk. She went to him, lifted him from the bed and nuzzled her nose in his warm face. His skin was soft, his eyes crusty: carefully, she wiped them clean. He sucked his thumb. Kyria Sophia had arrived by then, they had breakfast and the day began.

Leonard only returned at lunchtime. He looked a bit dishevelled but handsome as ever, the cold reddening his cheeks, his hair windswept.

Marianne had resolved not to nag him or ask him where he had been but when she saw him, her heart fell, and the words just tumbled out. 'Where have you been, Leonard? I was so worried about you.'

'No need to, Marianne. You can see that I am safe.' He seemed cheerful.

'But where did you go to in the middle of the night? Who were you with?'

'You cannot tie me to the tree and nail me down. I am as free as the sea and as dark, as turbulent,' and with those words he went to get washed.

There was a bad atmosphere between them that day. He stayed mostly in his study where she could hear the typewriter and the radio. She busied herself with her son and going to see Axel who was no less volatile, complaining about Sonja and her demands.

You want it all, you men, thought Marianne. What do I get in return? But she said nothing.

She held herself as a shield against them, angry with them, hating them, loving them.

She had not put a fresh gardenia in Leonard's room that day. In the afternoon she relented, picked the shiniest one from the potted plant on the terrace, and took it to him. As she drew out the limp one, and placed the new bloom in his vase, he caught her arm, kissed it and a truce was wordlessly sealed.

After months in the Athenian jail, Magda returned to Hydra. As the boat drew in, her friends gathered on the quayside. They were dressed warmly, defying the temperature. The sky was numb with cold, a slab of marble above a hostile sea.

Magda looked very different. Gone were the flamboyant clothes; gone was the chunky jewellery; gone was her shock of red hair; and gone was the bright make-up.

Alexis helped her from the boat, and Marianne hugged her. 'Magda, my big sister,' she said, 'it's so wonderful to have you back with us again.'

Magda smiled and squeezed Marianne's hands, her eyes were full of tears, her skin sallow as if she had aged ten years in four months.

Because of the cold, Douskos had moved the tables and chairs inside the taverna and that is where they sat, in a circle, facing each other, candles dancing and bending in jars at the centre of the table. A fire clicked and sizzled in the grate.

George was also out of jail and promising to drink less; Leonard was calmer now that he had seen the positive reaction to his latest novel, poems and songs; and Jack and Frieda were presenting a united front, determined to focus on – and save – their marriage.

The wine was brought, olives and dolmades; pitta and hummus in wicker baskets; feta and tomatoes shiny and glazed in their own juices; salamis and cold meats; grilled sardines crowned with lemon wedges; crusty bread carried in by Demi and wrapped in tea towels to keep it warm, like a swaddled baby, protected against the winter. Marianne had organised the lunch for Magda and the woman smiled her thanks to her friend. She said little, as if the imprisonment had robbed her not only of exuberance and life, but also speech.

'I am so happy to have you back here with us,' said Marianne. 'We have good times ahead. Axel Joachim will be very pleased to see Alexander. He's walking now and starting to say a few words.' Magda smiled. 'When Alexander returns, can you both live at the house?'

'Yes,' whispered Magda. 'My mother is on her way now to return him to me. We have the home and a small allowance. I'll sell Lagoudera, too, and live a quiet life, just my boy and me. That's all I want.'

While they were eating, Nick Katsikas came in and handed a note to George. They had a phone in the store now and the message was for him to ring his agent. George excused himself, and left the table. Charmian scowled at him: 'It's Magda's welcome home lunch,' she muttered, still angry about his arrest.

As always, the air was thick with conversation: Jack, Gordon and Chuck were telling each other about the books they were writing; Leonard was lending a volume of Lorca's poetry to Charmian who was telling him about *Peel Me a Lotus* and confessing to finding the mixing of information and description a challenge; Marianne was listening to Frieda and Anthony talk about the merits of acrylic painting as opposed to watercolour as a medium for conveying the rustic beauty of Greece; Norman was quiet as usual but absorbing what was being said.

Ten minutes later, George came running in, his face excited.

'That was my agent,' he said. The mixture of wine, coughing, and good news made him struggle to speak. '*My Brother Jack* has won the Miles Franklin Award and is going to be made into a television series.'

Applause broke out.

Charmian hugged him. 'Oh George, that's great.'

'What do you know, Charm? Thanks everyone. Jeez, this year is getting better and better.'

He coughed again and wiped his mouth with his hanky, concealing the blood from his wife.

'Can't believe it. ABC has bought the rights and they say it's going to be the biggest thing they've done for years. They're casting Nick Tate as David Meredith and Marion Johns and Chris Christensen as the mum and dad. I can hardly take it in.'

'Will you be adapting it?' asked Gordon.

'No, I think that's beyond my abilities. I've said I have someone in mind to write the script.' He turned to Charmian.

She blushed. 'Me?'

'Yup. I've told them. That's who I want.'

More wine was brought, the drinks were again on George and toasts were made.

'You know,' said George, standing up for his address, his eyes glassy with tears, looking around him, 'many of us here have come from imperfect families. On Hydra, we have made our own family. It is a slightly odd one, misshapen perhaps…'

There were cheers and whoops of agreement.

'…but it is a family nevertheless and I love every one of you seated here today. Sharing food and wine and conversation with you, is everything to me. Thank you. I appreciate you all.'

Charmian could not stop smiling. The thought that George, who she felt often underestimated her abilities as a writer, had asked her to write the script: it was amazing.

There were days when life on Hydra felt so good: friends gathered, laughing, talking, sharing. And, as if the day could not get any better, the door opened and in walked Alexis laden with suitcases, Magda's elderly mother and in her arms – Alexander.

The boy looked dazed and confused, even when Magda leapt from the table to hug him. He gazed around from Marianne to Charmian, all of whom he had known in the past but not seen in a while.

By now the table was covered in borrowed books; coffee cups rimmed with black; plates sticky with baklava and honey; wine glasses stained with their own filling and emptying, the air smoky and dense.

Although he and his granny came and sat at the table and were welcomed by all, the boy could not settle. He cried, tears scalding his red face and he threw his head back and wailed so the party gradually fell apart, Magda eager to take her mother and son home.

Back at their house, Charmian wasted no time in talking to George about the script. Shane was out with Baptiste, Jason was at Gideon and Esther's home, and Martin was in his room, working on his poetry, the newspaper and articles.

Fuelled by wine and excitement, Charmian and George talked animatedly.

'The thing is, what I really need you to capture is the complex relationship between David and Jack, the way the older brother feels that he is a redneck, a failure, measuring himself against his successful war correspondent brother.'

'I get that, George, but to what extent do viewers need to get the backstory, the parents, the differing ways they treated them?'

'Jeez, Charm, that's fundamental and the way that Jack has always idolised David. That's got to be in there. You have to decide when: either at the start or later as flashbacks, maybe. You're the dramatist.'

'But I also want to include Jack and Sheila and their romance.'

'Sure, and more about David's marriage, too, which I'll develop in *Clean Straw for Nothing.*'

She was thinking of Jack and Pat Johnston in real life and believed that they deserved to be portrayed. All the time, her mind was moving between the fictional characters and the real ones: to what extent was David Meredith just a vehicle for her husband to shout out his achievements as a war correspondent? Was writing fiction simply showing off? She recognised the details that were taken from their lives, not just the thinly disguised characters but also the places: George's parents' home in Buxton Street, Melbourne, and the Caulfield Convalescent Hospital where his mother had been a nursing sister. She hoped that he would be discreet.

Who am I to talk? she thought. My two recent books as well as all the journalism have stemmed from our lives. Ideas have to come from somewhere.

But she kept her thoughts to herself. She needed to get on well with George if they were to work together: no fighting or falling out, no acrimony. The focus must be on their writing, not their marriage.

And so long days, long nights, were spent working, writing, so that the tapping of their typing filled the house. Sevasty cared for the children, making sure they were fed, being mother and father to them, tutting: I would never neglect my children in this way.

Elsewhere on the island Norman gathered tin cans and chicken wire for his installations; Anthony painted and missed Charmian; Gordon and Chuck wrote and read their work to each other on candlelit evenings; Leonard wrote, sang, composed; Jack made good progress with his Middle East book; and Frieda and Carl continued their cycle of loving and painting. The island hummed with creativity as if they were all contributing to a collective force of artistry and inspiration, urging each other on. It was as if an energy hung in the air, somewhere between the sea and the sky, hovering above the land like a grapevine stretched across a trellis, whose fruit everyone was welcome to pluck and eat. And no matter how many grapes were picked, the vine just kept on giving.

One day when Frieda and Carl were in her studio, she seemed upset.

149

'What is it?' he asked her, stroking her hair with his thin fingers.

'Jack is sent a cheque every month from his publishers. It's not much, yet we thought we could manage on it if we were very careful but money is so tight. The cheque comes in, Jack orders books and periodicals that he says he needs for research and there are things the children need, and there is nothing left for my materials.'

Carl laughed. 'Frieda, why didn't you tell me before? I have the monthly allowance from my father's law firm and plenty to spare. There is hardly much to buy in Hydra, is there? Write down anything you want and I will put in an order to the art suppliers in Piraeus. I need to get some sent for me, too.'

'Thank you, Carl. Isn't your father kind to send you money every month?'

'Don't be naïve. He does so because he is bribing me to go back to Toronto and take over the practice. He's getting older now, his health isn't great, and he wants to retire but he won't do so unless I go back so it's a kind of emotional blackmail.'

'Why doesn't he just sell it?'

'He doesn't want to. He built it up himself and he wants his only child to carry on the legacy.'

'I see. Does it make you feel obliged?'

'Yes, of course. It is designed to do that and it works. His only son is bumming around on a Greek island while he wants me back there. How does one cope with guilt?'

'Don't ask me. I feel bad because I am living a lie and deceiving Jack. He is a good man but he doesn't make me happy. I shouldn't have married him. It was a mistake. I don't know what is going to happen. I wanted to give my children a wonderful family life but I have failed to do that. I thought that Hydra would heal our marriage but the bright light has only made the cracks clearer.'

Two large tears ran down her face.

'It will be alright,' said Carl, wiping them away. 'You'll see.'

A week later, he arrived at the studio with a large package.

'Surprise,' he exclaimed. 'Open up.'

She tore the brown paper away to reveal many delights: six large canvases, new brushes, their tips white and furry, and tubes of oil paints: cerulean, ochre, magenta, crimson, emerald, ivory and lavender.

'Oh Carl,' she exclaimed. 'That is so kind. How can I ever thank you?'

'Well,' he said, holding her so close that she could see the veins in his watery grey eyes, 'I can think of one way.'

xxvii

Their secret was out.

Leonard no longer belonged exclusively to Marianne.

Hydra no longer belonged only to the artists.

Film crews and photographers began to arrive.

One morning, when Marianne left Leonard to write, there was a group of young fans standing outside their door.

'Does Leonard Cohen live here?' a pretty girl asked.

'No,' Marianne said. 'You must have the wrong house.'

As more came, she began to feel as if she were pressed against a sea-wall, and the tide was coming in.

'A photographer called James Burke is coming to see me today,' said Leonard one day as they lay in bed and watched the daylight slide tentatively through the shutters and urge them into action. The winter had been harsh and, although not over, Marianne was beginning to feel that the sky was lightening a little, that it wasn't as granite and flint as it had been and that maybe spring was going to come after all. The previous day, she had seen narcissus and hyacinth shoots poking their green tips tentatively through the hard earth.

'That's good. Is he staying on Hydra?'

'Yes, just for a few days. He's from *Life* magazine and they are going to do a photographic piece on me, at the house and maybe at Douskos in the evening, seeing how we live here. You don't mind, do you?'

'Of course not. It's great that you're getting so much media attention.'

But deep inside her stomach she did mind. She worried that Leonard was slipping away from her and that she would lose him. She had recurring nightmares of him being whisked away in a boat and vanishing into the distance; or him being carried away by women and her being abandoned on the cliff edge, clutching her scarf around her head, calling out for him and not being heard.

As if sensing her need for reassurance, he rolled over and kissed her, on her ears, on her neck, on her brow and on her lips, as if to say that his focus was on her and that he was not going anywhere: she need not worry.

But there were still times when he would disappear for hours, day and night, and she would not ask him where he had been and with whom, for fear of annoying or, even worse, losing him.

James Burke was a tall man, well spoken, with a warm smile and round glasses. He and Leonard immediately liked each other. First, he took photos of Leonard outside the house, his dark hair against the white walls, standing at his wooden door, opening it with a key and also in his study at the typewriter, his head bent to the task and his back to the camera. Outside the window there was the famous cable cutting the view in two and James waited patiently for a bird to perch on the wire. There would be no article with these photos: the images had to speak for themselves but the readers would understand the allusion.

James walked with Leonard to the harbour where, for the sake of the images, they put the tables and chairs outside even though it was January. Everyone wore long sleeves and jumpers and the tables, usually scrubbed bare, were dressed in checked cloths as if they, too, were protected against the cold.

Leonard introduced James to his friends: Marianne had been with Axel Joachim to see Magda and Alexander, helping the boys to become used to each other again and she joined the friends at the taverna, the baby on her lap; Charmian and George came too, as arranged, as did Norman.

James clicked his camera over and over, while the friends shared retsina and red wine from carafes, baskets of bread and sautéed squid.

'Just behave as you would normally do when you're together and try to ignore me snapping away,' he said.

'Feel free to come and join us, Jim, when you want to,' said George, and so the photographer took a short break to eat and drink.

'Where's home for you?' asked Leonard.

'Nowhere and everywhere,' said James, tearing a lump of crusty bread and dipping it in olive oil which it absorbed like a sponge. 'I was born in Shanghai where my father was a missionary but I've lived in India, Afghanistan, China, all over.'

153

'That must have been amazing,' Charmian joined in.

'It was. I've photographed everything from snow leopards to earthquakes and monsoons. I go where the work is. Wherever I am, is home.' And after a short break he was photographing again, trying to capture and reflect their everyday way of life. As the images were black and white, he didn't seem to mind the lack of blue sky and sunshine.

'Where did you and Leonard meet?' he asked Marianne who was comfortable with talking to someone whose face was hidden behind a camera.

'In Katsikas' store,' she laughed.

'Would you mind posing there with your basket?' he asked.

'Sure.' So she left the baby with Leonard and walked there with James. Her light hair tied in a ponytail, she stood by the bottles of wine and vinegar, pretending to survey the goods. He clicked away, knowing that his editors would love the recreation of the day they met.

James stayed for a few days. He took pictures of the friends on donkeys trekking up the stony hillside, at the harbour, on a boat, and in the evenings, at the taverna.

Used to him now, the community chatted freely and ignored his snapping. Leonard played the guitar, everyone relaxed. James captured them in their circle, with the pine tree overhead, its dark leaves lit by the table candles so that the foliage appeared silver underneath.

The following day he photographed Norman painting; the one-belled chapel stamped against the sky; the harbour curved around the bay, and a lone goat standing in a gridded window as if he was framed by it.

Next came Charmian and George holding hands on the cobbled quayside; Marianne holding Axel Joachim up to the sun; and somehow James got himself invited into some of the grander houses where there were gilt mirrors and padded furnishings.

They became so used to James that they were sad to see him go, but when he packed up his equipment and boarded the boat to Piraeus, they waved him off.

'Thank you again,' he called. 'I'll send you a copy when the pictures are in.'

They had to wait a few weeks but there was great excitement when Leonard brought a copy of *Life* magazine to the taverna one evening.

There were thirty images used, a large feature, and it was delightful.

'Look,' said George, coughing and laughing, 'there's you and me, Charm, loved up as ever!'

'Hm,' said his wife, her face twisting. 'And they say the camera never lies.'

'Lovely one of you painting, Norman,' said Gordon, but the artist looked shy.

'Hey!' said Marianne. 'They even included the posing goat!'

But a few days later, a film crew arrived.

A Girl in Black was being made with Anthony Quinn and director Michael Cacoyannis, and a notice went up asking for extras. Martin and Shane Johnston had small parts. Months later they heard that it had been nominated for a Palme d'Or at Cannes.

And then there was *Boy on a Dolphin*, the first Hollywood film made in Greece. The local people watched with amazement as the crew brought landing barges, water-tankers and diesel generators to their shores, happy to make some extra cash from supplying them with food, drink and donkeys to get around on.

'Hey, what do you know?' boasted George one evening at the taverna, 'Mart's not only got a part but he's acting as interpreter for Sophia Loren.'

'That's amazing,' said Chuck. 'What's the film about?'

'Well, Sophia is with her boyfriend, an illegal immigrant from Albania, working as a sponge diver on Hydra...'

'Slightly more glamorous than Vasilis.' Charmian knocked back a glass of vodka in one go.

'...and she finds an ancient statue of a boy on a dolphin at the bottom of the Aegean.'

'Unlikely,' laughed Gordon, 'but interesting.'

'And then she is torn between selling it to Dr James Calder, played by Alan Ladd who is an archaeologist, and Victor, who is a dodgy dealer with a history of selling on works of art seized by the Nazis. It all ends happily; the people of Hydra celebrate and she winds up in the arms of Calder.'

'Ah,' said Charmian belching. 'Sweet.'

As if that wasn't enough, a little while later, Melina Mercouri turned up on the island to play a part in *Phaedra*. Jason never forgot the day when he tripped her up and wrestled with her in donkey dung.

This media invasion was greeted by people in different ways.

The Hydriots watched the events with some amazement and did not mind the extra revenue it brought them. The actors and crew shopped at Katsikas', rented rooms in local hostelries, had their hair cut at Demosthenes', and drank and ate at Douskos'.

Some of the artists were bemused and fascinated but for Marianne it was disconcerting. It confirmed her loss of Leonard and she felt side-lined. His songs were frequently on the radio now and there were often articles about him in the papers. In her mind, it marked a separation between them; they were destined, now, to travel different paths.

The *Life* feature and other profiles all told the world about Hydra so it was now common for tourists to aim for the island to seek Leonard out. Celebrities visited: Twiggy, Jackie Kennedy, Yoko Ono and John Lennon – with their long dark hair and matching sunglasses making them immediately conspicuous although they were probably hoping for the opposite.

For Marianne, the island had been an escape, a secret, *their* secret. How could it continue to be that now that everyone knew about it?

Leonard tried hard to reassure her. 'Just because other people come here does not lessen my love for you, Marianne.'

Put like that, what he said made sense but then when he disappeared for hours on end or when he locked himself away in his room and seemed to abandon her, she felt herself being edged to the margins of his life.

When they were alone together, that was when she was happiest, with no-one else to interfere in their love. Facing each other in the bed or on the terrace, his gaze, those lovely dark eyes, would be focused on her, not looking anywhere else but at her, and then she knew that she was the centre of his attention and that he loved her deeply.

When he came forward to kiss her and their lips met, it only proved his devotion to her.

She tried to train herself to enjoy these times and not think of the times when he would vanish from sight.

Treasure what you have, she said to herself, and be grateful for it.

Having lost a few days being photographed by James Burke, George and Charmian were keen to return to work on the script. Charmian moved between George's novel and her own adaptation coming to life on the typewriter. Mostly they agreed on the wording and angle but after a drink-filled break for lunch at Katsikas', problems sometimes arose.

'The thing is, Charm,' said George as they settled back to their studies at home, 'I want you to focus more on the contrast between the brothers: David, suave, sophisticated but arrogant and bullish, and Jack, rougher, more of an Aussie redneck, uneducated, coarse. They embody the new Australia as opposed to the old Australia.'

'I get that, George, but the problem is that we don't want to play into those stereotypes, do we? There is so much of that image already around.'

'That's not our responsibility, Charm. Stereotypes exist because there are those people, and I have to be honest about Jack and show that he is like that. It's not for me to worry about how the rest of the world perceives Aussies.'

'Of course it is.' Her face was red from the drink and the heat of the argument. 'You are one of the country's best and most famous writers and we want to show that those perceptions are too simplistic. It is more complex than that.'

'That's for cultural commentators and sociologists to worry about: not writers.'

'So writers have no responsibility? They just write whatever they want?'

George sighed. His chest was tight and he really didn't want to waste time arguing. 'They tell the truth at the deepest level possible and to their best ability. That's what writers do. To be honest, Charm, I have ABC breathing down my neck, desperately waiting for the script, and you are wasting fucking time talking about morality.'

'Morality? Identity? Reputation? They are trivial, are they?'

'I asked you to write the script because I thought you were the best person to do it but you need to remember that it is my novel and you are merely adapting it, not questioning the very essence of it.'

'And that's the crux of it. I'm just the monkey at the typewriter. You are the important writer in the marriage, doing the great work. We all know that.' She crossed her arms angrily.

'Jeez,' George shouted. 'You and your fucking chips on both shoulders from your childhood. I can't deal with it. Just adapt the bloody script, will you, or I'll find someone else.'

And he started coughing and spluttering so badly that his face swelled and blood spurted from his mouth like water arching from the spout of a stone lion.

'Take it easy, George,' she said, standing up. He could not breathe; he was clutching his chest as if trying to control it. Charmian bent to place her palm on his forehead: it was hot and he was shivering with fever.

'Bloody hell, George, calm down, I was just saying...' but he fell with a thud on the stone floor and the blood did not stop coming. He began, it seemed, to choke on it.

'My god,' panicked Charmian, 'George, George,' and she ran into the kitchen where the maid was preparing dumplings for that evening's stew.

Sevasty ran in, her fingers floury, and her face red. She was used to the couple's drunken antics and nasty fights, but she had never seen George on the floor, a river of blood flowing from his mouth and forming an ever-widening pool on the white tiles.

'Go and fetch Dr Benedictus. Run as fast as you can, Sevasty. Dr Benedictus!'

Sevasty wiped her hands on her apron and flew as fast as her plump body and thick legs would let her to the surgery. All down the hill she saw donkeys and goats and stray cats and an old friend of hers but they were a smudge as she raced, panting, panicking all the way.

As she ran in, puffing, trying to catch her breath, Mrs Benedictus was smiling beatifically as always. Sevasty's voice was garbled, the doctor's wife's calm. She said her husband was with a patient but that he would come as soon as he could.

It seemed to Charmian that the doctor took hours to arrive but, in reality, it was only twenty minutes. George was barely conscious, his eyes rolling in his head, spittle foaming on his lips, sweating and bleeding continuously. As she knelt beside him on the stone floor, stroking his hair, her tears fell onto his face. Please don't die, George. I love you. I hate you. I am sorry I questioned you. You are everything to me. She thought of when they first met. She thought of Martin, Shane and Jason. She thought of Jennifer. The tears fell fast now. It had come to this: two heavy drinkers collapsed on the floor.

Dr Benedictus arrived, his beard white and eyes shiny. He kneeled to examine George, unbuttoning his shirt to help him breathe. Nothing riled him. In his thirty years as a doctor on Hydra, he had seen it all: the bloody, cut faces of drunk and foolish Hydriots; stillborn babies; women whose husbands beat them up; the artistic community's ailments and injuries. It did not matter to him whether the patients were locals, expats or tourists: they were all people who needed tending to and that is what he did, a serene benignity on his face, his large hands careful, and that ever-present smile.

He could smell drink on George. He took his pulse, listened to his heart and knew that it was serious. Through a combination of Dr Benedictus' broken English, Charmian's limited Greek, and Sevasty's breathless, panicky translating, it was agreed that George should go to hospital in Athens. With the blood still streaming and George's difficulty with breathing, he had no energy to argue.

He was too ill for a mule ride so Sevasty found Tzimmi with his log cart attached to the donkey, and it was in this unceremonious way that George was taken down to the harbour, for the boat to Piraeus and then a taxi to central Athens. For years afterwards he would remember – and happily dine out on the tale of – how he was slumped, bloody and sweat-stained, in a rough cart, clutching a bag of clean clothes packed by Charmian and a copy of Conrad's *Heart of Darkness*, where all he could see was Tzimmi's donkey's arse opening and closing and the lumps of shit that emerged frequently and stenchingly from it.

Charmian offered to go with him but there was no room in the cart and George insisted that she stay behind and finish the 'goddam script!' To be honest, she was relieved. She could be with the children, finish *Peel Me a Lotus*, complete the script unhindered, send it off to ABC and stay on Hydra. She had never liked hospitals and that was why she had chosen to have Jason at home, with the aid of a Greek midwife who rubbed

Charmian's tummy with alcohol, then gave her two tumblers of ouzo to drink while Martin sat beside her reading *The Iliad* aloud.

George had refused to have a phone at home but there was one at Katsikas' store now and Leonard and Marianne had one, too, so she would be able to phone the hospital for regular updates and she and George would write each other letters.

George did not enjoy his time in the Athenian hospital. The stark white walls and absence of beauty made him homesick for his lovely house with its colourful rugs and mayhem. He thought of his friends at Douskos' Taverna and Leonard's playing and singing and the warm atmosphere, their faces lit by candles, under the giant pine tree. He even missed his fights with Charmian, their repartee, their discussions and the drink. One of the kinder young nurses, Angelina, whose dark hair and dimpled cheeks George fell for, managed to find him some paper and a pen so that he could carry on writing *Clean Straw for Nothing*. After much nagging, she also procured a small bottle of brandy and George rationed himself to one swig a day. But when George tried to slap her backside, she gave him a frown and walked away.

A succession of doctors saw him and he was eventually diagnosed with pneumonia, tuberculosis and Herrmann's Disease, which had damaged his kidneys. George didn't know who Herrmann was but he cursed the fucking bastard for identifying a putrid illness and giving his name to it.

Charmian worked better on her own. Without George's intervention and with the children at school, she wrote the script she wanted and within two weeks had it finished, packaged and posted at Katsikas'. She also made great progress with *Peel Me a Lotus*. As she neared the end of her book, the writing flowed more easily and she wondered to what extent the constant immersion in language, the atmosphere of Hydra and even George's absence were spurring her on. Certainly she felt that there was a new rhythm and energy to her writing as she wrote of: *Morning sounds. Children, donkeys, roosters, bells – goat bells, sheep bells, donkey bells, church bells, even...yes, the handbell of Dionysus the dustman...all the air swinging with bells.*

That completed, she turned back to her first novel, *Walk to the Paradise Gardens*. She found the transition from fact to fiction difficult. She had worried that George's next novel was too much about their marriage and its infidelities but now she faced the same dilemmas herself. In describing the turbulent marriage of Charles and Julia Cant, she kept finding herself referring to incidents that had happened to her and George. How could she justify using real life in *her* fiction when she had criticised him for doing the same?

As well as her writing, Charmian became more domesticated while George was away. She worked alongside Sevasty in the kitchen, ignored her disapproving tuts and head-shaking, and learned to make home-made pitta and baklava. The children were amazed when they came home from school to find that their mother had cooked and even laid the table. She felt her life was more complete and harmonious with George away and, of course, her needs were well met by Anthony and Nature Boy, the one more aesthetic and sophisticated, the other more carnal, the combined effect, perfectly satisfactory.

She even wondered whether she would be better off without her husband. She was certainly more productive, drank less, and it was good not to be fighting and wrestling every day: so exhausting, so draining. Then one of his letters would arrive and she would miss the old bastard.

My dear Charm (he would write)

Here I lie in this white sanctuary devoid of your beauty or that of the island. It is so dull here that sometimes I think I may have died and gone to boring old heaven, especially as the only nurse here with any humanity is called Angelina. And what a pretty little angel she is. I wouldn't be surprised if she had wings. She has supplied me with pen and paper and a bit of brandy which is keeping me going. She has also promised me chocolate.

The matron and the doctors are cold and business-like and lack the warmth and humour that we usually associate with the Greeks. They are giving me tests each day and this morning one of the sternest doctors stuck his gloved fingers up my arse. Jeez, that hurt! I felt like charging him and saying there are many people who would like to do that, mate! What gives you the right? Join the queue!

I miss you terribly, my little praying mantis. How is the script? Have you finished it yet? I bet you have put in all sorts of things that I didn't want you to, you little minx. Oh well. And the kids, how are they? Is Sevasty still shaking her head and being disgusted at us and our bohemian ways?

Give my love to our children and our friends at the taverna, Len, Mari, Mag, Norm, Chuck, Gord, Tony, Pete, Liv, Jack and Frieda.

I miss them all but especially I miss you, not just our spats and disputes but also our very deep, indisputable, love.

George.

Each time Charmian read one of his letters, the tears sprang to her eyes. She wondered: am I just used to him or is he right that this is love? Or, like her script, simply a version of it?

Marianne and Axel were sitting in the living room of the house they both owned. Axel Joachim was walking now in that unsteady, drunken way that toddlers do, bumping into furniture, looking as if he was about to fall as he tottered, so that Marianne had to keep jumping up to stop him from hurting himself. She noticed how bare and shabby the house was now, as if Axel had lost interest in it.

'Sonja's left? Why?'

'Who knows? She didn't like Hydra, couldn't settle, was homesick. I did everything I could for her but the woman was impossible. There was no pleasing her. Partly I see what she means. I've had enough of this place for a while. I need a change. There's nothing to keep me here.'

Marianne thought: pay attention to your son in front of you, but she didn't say anything. Axel flared up so easily that she tried to avoid provoking him.

'Where would you go to if you did leave?'

The little boy held his wooden giraffe, which he was now chewing. Marianne wiped the dribble from his chin.

'John and I are corresponding and he has asked me to join him in Mexico.'

'How is he now? Did he recover from that horrible mosquito bite?'

'Yes. He's much better now. He's great, busy with the occult and spirituality and horoscopes, and all sorts of interesting things.'

'He's an amazing man.'

Marianne remembered when he gave her a solid bar of gold and told her she could sell it and keep the money.

'But I may just go back to Oslo. There is nothing to keep me here. My writing's going through a bad patch and I think possibly being near home and family will root me again. I don't know.' He was dark under his eyes as if he hadn't slept.

'I see. What shall we do with our house, then?'

'We could rent it out. You don't need to live here now that you're with Leonard,' he said bitterly.

163

Marianne did not say: you left me first for Patricia, remember?

'That's fine. Let's talk more about it later. I have to go now. Come on, darling,' she scooped the boy up. 'We are going to see your friend, Alexander.'

Wheeling the pushchair across the island, Marianne wondered what the effect would be on Axel Joachim of not seeing his father very often. Well, he has me, she thought.

The February wind was biting and she tucked the boy's jacket closely around him, smoothed his hair down against the cold.

The women met at Katsikas' where the scrubbed tables and chairs were still indoors, by the warm fire.

Marianne hugged her friend. Magda still looked pale but the colour was slowly returning to her cheeks, if not to her hair.

'You know, Marianne,' her voice was quieter than before, 'your letters really sustained me when I was in prison.'

'You are my friend,' said Marianne, stroking the woman's arm. 'It was my pleasure.'

The boys on the rug played cautiously, as if they had forgotten each other and would need time to reconnect. Marianne had brought some wooden animals in her basket and the boys enjoyed arranging them on the floor: cows, sheep, giraffes, lions, rhinos, horses. 'Not very Greek,' laughed Marianne. 'My mother sent them, but we might see them all one day.'

'Do you think you will leave Hydra?' asked Magda.

'I just don't know. I feel Leonard slipping away from me, as if he is being dragged in the opposite direction. I do not know where our future lies or whether we will even stay together.'

'But he loves you so deeply. I can see it in his eyes.'

'And I love him, but he is being pulled towards fame and America. We have groups of fans outside our house every day now. He has phone calls with famous singers like Joni Mitchell and Bob Dylan.'

Anthony Katsikas brought them bowls of olives and tzatziki, baskets of bread and crisp whitebait with lemon wedges. The boys abandoned their animals and immersed pitta in dips. Then they were brought a Greek salad with feta, a white slab like a tile on the top.

The women drank red wine from large glasses; the boys had apple juice in tumblers.

'What about your plans, Magda?'

'I don't know. All I want at the moment is stability and peace, so I will certainly stay for a while. Who knows what the future might bring?'

'But you will not reunite with Paolo?'

'Never. I could not forgive him for what he did to me.'

'Have you heard from him?'

'Nothing. We seem to have been forgotten. He has moved on.'

Alexander choked on an olive stone and Magda had to slap him on the back. The boy's eyes watered but the coughing soon stopped. Axel Joachim stared at him in horror.

Anthony brought them watermelon wedges, the flesh blood-red and the rinds green and tough. Their crescent shapes reminded Marianne of the boats in the harbour.

'Yes, my ex is the same.' Marianne avoided saying Axel's name. 'He just told me that he may go to Oslo as there is nothing to keep him here.'

'Extraordinary. Some of these men are so selfish and like children. They don't accept responsibility for their own sons.'

'Well, we do not need them. We can manage on our own.'

'So true. We are stronger than we realise.'

By now the tables were covered in smeared plates, watermelon rind and wooden animals. The women wiped their sons' faces which were stained with olives, apple and melon juice, like a watercolour painting on the canvas of their skin.

'When you were younger, Magda, did you dream of a perfect family? Mother, father, two children, all happy, seated around the table, eating cake?'

'Absolutely. I remember the colourful drawings in picture books. It looked so perfect, like a dream. I thought: I want to live like that.'

'I think we should start a campaign to make picture books more like reality: a man, a woman, not married, the child only hers. She has a new lover; it isn't his child.'

'Yes, or maybe we could use Paolo as our inspiration: a woman, a man, baby boy, princess in the Hilton Hotel and the man runs away. The woman is in prison, away from her child. That is the reality.'

'Yes. Good idea. Then maybe little girls will not grow up with the crazy dreams we had and not be disappointed by life.'

They paid Nick and put the boys' jackets and hats on.

The harbour was still, a slight mist hanging above the water like soft breath. The boats were rocking slightly as if they were finding it hard to settle after a busy morning. Some were blue, some red, but with a different colour inside, like tissue-lined envelopes. A few fishermen were swilling out buckets and nets, ready for the next day's catch. The cobbles were caked in a light frost as if there was a chill that they just could not shake off. A gull perched on a rock and shrieked in protest at the weather, its beak open wide.

The women hugged and promised to meet up again soon, they looked forward to sunbathing when the weather improved. Then each took her son and walked away.

The rolling motion of the pushchair up the hill sent Axel Joachim to sleep, his cheeks pink from the breeze and his drowsiness. Marianne felt suddenly quite bleak. She was still reeling from Axel's insensitive comments earlier and it made her feel that she had failed. She had tried to create a perfect family unit for her son and it had not worked out. Then she had tried to recreate that family again with Leonard and although he loved the child, she felt that he too would slip away from their lives. Was there a man alive who could be a good father to her son? And, if so, where was he?

Her spirits were lifted by the sight of more green shoots peeking through the dark ground but again dashed by the usual group of fans outside their wooden door.

'We are looking for Leonard Cohen,' said a young girl, her hair plaited, a camera looped expectantly around her neck.

'He isn't here,' said Marianne sternly. 'Excuse me,' and she wheeled her sleeping baby home.

In his study, Leonard was singing into the phone. He waved at Marianne but continued his song.

Marianne transferred her warm-cheeked son into his cot, waved to Kyria Sophia who was doing the laundry and went back to see Leonard in his study.

'Yes, that's great. Thank you, Judy, let's see what happens. Bye,' and he put the phone down. 'That was Judy Collins in New York,' he said. 'She wanted me to sing her *Suzanne*.'

'Lovely.'

'How was Axel?'

'Selfish.'

'And Magda?'

'Bruised.'

'What's wrong, Marianne?' He held her in his arms.

'Your adoring fans are outside again and I feel that you are being pulled away from me like a boat on the shore and I am left standing on the quay. I don't want to lose you, Leonard.'

'That won't happen. I love you,' and he kissed her so softly, so tenderly, that she had to believe him. It was a while since they had made love, so many people phoning, writing, talking, and constantly interfering in their relationship.

They moved through to the bedroom where the shutters were closed in defiance of the cold. Kyria Sophia had lit one of her silver plates of coals in the room and they glowed orange and hot.

They undressed each other and slipped between the sheets, their movements as slow and deliberate as a dance. They touched each other as if rediscovering who the other was, as if the landscape they found themselves in had made everything unfamiliar, as if it needed redefining.

Leonard had forgotten how soft her skin was, her mouth warm and open, and caressing her breasts was like rediscovering a pleasure thought to be mislaid or lost for ever. He liked to run his hands up and down her legs and part them gently as if he were unwrapping fruit, peeling it, pushing apart the flesh to discover what lay within.

She liked to hold him, feel him hard like a thick plant stem in her hand, moving him and kissing him at the same time so that they did not know where they were or what day or even season it was.

And still they kissed, their mouths adept at finding each other even with their eyes closed so that they only felt and smelled each other and did not need to see.

Then he was within her and she dug her nails in his back and felt him give her all that he was, all that he could be and they both cried when they came for they knew how lucky they were, how privileged they were, to have each other. And along with that came her fear, her terror, that it might not always be that way.

Marianne sobbed, and Leonard licked the salt-tears from her face.

'Do not be afraid, my darling Marianne. We have danced on the pebbles in the moonlight and we are always free.'

Each time Carl came to Frieda's studio, he brought her a gift. Sometimes it was goat's cheese wrapped like a moon in fig leaves, or a tin of olive oil infused with thyme. Another day, a basket of peaches, their skin pink and their flesh white. Limited by the season, what Katsikas had in his shop or by what Carl could buy on his occasional trips to Athens, he took great care to choose presents that would please her: jars of honey, the comb trapped in its golden syrup; chocolates individually wrapped, like secrets, in tissue paper; three cakes of herbal soap in a sturdy, hinged box.

'There is no need to bring me presents,' she said, gratefully accepting them.

'I know, Frieda, but I want to express to you how much I love you,' and he kissed her lightly. 'I know that you're unhappy in your marriage and I feel deeply for you.'

'I have so much guilt about deceiving Jack. We married too young. Maybe we were carried away by the romanticism of the kibbutz with its orange groves and roaming chickens. On paper, we seemed the perfect couple, both from South African Jewish backgrounds, both passionate Zionists with a love of culture and a hunger for excitement.'

'It isn't the paper that counts. It is what happens when two people are together.'

'I understand that now, Carl. The evening at Olivia's party, I knew for the first time what that meant, to feel so connected to someone that you cannot believe that you are not physically joined.'

'I feel that with you, too, Frieda.'

'When I met you, it was like being struck by thunder. I wondered if it would be a fling or short passion which would then fizzle out, but you and I are in love. There is no doubting that, but what do we do about it? I feel so bad for you that you have to hide away from the other artists, as if you were a shadow.'

'I don't mind. I meet Anthony sometimes for a drink and a chat and also John. He shakes so badly now that I think he likes to watch me paint, almost as if I am doing it for him. I bring him gifts from Athens that he likes: cocoa powder and cereal.'

'Yes, you are kind, but you can't be part of our Douskos group.'

'I am willing to endure that for you. It is a small price to pay for your happiness. You make sacrifices, too. I want to be with you for ever, Frieda. I have never felt this way about anyone before. Whatever happens, we need to be together.'

'But how? It would destroy Jack to break up the family. We will soon have to leave Hydra as his money will run out. It was only ever meant to be for twelve months.'

'Where were you intending to go next?'

'We weren't sure. Maybe Great Britain. Maybe the States.'

'I have pressure on me, too. My father is constantly writing to tell me that he is too frail to run the legal practice and that he wants me to take it over. Keep it in the family. He does not rate my painting. He thinks that I am a wayward youth who has run away to a Greek island to get it out my system, paint my silly canvases, and that I will return and see sense, marry a boring girl who my mother approves of, have lots of kids and be a lawyer.'

'What can you do?'

'I don't know. Although we are such different people, I do feel some duty towards my father and I understand that a man who built up the company from nothing does not want to hand it on to strangers or sell it.'

'There is nothing we can do. We are both trapped.'

'Don't despair. I will think of an answer. I am working on it. But all our talk of the past and future means that we are wasting the present.' He closed the shutters in the studio and they lay together on the blue settee.

And he kissed her more passionately now, his tongue deep in her mouth, and he caressed her breasts through her shirt, then unbuttoned it, throwing it and her bra to the floor, and she undressed him too. She felt him stiff in her hands and she drew him to her.

They made love with every part of them, as if there was nothing more to give, and when they both came, they cried out and kissed while he wiped her tears away with his hand and they felt closer than ever.

The gifts created problems for Frieda. She did not want Carl to feel that she did not appreciate them by leaving them in her studio (she now had a crate of them), but what would she do with them? She had thought of giving them away but to whom? All the women she thought of – The Gardenia Dwarf, Polixenes, Mrs Benedictus – would question where they came from. She had thought of giving them to Evgeniya but it would seem very odd, and as the woman was amazingly dedicated to her husband in spite of his drinking and violence, it would feel somehow unethical, giving the fruits of an illicit affair to a devoted wife. Besides which, what would Evgeniya do with jasmine perfume and peaches?

Frieda would have to take them home but explain their presence.

One evening, when the children were in bed, she and Jack were in the living room. They seldom rowed nowadays. It was more an atmosphere of neutrality, like talking to a colleague. There was no emotion, they had passed beyond that, and there was an unspoken acceptance that their marriage was over. They both agreed that they had put too many expectations on Hydra as a healing force and, unsurprisingly, it had failed them.

'The monthly cheques just aren't enough,' said Jack. 'I've had to order more books for my research as I can't get to a library. Then there are the bills, the rent, things the children need. It doesn't stretch far enough. All I can think of is that we get rid of Evgeniya.'

'No, that's not a good idea. She enables us both to do our work and Esther adores her. Also, she is the breadwinner in her family and they need the money.' She sighed and avoided his eyes. 'Well, I've had a bit of good news. I've sold a couple of paintings.'

'Really? That's great. Who to?'

'Oh, just friends, but anyway, I've bought us all some treats that we can share, just to make life more pleasant for us and the kids.'

'Treats. What kind of treats?'

'Oh, fruit and olive oil, and soap which Esther would like, and chocolate and honey for Giddy, and I got you some goat's cheese as it's your favourite.'

'It's kind of you, Frieda but don't you think they are a bit frivolous when we need money for bills and I have no typewriter ribbon?' Frieda remembered on the kibbutz when there had been an argument over money. The committee had had to decide what to spend their limited funds on and when it came to a dispute between a new typewriter ribbon for Jack or a part for the tractor, the latter won. Jack resigned from the committee in protest and there was a bad atmosphere for weeks.

'Well, I did spend some of my earnings on new canvases and paints so that I can produce more and sell more.' Frieda could feel her cheeks burning. 'That makes sense, doesn't it? Investing in materials?'

'In a way, yes, but don't you think it is quite important that I am able to type, given that my advances from the publisher are supporting us?'

'Yes, of course.' Frieda wondered whether money issues would haunt her all her life. If their marriage did break down, she would be a single parent with two children and how would she manage then? She had no qualifications and had only lived on a kibbutz and painted. Jack was never going to earn much, and was clearly not great at managing it. If they had two households to run, they would surely struggle. Most of her cousins and friends from school had married wealthy businessmen in South Africa and now had houses with pools and maids and she had turned her back on all that in her quest for excitement. Had that been wise?

'Look, I'm not saying that you haven't done well to sell paintings but if you do sell any more, please can you bring that money into the home rather than buying soap and honey that we don't need?'

That night, Frieda could not settle even though Jack always slept in the other room now. At first the children had queried it but had come to accept it as the norm. She had mixed visions of Jack and Carl and her children's little faces, Esther's podgy and pink, Giddy's more fragile and pale, and she didn't know what to do or who to confide in. The thought of them eating gifts from her lover made her stomach turn.

She had wondered about telling her mother about Carl, but she would be upset. Frieda thought of telling Charmian but she would see the affair as wild and exciting and trivialise it. Also, when she was drunk, she had a habit of blurting things out and Frieda did not know if Charmian could be trusted. Frieda thought of talking to Marianne who also knew the perils of marriage but she did not know her quite well enough. No, she really was on her own and would have to manage.

The following day she saw Carl and told him about the situation.

'It's easy,' he said. 'I told you I'm good at finding solutions. Must be the legal training. My father sends me far too much money. It's to make me feel guilty. I will give you some each month. There's nothing here to spend it on. How many goat bells do you need?'

'But that will be like you paying for the relationship?'

'Don't be silly,' he laughed. 'I am just helping the person I love.'

171

And that is what happened. Every time his monthly amount came through, he gave Frieda a wad of notes. She stared in amazement at the huge pile, fluttering slightly at the edges like a baby bird plucking up courage to fly away.

'Thank you so much,' she whispered. She had never held so much money in her hands before. On the kibbutz, everything was communal and the kibbutzniks were allowed no money or possessions of their own. When her mother had sent her frequent packages of food and treats, she had had to share them out.

She had to think carefully about when to hand it over to Jack so as not to look suspicious.

Life was becoming ever more complicated.

She gave away some paintings to friends whose houses they regularly visited so that it would appear that they had bought them.

'I thought you might like a painting of the boats in the harbour,' she said to Charmian; and 'Would you like a picture of the goats eating rosemary on the hill?' to Marianne and Leonard; or 'Magda, I thought you would like my painting of the monastery? Please take it.'

They were all delighted and some, like Olivia who loved her gift of a painting of wild anemones, offered to pay.

'No,' said Frieda emphatically. 'It's my way of thanking you for making us all so welcome here.'

At night, her body burned with deceit. She had the terrible sense, lying there alone in the dark, with the moonlight slipping in through the slats, that this deception could not be sustained for ever and that when it was revealed, it would do so explosively.

Somehow, she was now sure that it could only end badly.

xxxi

By early March, a modest sun made a half-hearted appearance. Narcissi and wild hyacinths sent their stiff stalks above the soil as if to establish themselves and some buds opened, peeping out cautiously from long leaves and releasing their uncompromised perfume across the island.

Marianne and Magda often took their sons down to the beach, where the women could start to tan their winter-white skin. The friends sat in the bay, edging their cotton dresses above the knees, as if reintroducing their bodies to sunshine. It was yet not warm enough for swimsuits. They lay on towels next to where Alexander and Axel Joachim, beside each other, did not interact. They had spades and sometimes they dug them into the sand or picked up shells to examine but they acted as two independent entities. Occasionally, one boy would stare at the other, spade suspended in the air, and then return to his occupation and his narrow world.

'How are you settling back again, Magda?' Marianne's voice sounded deeper when they lay down.

'It's certainly an adjustment. Prison felt like hell. You saw it. It really was a nightmare and here we are by the beautiful sea. It is hard to accept. It's like when you've been asleep and your eyes have to adapt to the light. When I wake up each morning, I still think I am in darkness and then I have to get used to the beauty again.'

Marianne understood. In a way, it reminded her of living with Axel and then with Leonard. Before she was blind; then she saw the sunlight. Sometimes it was hard to accept that it could be the case, that it could actually be true. She could not believe that someone could love her that deeply.

'I know what you mean, Magda. When we have been through difficult times – and we both have – beauty seems more intense somehow.'

'That's true. After the ugliness of the prison, I can hardly bear the beauty of the sea.'

'When I was a child, Momo tried to balance the difficulty of my home life by introducing me to loveliness: the birds, white shells, the calm lake. She showed me that nature was a gift which could belong to me.'

173

It was a practice sun that lit the sea in March, warming itself up in preparation for summer: the water shone but not brightly, like silver that needed polishing. There were little sparkles on the surface that flashed and glinted but then dissolved, unsustainable. Small waves rose and peaked, like the emerging breasts of young girls, before flattening out again. The sand made a margin by the sea, of white mixed with shells and stones. All was still as the day opened itself to them. Even the gulls, usually coarsely vocal with their smoker's cough squawk, were silent, as if assessing the atmosphere and acting accordingly. One perched on a ledge near them, astonishing them with its size, looking out of proportion with its large head, sharp yellow beak and white body. Both boys looked up to stare at it if in awe.

'Bub,' said Axel Joachim pointing to the gull.

'Yes,' said his mother. 'Bird. Big bird, isn't it?'

'I am worried about Alexander.' Magda raked the sand with her fingers. 'He is very quiet and serious and at night he sometimes wakes up screaming and crying.'

'He has had a shock, that is all. He will settle back here again.'

As she spoke of Magda's son, Marianne also thought of hers. She wondered how he would be affected by losing his father and then maybe Leonard, too. All these connections and breakages.

'Anyway, I've reached a decision, to stay on Hydra. Alexander needs stability now.'

Yes, thought Marianne, we all do.

'And what about you, Marianne? Will you stay also?'

'I don't know. I am concerned by the reports I have read in the paper about the junta overthrowing the government. It's all very worrying.'

'You can't believe those stories you read.'

'Are you sure, Magda? The *Athens News* predicts that the military will take over the running of this country and it will be terrible. All foreigners will need permits, they say, to prove that we are not earning anything in Greece. All weapons and knives will have to be handed in. It will be awful, like living under a dictatorship.'

'It won't happen. The papers like to scare us.'

'Maybe you're right. My mother wants us to return to Oslo. She is getting older now and she would like to give Axel Joachim the kind of childhood that she was unable to give me. Leonard is becoming famous. I think he will end up in America but would that be good for us?'

'He loves you. You know that.'

'Yes, he does, but he loves his writing more. I am competing with it but the writing will always win. He likes life simple, bare; he is so selfless, so hardworking. He is almost like a monk.'

'Albeit a very sexy monk.'

Marianne laughed. 'That's true. I can never work out if he is selfish or selfless.'

'Both maybe. But what about you, Marianne? What do you want to do with your life?'

The question startled Marianne. She had not thought much about it. No-one else had asked her. 'I am still trying to work that out,' she said quietly. 'When I was a little girl, I danced and sang, and I wrote and drew. I thought I could do and be anything I wanted but now that I am an adult, I realise how hard it is to do those things and do them well. Maybe I am better as a support to others than as a success myself.'

'The typical situation for women: not important in their own right but only in their roles as daughters, wives, mothers. Looking after everyone else. Feeding them. Clothing them. Loving them. And when they are done with us they discard us like apple cores.'

Marianne agreed with her friend but did not want to reinforce her cynicism.

'Well,' she smiled warmly, 'let me serve you today.'

They sat in a circle to share their picnic, two women, two little boys. The sun glazed the blonde heads of Marianne and her son; she saw with sadness how the light illuminated Alexander's dark hair but was unable to lift Magda's grey. She remembered when she had first met Magda and her red mane was the first thing she had noticed, bright and strong; then the chunky jewellery and her lovely, colourful clothes. Now she looked drab and Marianne thought: the sun can make its subjects shine but it can also bleach them. Had the men in her own life made her sparkle or wiped her out?

From baskets and bags, Marianne brought out pitta, slit at home and made into packages, stuffed with falafel and salad; olives and gherkins in little boxes; tzatziki to moisten their meal with. Magda had cut the boys strips of carrot and cucumber, and plucked grapes from their stalks so that they sat heaped and translucent in a little bowl. The women drank white wine, the boys juice.

'Look,' said Marianne, grabbing her friend's arm. 'It's him again. He is always here when we are.'

They looked up to the promontory where a man in trunks waved, then lifted his arms above his head and dived in a perfect arc. The water foamed around him, the waves unsettled and then they flattened out again. The women could see his head above the surface, protruding like a seal.

'He's called Theodore,' said Magda, shyly. 'He is a sailor and I've known him for a while. He came to Lagoudera a few times.'

'How exciting,' teased Marianne. 'I think you have an admirer.'

'I'm not interested. Men have hurt me too badly. I am better on my own.'

'I know what you mean, Magda. They can be dangerous.' She wiped the mouths of the boys and packed the food away.

'Not Leonard.'

'Don't idolise him. He is an amazing man, so talented, but he has his flaws. Sometimes he disappears at night or for a whole day and he will not say where he has been.'

'He's probably just walking, thinking about his writing and his songs, getting ideas. He would never betray you.'

'I don't know. He has written a song about a Suzanne who he says was just a friend but there are lines that sound romantic to me; and there is this recent song, *Sisters of Mercy*, which also makes me doubtful. Who are these women and how do they bring him comfort?'

'I don't know, Marianne. Why don't you ask him?'

'Because it annoys him. He's both secretive and honest, open and closed. He doesn't like me to ask him lots of questions and he hates it when I am possessive and jealous. When he writes, he is in a kind of trance and I don't want to be the one to break it.'

'You have rights as well, Marianne.' She poured her friend more wine. 'You don't always have to bow to his wishes.'

'That is the dilemma. If you do what others want, then you keep the peace but you do not develop your own identity. If you fight back, then the atmosphere is horrible for you and your children. I grew up with my parents fighting. It is dreadful. I don't want that for my child.'

The swimmer was out of the water now and drying himself in a blue towel.

'Yes,' said Magda, her mouth twisting, 'but then you can end up being a doormat with everyone treading over you.' Marianne listened carefully to her friend's words. 'And you ask me why I don't want to get involved with a man again.'

Later, after they had parted company and Marianne was wheeling Axel Joachim up the hill, she still had the bitter taste of Magda's words in her mouth. Maybe she was right: maybe Leonard was determining their lives and Marianne was following sheep-like behind him? Maybe she was treating him like a God who set the agenda and she was merely a worshipper?

But when she rang the goat bell and Leonard came to help her carry the sleeping boy and his pushchair carefully up the steps to their home, all her fears dissipated.

'How was Magda?' he asked quietly when the boy had been transferred to his bed.

'Cynical and bitter. I hope that the old Magda will one day appear again.'

Leonard took her in his arms. 'If anyone can return her to the light, it is you.'

They kissed sweetly, gently. He ran his hands over her warm hair.

'And how are you? How is your writing?'

'Good news. Someone in Hollywood wants to buy *Suzanne*.'

'That is fantastic, Leonard.'

'Yes, and there is talk about making an LP. But I'm afraid that I will have to go to New York again. Judy Collins wants me to sing in one of her concerts.'

Marianne could feel herself swallowing her own objections. 'Then you must go, Leonard, of course, I understand.'

'I met up with Martin Johnston. He wanted to show me his work. That boy has serious talent. He's had some issues with his eyesight but, at last, it is being seen to.'

'That's good.'

'Yes. He has a very bright future ahead of him if George and Charmian take note and ensure he gets a decent university education.'

'Do you think they won't?'

'You know what Charmian and George are like. They are loving parents when they are sober, not fighting, and when they are not obsessed with their own writing, which is rarely. You've lived with two writers. You know how driven we are so that we shut everything else out.'

Marianne smiled at the truth of his words.

'If you have children, you have to tend to their needs, surely? Maybe that's why I have been wary about having them. I very much want to but I worry about whether I will be a father who focuses enough on them and not just on myself.'

'Axel Joachim adores you.'

'Yes, but you do most of the loving and nurturing. I am there for some sweet playing from time to time.'

Marianne thought: I do not think the children Leonard has will be with me, and it made her sad.

'Anyway, good news. Martin tells me his father will return tomorrow from the hospital in Athens. Charmian wants his friends to be there on the quay to welcome him and she has organised a party. I think that we should go.'

They gathered on the quayside, waiting for the blue boat to appear.

'At least he'll return in more style than when he left,' said Charmian, drawing a cigarette from her lipsticked mouth.

Marianne laughed. 'Yes, Alexis' boat is certainly more dignified than Tzimmi's log cart.'

Leonard stood beside her, his hat brim lowered and a scarf around his face to conceal him from the fans who gathered not far away, gazing over and wondering if it could really be him.

George's children were there, too: Martin, tall and solemn; Shane, willowy and blonde, her fingers linked with her swarthy boyfriend, Baptiste; and Jason, his eyes shiny with excitement at the prospect of seeing his father again.

Also there were Gordon and Chuck; Jack, Frieda and their children; and Norman, thin and pale.

They all cheered when they saw the sharp nose of the boat, edging like a dolphin into the harbour.

George waved and Charmian was surprised as tears sprung uncontrollably from her eyes. She thought back to that morning when she had gone down to the sea-cave to find her lovely Nature Boy. He was there as usual, in his tiny loincloth, sucking turtle eggs and then tossing the empty shells onto the rocks where they shattered into fragments, like broken china. He had wiped the gluey egg whites from his mouth and waved to Charmian. She was wearing a sarong, knotted at the waist so that it could be loosened as easily as his pants, nothing hindering their passion.

Like a magician, he undid them both, threw off her lacy knickers and the two of them fell to the rocks, where he fucked her, ferally. She felt the pelt on his skin and the knots in his hair. How she called out when they both came and the roughness scraped her back, but she did not care because it was real, so genuine, and she loved it when he kissed her, the dirt on him, his skin filthy with nature, his mouth salty with seaweed and the dregs of wine left in discarded bottles.

Afterwards they sat together on a goatskin and watched the embers of his fire, noticing how the pine logs glowed defiantly orange before collapsing into ash.

'Hello,' she called out when the boat was moored and Alexis tied the rope carefully around the bollard. 'Welcome home.'

Everyone clapped and the children whooped as George was helped off by Alexis. There were hugs and embraces for them all.

'Jeez,' he said, 'what a welcome.' He passed his bag to Martin and smiled broadly. 'Hello, Charm, how are you?'

'Fine, George, all the better for seeing you.'

He looked well, his skin pink and scrubbed as if it had been hidden under his rough, unshaven face all along and had now been revealed. He smelled of hospitals, of sterile dressings and liniment and his breath was fresh and devoid of alcohol.

They all walked up the hill to the Johnston house, breaking up into small groups as they went, the island feeling warmer from greeting George. The children competed for their father's attention. Martin was desperate to tell him about his new writing project; Shane and Baptiste wanted George to know how much in love they were; Jason, his eyes and hair shiny, just craved his father's love.

Back at their house, Sevasty and Charmian had sliced roast lamb and braised chickens, and there were bowls of gleaming vegetables: potatoes and onions; artichokes in olive oil; aubergines, their purple skins velvet and mysterious. Demi's loaves were dotted with sesame seeds.

George was disorientated but delighted to be home. It was great to see colour again after the white sterility of the hospital: Greek rugs hung on the walls; all their books stacked on shelf after shelf; vases with narcissi were placed carefully around the room and sweetened it, like perfume sprayed on a lady's neck and wrist. He reached out his hand out for one of the many bottles of wine but Charmian scolded him.

'What did the doctor say?'

'He said take your medicine, cut down on the drinking and smoking, and rest. Jeez, I'm going to obey him on two of those. Give me a break, Charm.'

She laughed nervously and turned away to serve food and drink to their guests: she was determined not to fight with him on his return.

Leonard came up and hugged his friend.

'It's good to see you, George,' he whispered. 'Back to the darkness, back to the light.'

'Well, in a way. Jeez, it was a bit grim but I shall make use of it in my writing. I've started a new story called *The Verdict*, another David Meredith one, but it will draw on my experience. You know, suffering for my art and all that shit. But, Len, what's this I hear about you becoming a star?'

Leonard modestly waved that away. 'I want to talk to you about Martin. That young man is outstanding, a very talented writer.'

'I agree.'

'When you were away, I had a look at some of his poetry.'

'That was good of you, Len, I appreciate it.' George swallowed a lump in his throat: it should have been him reading his son's work, not a friend. He listened to Leonard and tried hard not to be defensive.

'He has written some great rhyming verse in Ogden Nash style and some more lyrical writing derived from Homer. His memory is unbelievable. He can recite huge chunks by heart.'

'I know. He won a prize at school for Greek poetry and both he and Shane were awarded diplomas for their grasp of the language.'

'But now he has started this novella. It is so crazy that it is beautiful. It's about a mammoth who is dug up and becomes a professor!'

'Really?' George tipped back a bottle of retsina so that the coolness slipped down his throat.

'The quality of the language is amazing. He writes his serious articles, too. The boy is incredible. I think he should apply to Oxford.'

'Our friends in England, the Camerons, say the same. You think he is seriously that clever?'

'No doubt about it. He has a remarkable, sharp mind.'

'Well, thanks, Len, for giving him your advice.'

'You are welcome, George. Anytime. Writers should encourage each other.'

He went over to be with Marianne.

George hugged Norman. 'How's the art work going, Norm?'

The taciturn man nodded. He was even scrawnier and dirtier than when George had last seen him. He wondered whether, if artists became their art, Norman was slowly transforming into a thin scrap, as insubstantial as the litter he found on the roadside.

'Yes, it's going. You know how it is.'

Later, when George hugged Marianne he thought: I swear that woman gets more beautiful each day.

'So you survived, George?'

'Well, I had a nurse called Angelina, angel by name and nature.' Marianne could hear that his words were slurred. 'She saved me. Jeez, that woman was gorgeous. She brought me brandy and pen and paper and bits of chocolate. I tried to hug her but she always pushed me away as if I was a naughty boy.'

'You are a naughty boy! We all know that.'

'Hello, George.' Jack approached to hug him.

'Hey, Jack. How's the book?'

'First draft finished. I'm working on the editing now, checking some facts.'

'Good on you, mate.'

'Well, I have pressure on me. The money runs out in a few months' time although things are looking up. Frieda has sold some of her paintings.'

'Jeez, that's great.'

'Anyway, how about you? How are you feeling? You look well.'

In another part of the room, a group of friends were admiring Frieda's painting of boats in the harbour.

'Isn't it great?' asked Charmian, already worse for wear. 'She gave it to us. Look at the fucking colours. She is amazing.'

'I like the way you've done the reflections, Frieda, of the sky and the boats,' said Gordon.

'Yes, and the seagulls,' added Chuck. 'Some close by and detailed; others vaguer in the distance.'

Charmian grinned. 'You two lovers, you never seem to fight. Nor do George and me any more. We're going to be like you, harmonious. That time is over.'

'Would you like a painting?' Frieda asked the men.

'Sure,' said Gordon. 'How much do you charge?'

'I don't. I'd be honoured to...'

Jack came up behind Frieda and joined the group.

'Um, let's talk about it another time,' she said hastily. 'I think we need to get these children home.'

By the time the guests had left, Charmian and George were smashed. The children, as usual, had put themselves to bed, Martin having read Greek myths to Jason until the young boy's eyelids closed and Martin had crept out of the room.

'Let's leave the plates till tomorrow; Sevasty will help me,' Charmian said. 'Come to bed with me, George.'

Worn out by his first day back and all the travelling, he complied. They climbed in between the sheets and blankets and she rolled over towards him.

'Welcome home, George.'

'Thanks, Charm. It's good to be here.'

'I've missed you, you bastard. The fighting and the spatting over the script.'

'You finished it, I suppose?'

'Yup. And it's posted and they like it and it was so much fucking easier without you and your hang-ups.'

'You probably put in all sorts of things that I would have hated.'

'Yup.' She belched and laughed at the same time.

'Steady on, Charm. It is my novel.'

'Yeah, but you asked me to adapt it so then you had to let it go.'

'Little minx.'

She crossed her arms and lifted her nightdress over her head to snuggle up to him. Naked himself, he turned to caress her breasts and was overwhelmed at the shape and feel of them. He bent his head to take a nipple in his mouth and lick his tongue around it. Then he kissed her and their lips were so numb with wine that they could hardly taste or feel each other.

He felt himself half-stiffen and climbed on top of Charmian. She thought of Nature Boy and could not stop the comparisons from entering her head: the youngster was so much more adept at it, as if he had been born only to eat and fuck. He was an animal who did not analyse what he did. George was an ill man, out of practice.

Despite kissing his wife and trying to keep himself hard, he felt his penis flop and shrivel like a dying plant. She tried to help him. She curled her legs around his back, dug her nails so hard into his skin that he cried out in pain, kissed him so fiercely that he felt himself shocked as she nibbled his tongue.

'Fucking hell, Charm. You trying to put me back in hospital?' He sighed, defeated. 'No, no good.' He rolled off her and lay on his back. The room was hopelessly dark. He could feel his heart racing.

She bent to him and took him in her mouth but to no avail. His dick could not be revived. It was limp and small, like a hibernating animal. It felt pathetic to her, like a chewy sweet, to be spat out. She couldn't help it; she felt contempt. She hated him.

Before she knew it, George had fallen asleep as if following the example set by his penis. His snores were thick as if travelling through mucus.

She lay in the dark room and thought of Anthony and his elegant, chivalrous lovemaking and of Nature Boy, the rough manliness of him and his sheer, utter filth.

'So Leonard's in New York again?'

'Yes. He's singing in a huge concert with Judy Collins and he has interviews to promote his songs.'

Magda and Marianne were lying in their favourite spot in the cove. They had spread striped towels on the sand and their boys both had sunhats on to keep them from the sun, which shone with more confidence now, getting into its stride. The sea was sparkling, blinking and flashing silver like a lighthouse, as if being allowed to rest in the winter had strengthened it, enabling it to return with more vigour.

'Are you feeling abandoned?' They watched how the waves tickled the shore with their white fingers and then retreated. 'We both know how men desert us when they like.'

'Sometimes I think that we give our hearts and souls to these men and we are not always appreciated. Leonard is much kinder and more loving to me than Axel ever was, but they both have a habit of disappearing – in body and emotion. You know that Axel has left?'

'No, I didn't. Where's he gone to?'

'Oslo. We had to let Maria go. I feel bad for her. She has so many children and struggles for money. If we get tenants, we'll employ her again but we can't afford to pay her when the house is empty. It must be so hard for her, without a wage.'

'I'm sorry about Maria but don't worry about Axel. Men are not worth it,' said Magda bitterly. 'I am much happier on my own.'

Marianne wanted to say: you do not seem happier to me, but kept her thoughts to herself.

'I am worried about the government being overthrown. There has been more about it in the *Athens News*. Haven't you seen the extra police on Hydra?'

'Yes. You were right. I hear that they are raiding people's houses for narcotics and getting them sent to jail in Aegina. What is happening to this beautiful country?'

'I don't know, Magda. I read that a doctor in Athens who said that he believed in democracy was thrown behind bars.'

'That's terrible. Have you thought more about your future here?'

'I don't know what to do. If the expats are ordered out, I will have no choice. Already, we have to prove that we are not earning money from Greece itself. I had to fill in a form. You are still determined to stay here, even if things get bad?'

'I told you, Alexander needs stability. His life has been too difficult up to now.'

At that moment, Theodore waved from the promontory above them before diving in a perfect arch into the sea. The water foamed around him before flattening out again, his head a small dome in the distance.

'It is definitely you who he is waving at,' said Marianne. 'He is trying to impress you.'

'Do you think so?' asked Magda, blushing. Her excitement seemed to contradict her earlier claims of being happy single.

They both looked to the sea for answers as if the issues were too large for them to solve. Was love worth it, the heavy emotional price one paid? Where was it best to live? And how?

But the water offered no answers. It just did as it always did: pulled back, lifted itself into a ledge, rolled out again and collapsed upon the sand.

Marianne was still thinking about these issues when she collected her post from Katsikas': there were two letters, one with a Norwegian stamp and one American. She tucked them into the pushchair, which she was wheeling up the hill to Kala Pigadia while the little boy slept, his head flopped to one side.

She saw Maria coming towards her and felt bad. She had been such a good maid but to her amazement, Maria was friendly. The two women embraced and Maria smiled at the sleeping child. Maria looked so pretty out of her overall. Her hair was down, she wore an attractive floral dress and she smelled sweet. There was clearly no resentment against Marianne and she felt relieved. Maybe she had some paid work somewhere else.

In her limited Greek, Marianne said that she was sorry to have to let her go.

Maria smiled as if to say: it's really no problem at all.

At Leonard's home, Kyria Sophia helped her in with the pushchair and they let Axel Joachim sleep in that.

Marianne took her letters and some coffee onto the terrace. It was the first day since the winter that she had been able to sit out there. It was lovely to open it up again and have fresh air rather than be cooped up in the house. There were mounds of dead leaves blown onto the floor which she would ask Kyria Sophia to sweep up later. The whole terrace needed spring-cleaning.

Beyond the terrace the mountains rose, purple and strong. All of Hydra pointed towards the harbour, as if expectant. She remembered the first time she had visited Leonard's house and she had gasped at the view and at the kisses he bestowed upon her later.

She would keep his letter for last. She opened Axel's and read:

Marianne,

I am now settled in Oslo with my girlfriend, Lena. We seem to understand each other well.

Georg Johannesen, you know, the poet, has written to me from Budapest where he is living with his Jewish girlfriend, asking if he can rent our house to him from August through to the winter. Is that alright with you? I assume it is empty. We might as well make some money from it.

I told Maria that we don't need her at the moment. I thought she would be upset about the loss of income but she seemed fine about it. If we get tenants, she can do cleaning and cooking for them, I suppose.

Your mother has been making trouble, going to the Oslo bailiff's office, saying that I am not paying for my son. I imagine she wants to ruin my reputation. Please talk to her and try to make her see sense. When I can afford to, I will help you, but you have Leonard to support you now. I hear that he is making splashes around the world so he surely has some money spare?

My film Line *has been nominated for a Palme d'Or award in Cannes so maybe my luck will start to improve. It's about time.*

I am writing a new novel but some days go better than others.

Are you well?

Axel

Marianne smiled wryly. It would have been good if he had asked about his son. She drank her coffee. It was powerful, as if trying to strengthen her. She opened Leonard's letter:

My darling Marianne,

Last night I sang in front of 3,000 people at a benefit concert in New York. I tried to give everything to them. Judy Collins introduced me. It was by no means my best performance: my voice was dry and hoarse after the long journey, my guitar was out of tune, but the audience still seemed to like it. I was pleased that I had failed. It made me happy to recall how flawed I am and reminded me that I must keep on striving.

People appear to like my songs. Maybe they know that I feel the pain with them and it is real. They play them on the radio and John Hammond and Columbia want to bring out an LP of my music. They will include Suzanne, Winter Lady *and some others. Maybe* Sisters of Mercy. *I am writing a song for you. I have the image for the cover. I found it near here, the Chelsea Hotel (where so far I have spotted Andy Warhol, Bob Dylan and Joni Mitchell) in a Botanica. It's a Mexican image of the Anima Sola or Lonely Soul portrayed as a woman breaking out of chains and flames and her eyes are gazing towards heaven. I really like the symbolism of the spirit triumphing over the material, the abstract over the concrete.*

Donald Brittain and Don Owen want to make a documentary about me called Ladies and Gentlemen, Mr Leonard Cohen. *They would film in Montreal and Hydra. Would you mind them coming to see us?*

I miss you day and night. I do not sleep well when I am without you. The loneliness eats away at me and gnaws at my soul. I know that suffering is good for me and so I welcome it. It makes me write better and love you more but how I wish I was with you, the candles lit, sharing the good light with you.

How is Kyria Sophia? Is she still disapproving?

And how is that beautiful blonde boy? Please hug him for me.

To you, Marianne, I always send my heart.

I love it when it rains because the sea and the tears we have shed are up in the sky and coming down upon us and we are united.

Your loving Leonard.

Marianne dropped his letter to her lap and the tears streamed in straight lines down her face. So this was what it had come to, her on her own, linked to two men only by paper. She worried about her future. Was she going to trail all over the world with her child, following Leonard, living in his shadow and being grateful for the little time they had together, in-between gigs and adoring girls screaming at him? It wouldn't be good for Axel Joachim. Her mother missed them. Maybe Oslo was the answer?

She hugged herself, feeling confused, alone.

Not far away, in the wood behind the two wells, Shane and Baptiste lay among the wild cyclamens, dabbing the earth with their white snow. He had been gentle and he had been patient, which she appreciated but as time went on, she became more confident, too. She did not need him to treat her like a child.

They lay side by side, their heads touching, her blonde hair curled over his dark, and it was Shane who rolled onto and kissed him. Her white skin pressed upon his swarthy skin so that they merged, their mouths, their bodies, united. Their love and passion leaked from them.

Elsewhere Carl and Frieda were in her studio. They had made love and were reclining on the blue settee, a blanket draped over them. Their skin and eyes were shining with the aftereffect of sex. She stroked his face, the planes and shapes it made, chiselled, angular.

'I have something to show you,' said Carl. He went to his bag and drew out a folder of photographs. 'My father has bought me a place in Toronto,' he said.

Frieda leafed through them and was amazed to see a large detached house, red brick, so solid and rooted that it looked as if it were planted in the earth. It had many large windows and looked light and spacious. There was space around it, with a garden behind. 'It's amazing.'

'Lovely, isn't it? It's in a smart suburb near his law firm.'

'That is so generous of him.'

Carl laughed dryly. 'Don't be naïve, Frieda. It is all part of his plan to lure me back. Good job, great salary, lovely house. He still doesn't understand that I do not want to be a lawyer. I love my painting and – I love you.'

Tears fell soft and fast from Frieda's eyes. 'There is no solution,' she whispered. 'I cannot see a way forward for us.'

'I can. I need to speak to my father again and then I have a proposal for you. You will need to think very carefully about it. It will change both of our lives for the better.'

They kissed before he dressed and left but not before he had given her more money.

'More? That's fantastic, Frieda.'

She could not look at Jack as she handed over the wad of cash. It had become increasingly difficult of late for them to have any contact with each other, either physical or verbal. It was as if their eyes knew it was over before their minds did. They had begun speaking through the children: 'Ask Abba if he wants honey in his yoghurt', or 'Tell Mummy that Evgeniya is going home now'. There had been awkward moments when Esther had tried to join them together.

One day they were all on the terrace, the four of them together but apart. Gideon was admiring his rocks; Jack was reading; Frieda was sitting with Esther at the table, but her eyes were searching the harbour as if looking for answers there. Esther had drawn a family of four in a white house by the sea. They each had a triangular body with flapping, skinny arms and legs and were holding hands. Frieda could see from the features on each that it was their family. Esther was small with short dark hair next to Gideon, who was taller than her and with glasses. He was linked to Frieda, who was not much bigger than her son, but she had long brown hair and she held hands with Jack, taller with a big beard and moustache.

Esther tugged at her mother.

'Ima. Look. Mummy, Daddy, Gideon, me.'

'That's lovely, sweetie.'

'Let's hold hands, like the picture.'

'No, darling.'

'Yes!'

Esther's face had gone red and she looked like she was about to cry, something she had been doing a lot lately. The teacher at nursery had mentioned this to Frieda. To avoid upsetting her, Frieda and Jack reluctantly held hands.

'Come on, Giddy,' said Frieda gently. 'It will make Esther happy.'

Sulkily, he dropped the rock he was studying. It landed with a thud on the terrace.

And so they stood in a line across the tiled floor, imitating the drawing. Esther did not seem pleased, as if she could detect the pretence. She cried without understanding why, her little face red and hot with confusion.

'Now, then,' said Jack picking her up. 'Shall we see if Peter's in my beard?'

Although the child was consoled and Gideon was relieved to be released from the charade, Frieda was neither.

She knew at the point when she and Jack obediently linked hands, and could hardly bear to, that her marriage was definitely now over.

It began as a normal day. Everyone was in their set place, chess pieces on a board: Jack in his study, Frieda in her studio, Gideon at school, and Esther with Evgeniya. It was early afternoon, bright light, and the little girl had returned from nursery and eaten her lunch – salami, olives and salad prettily arranged on a ceramic plate, with a slice of watermelon as a treat. Afterwards, the maid had wiped Esther's messy face, the red juices having stained her chin and sticky fingers. As the sun was so much stronger now, she insisted that the little girl play in the shaded part of the terrace, while she went inside to carry on with her chores.

Esther was plaiting her dollies' hair when she heard raised voices and crashing plates. She had heard this cacophony before and knew that Nikos was there with Evgeniya. She could hear the maid's usually soft voice, now high-pitched and screaming, and a man's deeper voice, shouting. Usually she did not go and investigate, staying on the balcony, gripping onto her dolls for comfort, but she heard a terrific thud on the floor below and then saw Nikos' bulky body storming up the hill. Esther dropped her dolly, hair half-tidied, and ran into the kitchen.

Evgeniya lay on the floor: her dark hair flayed out, her eyes closed and blood pouring from a gash in her head, staining the stone tiles. Esther knelt by her side, tears welling, and called her name, 'Evgeniya! Evgeniya!' No response, no movement at all apart from the blood which still sprung like an ugly fountain.

Esther ran from the house, her heart thudding, not knowing where she was going. She did not know where her father's study or her brother's school were, but she could certainly find Demi's bakery in the harbour with her mother's studio behind it, so she ran there, her face hot, her white T-shirt and shorts sweaty in the searing sun, her legs running as fast as they could. Tears sprang from her eyes and streamed down her face.

Esther could smell the yeasty bread as she approached but bypassed the bakery and went round the back. She pushed open the studio door.

Her mother was lying on the blue settee with a man on top of her. They were both naked. It was difficult to work out which limbs belonged to whom as they resembled an octopus with sprawling tentacles. The room smelled hot with sweat and wisteria scent. It was not an odour Esther could identify. As soon as her mother saw the open door and her daughter standing there, she jumped up, grabbing a towel to cover herself with, which seemed strange to Esther as she had often seen her mother nude.

The man leapt up too. Esther did not recognise him.

'Sweetheart,' said her mother, smoothing her hair, her voice rasping. 'What are you doing here?'

'Evgeniya's hurt, she's lying on the floor, covered in blood. I think she's dead.'

'Oh my god.' They both hastily put on their clothes. Frieda whispered something to the man. He nodded and left without a fuss, avoiding the child's puzzled eyes.

Hand in hand, Frieda and Esther mounted the hill to the house in Kala Pigadia. The air was oppressively hot and they panted as they climbed. They passed Maria who was on her way to do errands at Katsikas' and Frieda grabbed her. 'Dr Benedictus,' she cried. 'Go and get Dr Benedictus. It's Evgeniya.'

The colour drained from Maria's face and she ran down the hill to obey.

When Frieda and Esther reached the house, Evgeniya was in the same position; her eyes were closed but she was breathing. The blood on the stone floor had formed a pool. Frieda kneeled down to her, 'Evgeniya, dear Evgeniya, we are here now,' but the woman did not answer. Frieda unbuttoned the maid's overall to help her breathe, dabbed her forehead with a cold flannel and tried to stem the flow of blood, but there was no response.

Dr Benedictus arrived with his doctor's bag and his usual air of calm benignity. He tended the cut, wound bandage around her head and he and Frieda helped her onto a chair, him speaking quietly and reassuringly in Greek as he worked. A bruise was spreading across Evgeniya's face like a flower opening. She had her eyes open now and was conscious.

The doctor and Frieda helped her to her feet and to the front door.

At that moment Jack came running in. 'What's happened?'

'It's Evgeniya,' said Frieda without catching his eyes. 'She had a fall.' She did not want Esther to know what Nikos had done. 'You stay here with Esther. I will help Dr Benedictus walk Evgeniya home.'

'Are you sure?'

'Yes,' said Frieda. 'Comfort Esther, please. She has had a terrible shock.'

For many years afterwards, Frieda remembered this as evidence that deception did not come naturally to her. Had she been more cunning, she would have let Jack help the doctor and she would have stayed with Esther to beg or bribe her not to say a word about what she had seen. But she did not. And then it was too late.

By the time Frieda returned from Evgeniya's house she could tell from Jack's face that Esther had told him everything. They were on the terrace, Esther on her daddy's lap.

'Who is he?' Jack said. His face was ashen.

'What does it matter who he is?'

'George? Leonard? Norman?' His voice trembled with anger.

Esther was crying and had now wrapped herself around Frieda's legs. She stared at her father as if he were a stranger.

'No, none of those men. Let's discuss it later. Not in front of Esther.'

'I want to know who it is.' Jack's face had swelled purple with rage and a blue vein on the side of his head protruded.

'He's called Carl.'

'Carl?'

'Yes. I met him at Olivia's party.'

'At Christmas?'

'No. The party before that.'

'Just after we had arrived? So all this time you have been pretending to paint in your studio, you have been screwing another man?'

'I have also been painting, Jack. You know I have.'

'Do I? Can I trust anything you say?'

Frieda was stroking the hair of her daughter, wiping the tears that sprang from her hot little face.

'It's alright, Esther. I'm sorry, Jack. What I did was wrong but I was lonely and unhappy.'

'This was supposed to be our year of healing, of sorting out our marriage.'

'I know but it hasn't worked. We both know that it's over.'

Jack collapsed, his anger dissolving into tears. It broke Frieda's heart to hear him howling, like an animal in pain. She cried, and so did Esther.

Gideon came back from school and onto the terrace. He looked at them all weeping. To Frieda's shock, he walked calmly over to his rocks and started cleaning them.

'Hello, Giddy,' she said. 'I'm afraid there's been some upset today.' He did not answer or look up.

'I was going to give you good news,' Jack said when he had stopped crying. 'My publisher likes the book and is offering me another advance to do research in the States.'

'That is great, Jack.'

'I was going to suggest that we all moved there. Before I knew that...'

'Of course you must go. It is a great opportunity for you.'

'But what about you and the children?'

'I don't know. I need time to think. Can you give me an hour?'

He nodded. Frieda turned to Esther. 'Sweetie, stay here with Abba. I am going out and will see you soon.'

'Come, Esther, love,' called Jack softly, wiping his face. 'We'll have a story, shall we?'

On her way to see Carl, Frieda noticed how the island had painted itself yellow and sweet for spring. Narcissi and blossom seemed girly, innocently pretty. It seemed tragic to her that as her marriage was dying, the island was being reborn.

She pushed open the door of Carl's house and called to him. He was upstairs in his studio, a paintbrush in his hand. The canvas he was working on was covered in blue and yellow swirls and it conveyed to her the sea and sun. It felt strangely optimistic.

'Frieda!' He put down his paintbrush when he saw her tear-stained face. 'How is Evgeniya? Is she alright?'

'I think so, yes. The doctor came and she has gone home now. But, of course, it has all come out about us. Jack knows.'

'Oh god. How did he react?'

'Angry, shocked, and then very upset. It was terrible to see him like that. But it was strange: it's the first time in years that we have had an honest conversation where we have both spoken the truth, actually looked at each other.'

'Shit. What now?'

'He has been invited to go to the States to research his next book. But what about you and me?'

Carl took Frieda in his arms. 'This is what I have been trying to sort out with my father and we have finally come to an arrangement. I was going to tell you later.' He wiped his paint-stained hands on a cloth and faced Frieda. 'He has agreed to me being a senior partner in the firm but on the condition that I will be allowed time to paint.'

'That is wonderful, Carl. Such good news for you.'

'For us. Come with me, Frieda. I have never loved anyone the way I love you. You saw the photos of the house. It is beautiful. I will support you and you will never have to worry about money again. You can paint all day long if you want to.'

Frieda's face brightened. She felt her body tingle. 'And your parents would accept that?'

'They would have to. That would be part of the agreement.'

'Gosh. This is incredible. Today has been the strangest day of my life. An hour ago, I thought everything was over. Now the future seems full of exciting possibilities.'

'It is. And you'll love Toronto. It's a great place.'

'And I could really spend my time painting?'

'Absolutely. I want to support you. You are so talented.'

'And I'm sure Toronto has good local schools?'

'Schools?'

'Yes. For Giddy and Esther.'

The smile fell from Carl's face. 'No, I didn't mean them.'

'What?'

'I am asking you to come with me. You know I never wanted kids.'

Frieda laughed drily. 'You think that I would leave my children?'

'They were never part of the deal.'

'The deal? Listen to me, Carl. There is nothing in the world, nothing, that would induce me to abandon my son and daughter. Not you, not anyone. Do you understand? I am not interested in any deal, no matter how big the salary or the house, if it means losing them. Go to Canada. Live out your deal. And never, ever contact me again.'

With those words, she stormed out of the house and into the inappropriately bright light.

She went into Katsikas' store and asked to use the phone.

'I need to ring South Africa,' she said.

Back home, there was a strange serenity in the house. Nothing had changed, as if the three of them were frozen in a tableau – Gideon busy with his rocks, Esther on Jack's lap, having a story and a cup of juice, her face still tear-stained.

'I'll prepare us a meal,' said Frieda. 'Evgeniya won't be back for a few days.'

As she boiled pasta on one ring and fried onions, minced beef and tomatoes on the other, Frieda thought: what a fool I have been. The family I so badly wanted is broken. And it is me who has broken it.

They sat together, the four of them on the terrace, and shared their meal. They talked quietly, a calmness that had been previously absent. Is that because we know it's over? she wondered. There is nothing to fight for or about.

The children stayed up until the sky darkened and the sun slipped behind the mountain like a coin being slotted into a machine.

Only when the kids were in bed did Jack and Frieda speak, albeit in low voices.

'I am deeply sorry for the pain I have caused you, Jack,' she said. 'I suppose it wouldn't have happened if we had been happy together.'

'We expected the island to heal us but it couldn't do it.'

'No.' Tears slipped down her face. She had never felt sadness like it. 'It is the end of the dream.'

'We were full of optimism on the kibbutz that our love would last. But it didn't.'

'No. I'm sorry. I wanted it to.'

'I'll go to the States alone. What will you and the children do?'

'I phoned my mother and asked if we can go and live with her for a while in South Africa. She immediately said yes .'

'When will I see Gideon and Esther again?'

'Whenever you are able to. I will never stop you seeing your children.' She recalled what Carl had asked of her earlier that day. 'I know how much they mean to you. One thing I didn't understand. How did Maria know where to find you in your study? Nobody knows where you write.'

Jack looked down. 'She came to the room a few times. It didn't mean anything. I was just lonely.'

'And you paid her?'

'I gave her some money, yes. She was very hard up after Axel and Marianne let go of their house.'

'So that's where our money went to. Were there others or just Maria?'

'I paid a few maids – Agappe, Elena.'

'What? That is really shocking.'

'Not really. I was unhappy. The maids are badly paid. They always need a bit of extra income. And how can you call that shocking when you were having an affair for most of the year? Talk about hypocrisy.'

His honest words made her cheeks burn.

So some of the money Carl had given to Frieda, and which she had given to Jack, may well have gone to Maria and the other maids: her lover had been paying for her husband's women.

Frieda would have laughed had it all not been so utterly, utterly sad.

Once again, Marianne stood on the quayside, waiting for the boat to come in. Standing at the arrivals and departures, she thought: how many more will there be? And will there be a final departure and no return?

Axel Joachim, in his pushchair, was pointing at the gulls who waddled, large and comical, over the cobbles, but when he saw the boat and Leonard waving, he called out, 'Cone! Cone!'

Marianne was amazed that the child recognised him, now that he always shielded his face with a hat. A group of tourists nearby had their cameras ready. Some policemen stood in a circle, talking in low voices. Costas and Constantino were part of the group of police but their previous friendliness had vanished as they distanced themselves from the expats and stared in the other direction. Earlier, Marianne had been asked to show her papers and then, satisfied, they had walked away.

Leonard and Marianne embraced and he ruffled the little boy's hair.

'Let's get you home,' she said.

As they walked, each with a hand on the pushchair, Leonard told her his news.

'First I went to see my mother in Canada. Masha sends her love. Then to the States. The concerts went well, thousands of people there. Although I sometimes had problems with my guitar strings, I don't think they noticed. The record is going ahead and I have had so many more ideas for songs. I have been bleeding my heart onto the page. How has everything been here?'

'I hardly know where to begin.'

They walked slowly up the hill to their house. It was nearly Easter and the locals were decorating floats with white flowers; one had an effigy of Christ on it. A sheep had been slaughtered for the festivities and two men inserted a metal rod through its centre. Marianne saw the animal's glazed eyes and the way its bloody body remained rigid. The island seemed coated in lemon and vanilla as if in preparation for this sacred day.

'Jack and Frieda have separated and he is going to America.'

'No. Why?'

'It seems that she was having an affair with Carl, a painter.'

'I know Carl. From Toronto. Lovely man, talented artist. I spoke to him at Olivia's party and I gave him a copy of *Flowers for Hitler* as he seemed interested in poetry. He kept himself to himself. I invited him to Douskos' but he didn't seem keen to attend. How sad.'

'And Maria has been sleeping with Jack.'

'What?'

'It's true. For money, after Axel and I didn't need her.'

'I can't believe it.'

'Honestly. I bumped into Maria one day and she looked really pretty and glowing. I thought she must have found another job but I had no idea what it was. Now I know.'

'But how did Jack and Maria know each other?'

'Apparently, he dropped in on Axel one day to talk about writing and Axel was out. Maria made him coffee while he waited and that was how it started. Jack slept with other maids, too.'

'Extraordinary.'

'Yes. And Magda seems to have an admirer, a sailor named Theodore.'

'Really?'

'And Axel has written. He and Sonja have split up but he is now with Lena. So, plenty going on.'

'I feel like I have been away a year. It has all changed. There were so many policemen in the harbour.'

'Yes. They demanded my papers while I was waiting and asked lots of other questions, too: what I do here, how long I intend to stay.'

'There has been a lot in the American papers about it. The colonels have overthrown the government, the military junta is taking over and the whole country is changing. King Constantine and his family have been banished.'

'And that's why the police are around?'

'Yes. I'm afraid so. The junta has even said that it is now forbidden to play music by Mikis Theodorakis because he is considered communist. It's crazy. If anyone disobeys, they will have to go before a tribunal. It's no good, Marianne. This is only the start of it. Do you want to bring Axel Joachim up in an atmosphere like this, in a dictatorship?'

'No, I don't, but then where should we live? In the States where you will be heralded and we will be in your shadow? My mother wants us to go back to Oslo and live with her.'

'It has to be your decision, Marianne. I will support you whatever you decide.'

They had reached their house. Leonard carried the sleeping Axel Joachim to his bed and then half-closed the door.

On the terrace Marianne brought them iced tea in thin, frosted glasses.

'I think our time on Hydra is coming to an end,' she said.

'You really feel that?' He looked away from her and towards the mountains.

'Everything seems to be pointing that way. You are more in demand abroad; our friends are leaving; now the police are invading our island. Maybe the dream is over?'

He looked into the distance as if he did not want to admit the inevitable.

'Whatever happens, Marianne, you are the sun and the moon to me, day and night: you always will be.'

His words were beautiful but they did not answer her concerns.

In the past, when he had been away, they had fallen into bed as soon as they could but, this time, it did not happen. The child was asleep, they had the option, but the desire did not come, as if they instinctively knew that it was over before they could bear to say it.

So, this was it. She had known all along that it would end, that the relationship would not survive and, as they sat and drank their iced tea and watched the purple mountains, she knew. They both did.

That night, when the friends met at Douskos' Taverna, the atmosphere was different. Even the giant pine tree which covered them seemed less effective, its leaves lacking their usual sheen, and the candles flickered as if their flames were having difficulty staying alight.

'I want to thank you,' said Frieda, struggling to keep her voice from cracking, 'for the kindness you have shown us over the year. It has been an amazing experience and we have learned so much.'

'Where is Jack tonight?' asked Gordon, Chuck, as ever, by his side.

'He sends best wishes to you all. He leaves for America in the morning. He has an advance for another book.'

'And you?' asked Chuck.

'I am taking the children to my mother in South Africa and we will see what happens after that.'

Her friends looked sad for her.

'Well, we have good news,' said George, trying to lighten the mood. '*My Brother Jack* has aired on ABC, script written by my lovely wife here,' Charmian smiled awkwardly, 'and her book *Peel Me a Lotus* is now in print.'

The friends raised a glass to them and there were cheers and shouts of 'Well done!'

'And as for our friend, Leonard,' continued George. 'His first LP is soon to be released, books in print, his songs often on the radio.'

Leonard nodded his thanks.

'What we have had here, my friends, has been a dream,' George said. 'But dreams come to an end. You wake up, rub your eyes and then you realise that what is facing you is the military junta, debt, and film stars invading your space. This island that we have lived on and loved has been generous to us in its honey, its sponges and its welcome. But now we have woken up. It is time to get out of bed. It is time to leave and we know it.'

Charmian was crying, fat, clear tears running down her face. She would have to desert her home, Nature Boy, Anthony and her friends, the sky, the sea, the gorse-covered hills.

'It will break Shane to leave Baptiste,' she said. 'She loves Greece. It is her home. She was christened by the church and baptised by Baptiste. It will destroy her. But Martin will go to university in Sydney and Jason to school. They will adapt, I think. But I am not sure about Shane.'

Leonard did not comment. He was still upset that they would not let Martin try for Oxford.

'I am going to America,' said Norman. 'Maybe they will appreciate my sculptures there.'

People smiled kindly but they doubted it.

'I have known such joy on Hydra,' said Marianne, looking at Leonard, 'and also great pain.'

'Yes,' he whispered. 'Hydra has been both a destroyer and a creator.'

'Who would have thought,' said Gordon, 'that this lovely country would be overtaken by these awful people? A culture that was all about art and democracy?'

'Tragic,' agreed Chuck. 'This beautiful land is tarnished for ever.'

'What surprises me,' said Charmian, her words becoming more slurred the more retsina she drank, 'is that the Greeks, who have had a history of battles, seem to be so meek in accepting this new regime. What has happened to their fighting spirit?'

'Jeez, Charm, they have no fucking choice, do they? Do you want to pick a fight with the military? One politician was thrown into the sea and another loaded onto the ferry, just for debating!'

Douskos was not thrown by their arguing: he was used to it. Calmly, he brought them grilled squid and octopus in lemon juice; spicy lamb slices; dolmades like little cigars; tyropittakia; a Greek salad, with tomatoes and cucumber shining like jewels; cacik; olives, tiny as bullets; and bowls of dips and warm pitta bread.

'The last supper,' Charmian said. 'Thank you all.'

The atmosphere that night was one of celebration and mourning. There were tears of joy and tears of pain.

'I have never known friendship like this,' said George, his voice cracking. 'You have been my second family. Thank you, to all of you.' He raised his glass high.

'To be with people who understand the creative process, who are interested but do not pry, who encourage but don't push – that has been amazing.' Gordon smiled. 'We hope that we will find a similar community elsewhere but it is unlikely.'

'Agreed,' said Chuck. 'We have been among people who understand us and have allowed us to be who we need to be.'

'I have really appreciated your love of my sculptures,' Norman said quietly. 'That exhibition you came to boosted my confidence. It was wonderful.'

'What about you, Leonard, and Marianne?' asked Charmian.

'I am being called,' he said, 'to devote myself to my writing, and that is in America.'

'My mother wants Axel Joachim and me to live with her in Oslo.' It was the first time that Marianne had admitted this in public and it was as far as she could go: she could not say that she had decided to do so.

Leonard reached over and held her hand. Should she change her mind and follow him where his career led? Would that be good for her child?

As the sky darkened, the candles struggled to exude light, bending and twisting in their glass cages as if they couldn't settle. Douskos cleared away the plates and brought them baklava, sticky and syrupy, kataifi like little bird nests, and chocolates rolled in icing sugar. He also placed pots of strong coffee and tiny cups in the centre for them all.

It seemed to Marianne that what they were witnessing was a celebration of their time together but also a candlelit vigil for its passing. She thought of Mikalis sitting in his cottage and howling sea dirges and she understood his loss.

She felt that part of her was being ripped away.

'I'm not leaving,' shouted Shane. 'You can't make me.' Her face was hot and her eyes brimmed with tears.

'Darling, we are going back to Australia as a family.'

Shane laughed. 'A family? When have we ever been that?'

Charmian hung her head. 'Look, I understand...'

'No, you don't. You don't understand at all. You dragged us from Australia to Britain where we did our best to settle; then you took us to Kalymnos where we had to learn Greek. Then you uprooted us to Hydra. We aren't your books which you can just pack up in a crate and ship abroad. We are people. We have feelings. I am not leaving Baptiste and that is final.'

'I am sorry, Shane, but you are seventeen and you will have to go with the rest of us. Things are changing on Hydra. You see the police everywhere? We have to register with them and account for every movement. It is no longer the right place for us. Martin will go to Sydney University and you will return to your old school in Melbourne. Jason can go there too. I have already spoken to the principal.'

'You can go if you want to. I'm staying here.'

Charmian laughed. 'Where? Who with?'

'Baptiste.'

'He is a schoolboy. He can't support you. You need to come with us.'

'NO!' she shouted and ran out of the house and into the street, her blonde hair flying behind her.

Panting, she ran all the way to Baptiste's house where he was helping his father to paint window frames. His mother was feeding the chickens; all the other children were in the yard, playing. That is family, thought Shane, a proper family. She and Baptiste exchanged words in Greek, he dropped his paintbrush and went off with Shane. They walked, hand in hand, to their favourite spot, the woods behind the monastery where the cyclamen had now given way to wild narcissi, as if they had prepared the ground for them and left them ready for the next season.

The couple lay among the white and gold flowers, like milk and honey sweetening the air. Shane wept. Baptiste held her in his arms and wiped away her tears, thinking that he had never seen anyone so beautiful. Unlike the dark-haired, olive-skinned girls in Hydra who felt more like sisters than potential girlfriends, Shane was like a sea-nymph washed up on shore. Her golden hair, her lightly tanned skin and her shiny eyes touched something inside him and he carried her image in his head, every day and night.

With tear-stained faces, they made sweet love, pressing themselves among the spring flowers, as if they, too, were of the earth. It was tender and gentle – their kisses, their stroking of each other's skin, his entry into her. Every action had added meaning and they both knew it.

Inside the Johnston house, the rugs had come off the walls and were being rolled, ornaments and crockery were being wrapped in brown paper and the books were packed in box after box.

George and Martin worked at dismantling the studies: Jason was sorting out which toys he wanted to keep and which he could bear to give away to Sevasty for her children.

The house was calm on this occasion, a quieter atmosphere than usual, a sense of shared purpose. Everyone knew what they had to do; they were in the same place at the same time yet all were quiet in their own thoughts, engaged in their own tasks.

For Charmian, although she was sad never to feel Nature Boy or Antony's skin beside her again, it was time to move on. Her new novel was progressing well and with the success of the television adaptation, Australia was the right place for her to be. George felt that the second volume in his trilogy would be explosive and he needed to be home to see that happen. Besides, their community was breaking up and who wanted to live in a country where free speech was abolished? Martin was looking forward, with some trepidation, to being a university student. He wondered what it would be like to adjust from a small Greek island to a large Australian city. However, he would continue his writing. Just that day, he had heard that *The Herald* had accepted his poem *To Greece Under the Junta* for their next issue. And Jason was wondering whether he was Greek or Australian and whether Sevasty's sons would appreciate his model dinosaurs.

They were not the only ones whose homes were being dissembled. The island had now fragmented.

The locals carried on doing their jobs; the expat artists were sadly waving their idyll away, and in the harbour, the policemen were checking the papers of all those arriving and departing, only once abandoning their solemn duties when Jackie Kennedy came to visit Onassis on his yacht and needed their protection.

Leonard was packing, too. His heart was torn between Marianne and his work but the writing had to come first.

'Come with me, Marianne,' he whispered. 'You and Axel Joachim could be with me.'

She shook her head. 'It will not work out,' she answered sadly. 'You will be focused on your writing and music and we will be following behind you, lost. Axel Joachim needs stability in his life and I think he will have that back in Oslo.'

She relayed this to Magda as they sat in their favourite cove on the beach, their boys beside them, hitting the sand with wooden spades.

'It is so sad,' said Magda. 'You and Leonard love each other so deeply.'

'That is true but I always knew that it would end. It was almost too good to last.'

The sea was strong today, unequivocal in its deep blue, as if it sensed the mood on the island and knew it had to be constant.

'Is there no way you can see of making it work?'

'How? His career is taking off and I am happy for him but he will be a famous singer-songwriter with all the girls swooning after him and I will be a nobody, chasing after him, with a baby in my arms. No-one will be interested in me. All the attention will be on him and his music and I will be a hanger-on. It's not what Axel Joachim needs. He craves security and why shouldn't he have it?'

'So what will you do?'

'Go back to my mother, although she has also kept the Larkollen house so maybe we can have holidays there.'

'That sounds lovely, Marianne.'

'Yes. I tried to give my own son something better but I failed. He has moved from home to home, his father has abandoned him, he has a deep connection with Leonard who he will now lose, and we will start again in another home, another country.'

'You have done your best, Marianne.'

At that moment, Theodore waved and dived again in a perfect arc into the receptive sea.

'Theodore has invited me out for dinner,' said Magda coyly.

'How lovely. I told you that he was your admirer.'

'I don't know about that. I don't think I would ever get involved with anyone again after what happened.'

'But you'll go on a date with him?'

'Well, maybe just the one.'

As evening fell, Shane had still not returned home.

'I'm worried about her, George.' The house was bare, most of their belongings in crates.

'Jeez, Charm, the girl's seventeen. She knows the island better than we do. She'll be fine.' But Charmian was still concerned and she looked out from the terrace to see if she could spot her daughter's golden hair: she could not.

'She'll be with Baptiste,' said Martin.

'I know that, Martin, but where?'

'She likes the woods behind the monastery,' said Jason and his brother glared at him: that was supposed to be their secret.

'I'm going to look for her,' said Charmian, wrapping a shawl over her shoulders, and she left.

The air was cool as dusk descended. Charmian thought as she mounted the hill: now I am being the mother that I should always have been, not crossing the island to see my lovers but to ensure that my daughter is safe.

The monastery buildings stood white and stark against the darkening sky as if symbolising hope. As Charmian walked behind them, she was anxious about what she would find.

Shane and Baptiste were still there among the narcissi, their creamy blooms like candles. They had made love twice and now he was sitting up with his legs open and Shane was tucked between them, leaning her back against him. They were dressed but their faces were pink and Shane's hair was dishevelled. They were speaking in low voices, sharing the bottle of retsina that Baptiste had taken from his family uncles store.

'You know I love you, Shane,' he said softly, stroking her hair.

'Then let me stay with you.'

'You can't. I am at school. Then I will have to run the store. You need to be with your family and receiving an education.'

'But will you still love me?' She wiped the tears from her eyes.

'Always.'

She would remember Baptiste for the rest of her life. How could she ever love like that again?

She felt resigned now. His soft words, the narcissi, the half-light: all had come together to make her accept the situation they were facing. Her life and Baptiste's would go in different directions, but he would always remain her first love.

To their amazement, her mother appeared round the corner of the building. The lovers sat up straight.

'Mum, what are you doing here?'

'I was worried about you, wanted to make sure you were alright.'

Baptiste nodded politely at Charmian.

'Baptiste,' she responded.

Charmian never forgot the sight of them, young and innocent as the flowers around them, as if they were wood-nymphs from a fairy tale, escaping their parents, running away, devoted to love. It moved her: may life be good to you both, she thought.

Baptiste said something to Shane in his hypnotic voice, and she agreed. He stood up, wiped himself down and walked away.

Mother and daughter held hands as they descended the hill to their home. Night fell suddenly, as if it had been ready earlier but had agreed to hold back for a while. The air was still sweet but cool. The outlines of the houses were lost in the darkness but in the distance the lights of the harbour still glimmered.

Charmian took her shawl and wrapped it around Shane's bare shoulders. Shane let her. She liked this, her mother coming to find her, holding her hand, shielding her against the cold. She hardly recognised this protective woman. That was what she had been longing for.

They walked in rhythm with each other, heard some rustling in the bushes, a bird maybe. Smells of delicious food emanated from the houses they passed, and some people had lit candles in their windows, the hour of evening electricity over. As they passed Mikalis' cottage, they heard his wailing.

'I love Baptiste,' said Shane as they walked.

'I know that, darling.' Charmian did not say: you will get over him, you will have other men. Somehow, she had lost her confidence in that realm.

'I will never love anyone like that again.'

Charmian squeezed her hand and wrapped the shawl more tightly round her daughter's young shoulders.

'Whatever you are going through, I am there beside you,' she whispered.

Shane remembered that as the night she lost her lover and found her mother.

Frieda's lover and husband left on the same day.

Carl took the earliest boat, before daylight broke. It occurred to him, as Alexis steered him to Piraeus across calm, sleepy waters, that his whole stay on the sunny island had been shrouded in darkness and secrecy, so why should he not leave like that, too? He had never loved anyone, connected with anyone, the way he had with Frieda. In spite of their different nationalities, different religions, they had spoken the same language, in words and in paint.

As the waters lapped around him, and Hydra shrank from view, it seemed clear to him that she had made a mistake in not coming with him to Canada. He had offered her security, time to paint and a beautiful home. What more could he have done? He recalled the way she wound her dark hair in a plait around her head, her perfect, petite body, her canvases covered in bright, strong brushstrokes. He thought of her blue settee and the shuttered room in which they had made love so many times, her affection and her skill as an artist and lover gaining confidence daily. How they had adored each other in that studio with the hot, crusty smell of Demi's bakery and the heady scent of the wisteria over the doorway. He had not seen Frieda again since their argument, but she had slipped a poem under his door. He drew it now from his trouser pocket:

We loved each other
In that white space,
The shutters down, the boats beyond.
We ate peaches,
We drank wine.
We thought that it would last for ever.
I cannot live with you
Nor without you.
As the light fades on our Greek dream,
You will go your way
And I will go mine.

And in the harbour, the boats will still rock
In the morning breeze.

The previous night, John, Anthony and Carl had sat in his house and drunk their goodbyes, surrounded by wrapped canvases, ready for shipping. It was an understated farewell with the woman he loved absent. John's tremor was worse than ever and he had more or less abandoned his drawing – or it had abandoned him – and Anthony was morose at the prospect of losing Charmian. In a way, it was a fitting adieu: a secret, hidden drink on a secret, hidden island, which he had never really known. Carl stared miserably into his deep glass and thought: here we are, three failed painters, one who can't stop shaking, one who can't pay his bills, and another who has abandoned his dream.

Now, as he let the boat take him away, listening to the slap of the water against the wood, he searched the sky for glimmers of sunlight but found none.

Three hours later, Jack left. The previous evening, he had run around the island with a knife in his hand, looking for Carl. No-one seemed to know where he lived or much about him. Not usually a violent man, Jack had decided that he would kill Carl if he found him but he could not trace him. While the others were packing, Jack ran from taverna to quayside, to monastery to chapel looking for the bastard but he could find no trace of him. When he thought of Carl with his wife, it made him livid.

He remembered his high school days in Cape Town, where he had been moved up two years because he was so clever. There was a boy in the new class, Trundy he was called, who mocked Jack and called him a 'Jewish swot', jeering and laughing at him whenever he spoke. Jack could feel the rage build up inside him and then his self-hatred when he failed to tackle Trundy either verbally or physically. He had wanted to respond but something had always stopped him, maybe his genteel upbringing or his fear that the attack would fail.

The previous evening, he had roamed the cobbled streets of Hydra, brandishing his weapon. He did so in search of Carl and of Trundy but, of course, he failed to find either of them. So he had slunk home again, tired with despair and endured a sleepless night.

As he kissed his children goodbye, Gideon lifted his face but said little.

Esther clutched her fingers tightly around her father's neck and kissed him. 'Abba,' she wailed, 'don't go.'

'Sweetie,' he said bravely, 'we will see each other again soon.'

Frieda prised the child away, feeling her pain and guilt ever more keenly. 'It's alright, Esther, darling.'

What the hell had she done? What an idiot she had been. She had failed to give her children a happy family life.

Jack picked up his suitcase, looked at Frieda, but did not hug her, and left the house.

Gideon carried on labelling his rocks. Esther and Frieda sat on the terrace and covered each other in kisses and tears.

'It's okay, sweetie. You will see Abba again, I promise you.'

Later that day, the front door opened and Evgeniya came in. Esther flew to hug her and the maid looked overwhelmed with joy. She was as chubby as ever but her face was pale and she had a bandage around her head.

With Evgeniya's limited English, and some reluctant help from Gideon, they found out that she had gone back to Nikos, that he was always angry with her when she wouldn't give him money for drink and that everything was fine now. No, she said stoically, she wouldn't tell the police.

Her brave smile turned to tears, however, when Frieda told her that they were leaving. 'Jack,' she made a gesture with her hands, 'gone. America.'

'America?'

'Yes, and we,' she indicated the three of them, 'South Africa.'

Evgeniya looked confused.

'Giddy,' said Frieda. 'Can you help to tell her, please?'

The boy did not look up but spoke in perfect Greek. He sounded like a native, Frieda thought, his voice more singsong and expressive in Greek than in English or Hebrew. Evgeniya clearly understood him because she hugged the mother and daughter and the three of them stood on the terrace and wept while Gideon cut out sticky labels with tiny scissors.

Evgeniya said some more words to Gideon and he translated. She told Frieda and Esther that she had lost a baby girl who had lived only for a week and that Esther had been like a daughter to her. They hugged and cried more, Frieda gave the maid a money gift, and then Evgeniya, head bandaged and bowed, her face damp with tears, left.

It was strange to be in the house, just the three of them. Gideon was silent, head bent to his task while Esther clung to Frieda, following her wherever she went, frightened, needy.

'I miss Abba,' she said.

'I know,' said Frieda, 'but you will see him again before too long.'

'I miss Evgeniya,' said the little girl.

'I know, sweetie. She is very special.' Frieda did not promise that Esther would see her again She was not willing to lie any more.

That night she let Esther sleep in her bed. The little girl gripped onto her the whole night long, and Frieda wondered who was comforting whom.

They packed up the house: Esther's dolls and the clothes Evgeniya had made them, Gideon's rocks and fossils and a few of Frieda's possessions.

Frieda gave most of her paintings away to friends. Jack had already shipped the books. Frieda kept one, the first edition of *Flowers for Hitler* that Leonard had given to Carl and he had given to Frieda. It was inscribed in Leonard's large, curved blue writing: *a good winter on this Rock, Leonard*, with *Hydra* written in Greek and the date: 1965. She would treasure it all her life.

By the end of the next day, the house was bare. Frieda looked out of the window at the well, the crazy chickens in the yard, the almond blossom dotting the sky. She felt hollow and alone, fearful for the future, for her, and for her children.

There was a knock at the door and when she opened it, Marianne was there with Axel Joachim.

Esther's face brightened and she threw her arms around the little boy.

They sat on the terrace where the spring air was now spongy and warm.

'I have baked you some of my biscuits,' said Marianne.

'We remember those,' said Frieda. 'When we first arrived a year ago you brought us some. We wondered why we were all so mellow that first day! Thank you, Marianne.'

'Well, there is a magic ingredient. Just a little. Will you come to Passover at Leonard's tonight?'

'I am not sure. Without their father there, it might upset the children.'

'It may do them good. We will be there, too.'

They sat on the terrace where Esther played with Axel Joachim, holding his hand while he tottered unsteadily across the floor. Gideon's head was bent to his rocks.

'What a lot has happened this year,' said Frieda.

'Leonard says that Hydra creates us and kills us.'

'Is it fair to blame the island? Is a piece of rock in the sea capable of that?'

'I don't know. I think we all came here to escape, but we have found that there is no escape.'

Tears ran down Frieda's face. Marianne embraced her and realised that she, too, was crying, the tears of the women moistening their own faces and each other's.

That evening, they sat once again on Leonard's terrace, Elijah's mountain behind them and Elijah's cup in front of them. It felt strange to Esther and Gideon that Jack was not there and the little girl wondered why, if an invisible prophet could make the effort to come and join them, her father could not. Maybe he would fly in and surprise them, after all. She crossed her fingers and really hoped so, but he did not arrive.

Leonard had once again laid the table with the Seder plate at the centre but this time he did not explain or introduce what everything meant, partly because Marianne now knew and because, anyway, he felt more subdued. They read from the *Haggadot* but he left chunks out, feeling that he could not fake the joy at the exodus that the passages required.

When he looked across at Esther and Gideon flanking their mother, maybe making sure that she, too, did not leave, it broke his heart. He thought of his own lost father and how he had been searching for a replacement for him all his life. He saw Axel Joachim sitting on books to make him higher at the table, now without a father. Fatherless children: all of them. When Leonard read *Blessed art thou, O Lord, our God, King of the Universe…* the words stuck in his throat. Maybe God would be the father to protect them all.

As the only adult male at the table, he felt responsible for them. He looked around as they ate their meal quietly: Marianne, so beautiful, her face a series of planes catching the light; Axel Joachim, whom he loved like a son, his face vulnerable and small; Frieda, still lovely, her long hair wound in a plait around her head, her face drawn; Gideon, quiet and down; Esther, sweet and chubby, her eyes still shiny with hope. What lay ahead? Where would they all settle and to what?

After the meal, they did not sing the songs that they had enjoyed the previous year. Without Jack with his strong voice and fluent Hebrew, Leonard did not feel he had the strength to carry it off, nor the gusto it required.

At the end of the evening, Leonard carried Axel Joachim to his bed, still clutching his toy giraffe. Its ears were shiny where the boy had sucked them.

Frieda thanked Leonard and Marianne for the evening, hugged them tightly, and then she and her children started the long walk home, feeling their way in the unforgiving darkness.

The following morning, Frieda, Gideon and Esther left their whitewashed house. As they walked away, they turned to take one more glance at the well in the cobbled courtyard, the manic chickens, the almond blossom offering its dainty confetti sprigs to the sky, and the bronze lion's head knocker. Magda had kindly agreed to oversee the shipping of their belongings and so the three of them walked to the harbour with only a few bags of clothes: Frieda had her *Flowers for Hitler* from Carl, Gideon his favourite gemstones, and Esther, three dollies. Mother and daughter linked fingers, Gideon trailed behind.

Seeing the island for the last time made everything even more beautiful and yet not quite real: the smatterings of crocuses, hyacinths and narcissi blanched by the sun. Frieda felt that she was in a film, or maybe had been all year, watching the lives of other people on a screen and wondering whose lives had been depicted: surely not theirs? Had she really been married to Jack? Had they honestly come here with cautious optimism? Had she risked everything for an affair? Had it really fallen apart? She hardly recognised herself from the woman who had arrived a year ago.

Down in the harbour, Douskos was sweeping his yard, The Gardenia Dwarf by his side so that Frieda had the strange feeling that they were arriving, not leaving, and that it was starting all over again. Nick Katsikas came running out to see them. He handed Frieda a package addressed to Gideon and Esther Silver, written in Jack's large script.

'Here, children,' said Frieda, recognising the handwriting. 'You need to open this, not me.'

Inside was a book for each child: *The Golden Treasury of Verse* for Esther with bright, glossy pictures of green fields and rainbows, and a book on fossils and gems for Gideon with illustrations and detailed facts. He almost smiled. Inside, Jack had written a loving message for each child and the words: *See you soon, Love Daddy*. Frieda noticed that she was not mentioned and she wasn't surprised. She could smell his bitterness towards her from the envelope.

The three of them walked down to the boat where Alexis waited.

Amid the crowd of policemen were some familiar faces: Leonard, Marianne and Axel Joachim; Charmian and George; Olivia, Michael and Melina; Gordon and Chuck; Norman; and Evgeniya. Esther flung herself at the maid and felt for the last time the comfort of losing herself in the warmth of her curves. The bandage had gone now but her bruise had flowered from purple to yellow and her forehead was still swollen.

There were hugs and kisses, promises to keep in touch and assurances that they would meet again, which everybody said and nobody believed. Frieda thanked them all for their kindness and they said that her paintings would remind them of her always. She smiled wryly at her own deception.

Frieda and Gideon climbed into the boat and Alexis lifted Esther in. Looking up at the quay, with their friends gathered there, mother and daughter cried but Gideon did not. Frieda put her arms around her children and as the boat sailed away at the start of a very long journey, Hydra gradually shrank to a line in the distance, and was then swallowed up by the sea.

The friends dispersed and Marianne and Leonard wheeled Axel Joachim home in his pushchair. Their house seemed different although most objects were not packed away, just Marianne's summer dresses, Axel Joachim's toys, and a few treasured possessions. But somehow those small adjustments altered the home.

The Johnstons spent their last evening together at Leonard and Marianne's house. Kyria Sophia had made a wonderful meal: roast lamb baked in Demi's oven, infused with juniper and surrounded by onions, potatoes and carrots, with a huge Greek salad. There was crusty bread from Demi, too, and a selection of sticky, syrupy sweets for dessert. As the maid brought out the food and collected in the dirty plates, she was close to tears.

They sat together on the terrace and Charmian looked round proudly at her three children, all gathered in one place. Shane had been very difficult about coming, wanting to spend her last night on Hydra with Baptiste.

'Please, Shane,' her mother had pleaded with her, 'it is a big moment in our lives and we need to face it as a family.'

Shane crossed her arms and pouted. Her mother had suddenly been converted to this notion of family unity, and this hypocrisy annoyed her: being a collective when it suited her but at other times being happy for the five of them to go their own way. It was always on her terms: so unfair.

But what was more painful than her mother's audacity was the sense Shane had from Baptiste that he was willing to lose her. She had moaned to him about her mother's demand for this last evening's meal and he had taken Charmian's side, agreeing that family should always come first. It seemed to Shane that although he professed to love her, he had already begun to let her go.

In the end, he was not really her devoted Greek lover. He was a local island boy who would follow his family blindly into their store and become a clone of them. He would marry, have children and visit his parents each week for lunch, dutifully taking them a gift from the shop.

Yet although she tried to dislike him, she found she couldn't. His dark hair, swarthy skin, his large hands, the taste of his mouth: they were all so utterly delicious that even the thought of his name made her hungry for his presence.

So yes, Shane was at the meal but reluctantly so. Martin and Jason were more compliant and had agreed to come.

'What a lovely meal,' said Charmian. 'Thank you.'

'It's great to have you all here,' said Leonard, lifting his glass.

'Jeez, Len, thanks a bunch for having us.' George coughed as he spoke. Charmian watched him with concern. After his stay in hospital, he had seemed better but since then he had regressed. George reached for a cigarette now as someone else would reach for medicine, as if it were the solution. He lit up, the tip glowed orange, he inhaled and coughed some more.

'Take it easy, George,' said his wife, but without conviction.

'Well, it makes sense,' said Leonard. 'Your house is all packed up and here we are, still a home.'

Shane and Jason had left the table to play with Axel Joachim. Shane would rather be with him than with those adults and Jason felt the same. Martin had gone indoors and was looking at Leonard's bookshelves, drawing out volumes of poetry that interested him and reading.

'Do you think you will come back and live on Hydra again? After all, you own the house, don't you?' asked Charmian.

Leonard looked at Marianne. She was so beautiful this evening, dressed in white cotton, that he could hardly bear to gaze at what he was about to lose.

'Who knows? Life will lead us and we will follow, into the darkness, away from the light.'

'Marianne, are you looking forward to returning to Oslo?'

'In a way, yes. I am pleased that my mother will have a chance to know her grandson and maybe she and I can build a better relationship, but of course, we gain and we lose.' She looked at Leonard and tears filled her eyes. He reached his hand across and held hers.

'We have been blessed to live on this beautiful island.' Charmian looked across at the mountains as she spoke. Dusk was just falling, coating the landscape in a haziness, like gauze thrown over it. The edges of the harbour were less defined, the boats, dabs of paint and the almond blossoms, impressionistic.

'Jeez, it's been amazing, hasn't it?' The drink and tiredness were beginning to show on George. 'All these incredible people, time to write. Unbelievable.'

Marianne looked over to where the children were playing on the tiled floor and wondered about them. Had it been good for the younger people? Yes, they had had camaraderie and community but they had also witnessed family break-ups and disharmony.

Kyria Sophia brought them coffee and Marianne noticed that her eyes were red.

Leonard went inside and found Martin. 'Have you found any poetry that you like?'

'Oh yes, so much. What do you recommend?'

'Well, I particularly like Yeats, Lorca, Shakespeare sonnets. And have you read any Maya Angelou? She's an amazing new Afro-American poet, who writes so powerfully about the lives of black people and women. I also love the lyrics of Bob Dylan and Joan Baez.'

'That's great, Leonard. Thank you. I will follow those up.'

'What are you writing at the moment, Martin?' The young boy tended to avoid eye contact but when he did look up, Leonard saw that his eyes were etched with pain. He was thin and pasty in spite of the bright sun. Leonard thought: if I ever have children, I will do everything I can to focus on them and engage with their ideas.

'Exploring the whole issue of belonging and identity. In Greece I feel Australian and I guess in Australia, I'll feel Greek.'

'Being on the outside is not a bad place for a writer. We are well placed on the margins, looking in.'

'I suppose so, but we can't be too far away or else we cannot see.'

'So true.' Leonard nodded. This young boy was wise. He saw the truth about life that many did not: the depth, the complexity, the contradictions. He wondered whether his use of the word 'see' alluded to his myopia as well as metaphorical perception.

'I'm working on a long poem called *Microclimatology* which will be written in sections. It will make references to Hydra: the driftwood, the cats, the wild thyme. And even Donkey Shit Lane is in there.'

They both laughed.

'That's good. I'm pleased that name gets its well-deserved glory in a poem. Seriously, Martin, if you ever want to send me some of your work or correspond with me, I'd be happy to help if I can.'

'Thank you, Leonard. You have been very kind to me. Some writers are so obsessed with their own work that they can't engage with anyone else's, but you manage to do your own and also have time to take an interest in others.' They both understood what he meant.

Leonard patted him gently on his shoulders and went back up to the terrace.

The coffee cups were empty and Charmian and George were back on wine. They spoke in low voices.

'That boy is amazing,' said Leonard, rejoining the group.

'We know,' said George, coughing.

'We realise that.'

For a rare moment, Charmian and George agreed.

'His chess, his writing, his politics. He is an outstanding young man.'

'He'll thrive at Sydney University,' said his mum, sounding to Leonard as if she wanted that topic closed. 'It's getting late now. We need to get these kids to bed. Will we see you at the harbour in the morning?'

'Of course,' said Marianne.

After they had left, Marianne and Kyria Sophia cleared the dishes away. Leonard typed in his study and the little boy slept, undisturbed by the tapping of keys and the sounds of crockery being put away.

When it was time for Kyria Sophia to leave, Marianne hugged her to thank her for her help and said that she would see her the next day. Closing the door after her, Marianne wondered if she was managing these last few days by deceiving herself – that it was all going to carry on as before.

On the morning that they were due to depart, Charmian awoke early. She strolled down in the subtle sunshine to the cove Nature Boy inhabited. Of course, he was there. She wondered if he ever left. He had already lit a fire that day and was cooking meat on it.

How could she bear to leave Hydra without seeing him one last time?

She loved it that their exchange was all done without words. She did know some basic French but language wasn't necessary. As soon as Charmian arrived, they kissed. His skin was dirty with seaweed and the skin and guts of an animal he had just killed: a bird, maybe, or a rodent. Soon, his hand was inside her, grabbing her breasts roughly the way she liked, and he loosened his loincloth, lifted her dress and they were on rough ground, the rocking of him inside her grazing her back. She cried out and she moaned and they kissed some more, his mouth salty and dirty.

Afterwards they lay naked in the sun and he caressed her hair with his fingers, almost parental. How did this young boy understand her so well? How did he know exactly what she needed? He was probably only in his twenties but he had an instinctive understanding.

After she had dressed, she kissed him again and whispered, 'Au revoir, Jean-Claude, et merci beaucoup,' and he knew that he would not see her again. She strolled up the hill, still tingling from his touch and the smell of him while he took a stick and flipped the meat on his fire.

Her mind was racing as she walked to Anthony's house. How could it be that a feral, young boy who was probably illiterate could understand her better than an educated man like George? Did it mean that she was more animal then cultured? Or did one side of her need the other to counteract it?

The island was pretty today, the ground dabbed in hyacinths and crocuses, like spilled paint. A pigeon flapped its cardboard wings and landed in front of Charmian, surprising her with its size. She sidestepped it and walked on, aware of the sunshine massaging her back with its gentle warming. After the harshness of the winter, she appreciated the subtlety of a Greek spring: lemon-white and hazy.

Anthony was in his studio, painting a harbour scene. As he usually did portraits, she was pleasantly surprised and liked it: the water crinkly and reflective; the boats brightly coloured; a half-completed sky. They embraced and she could smell last night's heavy drinking on his breath. She perched on his sofa while he worked and remembered their lovemaking on its threadbare surface.

'I couldn't leave without saying goodbye to you, Tony.'

'You're going so soon,' his paintbrush frozen mid-air.

'This afternoon. We're all packed up.'

'I can't believe it.' He put his paintbrush down and sat beside her. His shirt was stained with paint and his dark hair was tussled.

'I know. I wish you could come with us.'

'To Australia? How could I? What would I do there? I don't think George would be very happy about that, do you?'

'It's not realistic, I know that, but I don't like the thought that we may never meet again.'

'You are very special, Charmian. Always remember that.'

They kissed but it did not flow into sex and she didn't mind. She was still carrying the scent of Nature Boy on her skin.

'Thank you for everything, Tony.'

'Goodbye, Charmian.'

Walking back to their house she thought about their time in Greece. It had been so fruitful in so many ways and she wondered what the next stage held. She dreaded the next novel in George's trilogy and the humiliation it might bring. She also saw her future as lonely: no Tony, no Nature Boy, no island with the sea lapping tenderly at its rocky edges.

Their house looked bare and soulless. The rugs were down from the walls, the crockery all packed, the books off the shelves and a sense of all things ending. George was drinking, bottle tilted; Jason was drawing a picture of Hydra, the many-headed serpent; and Martin was reading.

'Jeez, Charm,' George looked up when she entered. 'Where the hell have you been?'

'I had a few things to see to. Where's Shane?'

'Gone to say goodbye to her lover boy.' He exploded into a bout of coughing and wiped the blood from his mouth.

'She needs to be back here soon. The boat leaves at three.'

Shane and Baptiste were in the woods behind the monastery, caressing. Her Greek almost as good as his, they confessed their eternal love for each other and were thankful. She thought of asking him why he had been more loyal to her parents than to her but decided not to. Why waste their last hour together fighting?

For the final time, they made love, pressing their bodies upon the receptive flowers and Shane wished that the earth would open up and receive their weight and they could live below ground for ever.

She thought about the journey that she and Baptiste had been on: how shy and virginal she had been at the start, how he had led her gently through the early stages of lovemaking, and how he had given her confidence in her own beauty and appeal. She would always remember him and be grateful to him for that. Any future relationships she had, and she doubted that she ever would, would owe everything to him.

After they had dressed, they sat up among the wild flowers and looked at each other. She thought: he will work with his father and uncle at the store and maybe run it himself one day. He will marry a pretty, dark-haired local girl and have lots of chubby, rosy-faced children and chickens in the yard. When Baptiste looked at Shane he felt less sure of her future: the locals all gossiped about her family, how they drank and fought and neglected their children. He wondered whether her life would be happy. He hoped it would be; somehow he doubted it.

He drew from his shirt pocket a turquoise ring, lapis lazuli. It caught the light as he tilted it, as if the sea and sun had been trapped in that stone. Shane gasped and he slipped it on her finger, not her engagement finger but the middle one, to show that it was not a proposal but a token of gratitude and love.

'*Se efxaristo*, Baptiste,' she thanked him, and he knew that it was not just for the ring.

When Shane returned to the empty house, her face was tear-stained. Her mother hugged her and each woman could smell sex on the other's skin.

Sevasty served them one last family meal. It was simple because most of their crockery was now packed away so she just made a platter of cold meats: salami, lamb, slices of chicken, a basket of bread and the ubiquitous Greek salad, the olive oil trickling over the crumbling cheese.

They sat together on the terrace, the five of them, all conscious of how strange it was, not only the fact that they were leaving but the way they were united, playing at families, thought Shane, pretending as children do with plastic teacups and empty plates.

As they sat in their uncomfortable circle, like schoolchildren forced to work in a group with those they did not know or like, George made some attempt at unifying comments.

'Jeez, this time has flown by, hasn't it?' and, 'Well, as our Greek adventure nears its end...' but no-one responded.

Shane thought of her last love-making with Baptiste as he leant his weight carefully upon her on the narcissi mattress in their favourite wood. She wondered whether there were any other men who could make her feel that way or did everyone have only one soulmate in the world and she had just lost hers?

Charmian was thinking of Nature Boy, his hands caked in pigeon flesh and the way he ripped their clothes off, and then she smiled at the contrast with dear, genteel Tony, and his paint-stained, careful hands.

Martin remembered the words that Leonard had spoken to him: carry on writing; don't be afraid of the dark; all writers are outsiders. He would never forget the wisdom and the kindness and it helped to make him feel stronger as a man and a writer.

George was thinking about the character of Cressida in his novel. How close could he make her to Charmian without annoying his wife? The infidelity; the pretence about her perfect childhood when it was so clearly a long way from that; the way she had of floating above the world, always out of reach – he had to include them. Those images were too good to waste.

Jason, the only one in the family who had never been to Australia, was thinking about the book his parents had given him about the wildlife there. He wondered if he would ever get to see a koala or a kangaroo, and whether the kids in school would laugh at his Greek accent.

And Sevasty thought, God protect that family: I fear for them.

Down at the harbour, once again, they gathered, the friends: Olivia and her family; Norman looking like he hadn't eaten for a week; Gordon and Chuck harmonious as usual (did they ever fight? wondered Charmian), John

226

Dragoumis; Marianne, and Leonard carrying Axel Joachim. This time Nick and Anthony Katsikas were there too, as well as Polixenes and The Gardenia Dwarf, looking exactly as she had done a year before: dressed in black, a fresh bloom tucked behind her ear. It occurred to Charmian that, whereas their lives had changed beyond measure, the locals seemed more or less to be the same. The smiling Benedictus family was there too, as was Baptiste, and wiping the tears from her eyes, Sevasty.

'Remember,' Leonard whispered to Martin, 'you can always send me your work. Don't stop writing,' and the boy looked pleased that those were the last words spoken to him on that complex piece of earth.

There were hugs and farewells, and the family of five climbed into the larger boat that Alexis had arranged for today. The last image the bystanders had of the family was George raising his hand and waving; Jason smiling beatifically; Martin looking down shyly; Charmian's wide-brimmed hat, defined against the sky; and the ring on Shane's finger, catching the light, until the boat vanished into the distance and no-one could distinguish between the flashing of the lapis lazuli and the surface of the sea.

The only remnant of them was the sound of George's coughing and even that eventually faded.

xxxx

So Leonard left his home just as it was, a shrine to their love. Yes, he packed some clothes and books and had his green typewriter shipped to the States, but as he owned the house, he thought he may well return. Marianne had packed up everything she and Axel Joachim owned and would have it all shipped to Norway. For the journey, she had little with her: a rucksack with some clothes for them both, Momo's white shells and a few of the gifts from Leonard – the tortoiseshell comb, the silver mirror, the tiny scissors that opened like a bird's beak, the cheque on which he had written that he paid Marianne his heart.

Tenants now lived in Marianne and Axel's old house and she couldn't even think about selling it. The last letter she had had from Axel told her that Lena was expecting their 'first child'. She had been tempted to write back: no, Axel, it is not your first child, you already have one, but she stopped herself. It would only invoke a vitriolic response and that was the last thing she wanted at this difficult time.

Magda had taken Axel Joachim for the morning and would meet them at the harbour at two.

'You were a good friend to me when I needed you,' Magda said, when Marianne protested. 'Please let me do something in return.'

Marianne and Leonard made love for the last time that late spring morning, the shutters open to the day and the light spiralling in. Each kiss, each touch carried with it an added poignancy. They treated each other gently, feeling the naked body, lips and tongue of the other as if committing that sensation to memory, knowing they would never have it again. Caressing her breasts, feeling her satin skin, was almost more than Leonard could endure. They took their time, affording themselves this luxury. They cried and kissed again, the salt tears dripping into each other's mouths.

'You have given me so much,' he told her quietly, as they lay there, still, not wanting the experience to end. 'At first, I admired you for your beauty. When I saw you that first day at the store, among the sacks of flour and grain, I thought how can a goddess walk among the ordinary? But then it became something else. I saw the way you looked at the moon. I watched you honour the spring flowers. I observed you dancing at night on the small, wet pebbles and that is what you have given me, Marianne. You opened up love for me to dream of.'

'When I met you,' she spoke through her tears falling on her lips, 'I was so unhappy with Axel. I did not think that anyone could love me or value me as you have done, that anyone would see me as special. I thought perhaps that my time of love was over and that I was worthless.'

'That could never be true. I have loved you and I have loved your child. When I close my eyes, I see you at a table, your son at the other side, and I am carrying flowers, wet with dew, and I want you to open yourself to me as I have entered the cave of your soul.'

'I am frightened of the future, Leonard, a future without you. I do not want to live a life that does not contain you.'

'I have promised that I will provide for you and Axel Joachim when you are back in Oslo and for ever. If you need anything at any time, I will send it.'

'You are kind, Leonard, but I do not only need money. What I want from you cannot be posted or transferred to a post office account. I will miss you: your words, your skin, the darkness of your hair, the way you sing to me in your deep voice with the guitar purring beneath you. But I know that I cannot be with you, seeing you with other women throwing themselves at your feet and me, the little wife, carrying my child and wishing you would turn to us.'

'That is your decision, Marianne. You know that I will carry you in my heart for ever.'

She slipped on her lemon cotton dress and sat in a chair on the terrace. Honeysuckle and jasmine twisted around the railings, releasing their sweetness into the fresh air. Leonard sat opposite and sketched her. He drew her in pencil to begin with – her short hair, her smooth, open face, her delicate nose, her soft neck. Then, with a yellow pastel, he shaded in her dress, blending it with white for her hair so that it looked bleached by the sun.

'Your mother must be pleased that you are going to live with her again.'

'Yes, she is, but I do not know if we will stay in Oslo. Maybe I will take Axel Joachim to Larkollen to Momo's house so that he can gather shells and watch the water and experience what I did as a child.'

'We have to be wary of returning, of expecting something to be the same as it was. We have to have new encounters, not try to replicate the old.'

'I understand what you mean, Leonard. But maybe I can find the good parts of my childhood and open them up for Axel Joachim?'

'Maybe, but he will respond to life as who he is and with what he has. He cannot relive it through you.'

'Yes, I see. Maybe I was hoping that my childhood could be improved if he finds it again, that I could be healed through him.'

Leonard did not answer; he had led Marianne to her own revelation.

'I will let him live as he is.'

Beneath the dress, Leonard could see the curve of her breasts as if he could see through the material. He wished that he could slip the dress over her head and make love to her again and again, every day for the rest of his life, without end.

'Are you going to visit Masha again?'

'Yes, I will. She is very lonely.'

'So maybe we are all returning home to our mothers, in one way or another.'

'It could be.' He was drawing her slender legs now and her bare feet, the toes perfect, her shins smooth.

'Were we wrong, Leonard, to try to escape, to search for something else?'

'No, I don't think so.' He drew the mountains behind her, roughly colouring them in purple and grey. 'We have drunk the wine in the sunlight and the barrel is now empty.'

For the sky he shaded it blue with white and rubbed some ochre in.

He propped the drawing on a chair while they ate their lunch so that he had two versions of Marianne beside him. Kyria Sophia brought them their last meal: baked artichokes, which opened themselves out like waterlilies on a pond of rice, followed by kouneli stifatho, and a courgette-ribbon salad. Too full of food and emotion for dessert, they drank coffee from Leonard's tiny ceramic cups. Marianne rubbed her finger over the rim of a saucer and thought: I will miss every detail of Leonard and his life. Now I am touching everything for the last time.

'You know that we will meet again,' he said as if reading her thoughts. 'This is not the end. It is the start.'

'It is the end of our love affair on Hydra,' she whispered.

'I do not recognise this notion of beginning and ending, Marianne. Did our love start on the day we met and end on the day we leave Hydra? No. You cannot say when it began; you cannot say where it will end. My love for you is beyond all conventional ideas of time. It exists and always will.'

Walking down hand in hand to the harbour, they saw how the island had rid itself of any hint of winter as if it refused ever to have another. The earth was clean and fresh, the air dotted with almond blossom and the sky stretched wide and open – a perfect day for a wedding. Marianne thought of the pop-up books that children read, where you open the covers and allow the world to emerge.

Down on the quayside the ever-small expat community gathered for the last time: Norman, John, Gordon and Chuck, Anthony, Olivia and family, Kyria Sophia dabbing her eyes with a tissue; and then Magda arrived with the two little boys, each glumly holding one of her hands, and Theodore shyly behind her, lacking the history and the bond that the others had. A group of Leonard's fans stood a way off, taking photos.

'Mama! Cone,' called Axel Joachim when he saw them.

Marianne picked him up and kissed him. Leonard ruffled his soft hair.

The friends hugged and there were tears, especially between Marianne and Magda. 'I will never forget your kindness,' said Magda. 'When you visited me in prison, wrote to me, you gave me hope. You have a good heart,' and she slipped an amber necklace around Marianne's neck.

'Thank you, Magda. I shall treasure this as I shall always treasure our warm friendship and the way we have sustained each other.' They embraced and sobbed. 'I will write to you.'

Marianne and Axel Joachim were helped into Alexis' boat and Leonard, his guitar strapped around him, stepped into another. When he looked up, he recognised the face of the boatman, although more gaunt and yet redder than when last he saw it.

'Mikalis!' he said with glee. 'How lovely to see you again.'

Mikalis nodded as if to say yes, I am on the boat again, but I am not healed.

Marianne and Axel Joachim looked over expectantly to Leonard's boat. He had promised a surprise.

The two boats began side by side, their curved wood touching, and then they moved apart, arching away. Leonard took his guitar and began to sing to Marianne. She listened, tears running down her face.

And Leonard sang his new song, *So Long Marianne*, to her.

She heard his beautiful, velvet voice move further away from her as the boats carved the water on their different journeys. Marianne saw Hydra and its red-rooved houses slip slowly away. She saw the single-belled chapel on the hill, and the monasteries shrink into the distance, as if they had never existed; it had all been a dream.

Holding Axel Joachim tightly she wondered what lay ahead for them, whether the future would be a disappointment after Hydra, whether she would ever have the capacity to love anyone the way she had loved Leonard.

Marianne listened to his words disappearing into the horizon and when she looked up, he was gone.

She gazed down at the sea, and she saw that it was dark, almost black, but when she peered more closely at the water, she could just detect a slight hint of blue, as if a painter had taken a thin brush and skimmed the surface, very gently, with light.

Subsequently...

Every limit is a beginning as well as an ending. Who can quit young lives after being long in company with them, and not desire to know what befell them in their after-years?
George Eliot, *Middlemarch*

Leonard Cohen had an international career as a musician, singer and composer. He lived in the US, had two children, Adam and Lorca, three grandchildren, and kept in touch with Axel Joachim. He died in November 2016, four months after Marianne.

Marianne Jenson moved back to Oslo (although she kept her grandmother's house in Larkollen) and in 1979 married Jan Stang. He had three daughters from an earlier marriage. She was involved in Buddhism and painting, although she worked in the oil industry. She died in July 2016 and Leonard Cohen wrote a letter which was read to her before she passed away, saying that he was not far behind her.

Axel Jensen had two daughters with Lena but after they separated he married Pratibha in India. For the last ten years of his life, he had a debilitating illness, and friends, including Leonard Cohen, helped to pay his medical bills. He died in 2003.

Axel Joachim Jensen had an unsettled life, fulfilling his mother's worries about him. He went for a while to Summerhill, the progressive school, which he did not like. He was close to both Leonard Cohen and his mother's second husband.

George Johnston and Charmian Clift moved back to Sydney where they continued to write, but their drinking and smoking took their toll. Charmian took her own life in 1969, aged 45, on the eve of the publication of her husband's novel *Clean Straw for Nothing*, and George died of tuberculosis in 1970, aged 58. Shane Johnston committed suicide in 1974 aged 26; Martin, accomplished as a poet and writer but an alcoholic, died in 1990, aged 42. Gae Johnston, from George's first marriage to Elsie, died of a drugs overdose in 1988, aged 47.

Norman Peterson moved to the US, continued to work as an artist but eventually committed suicide under Brooklyn Bridge.

Magda Tilche married the sailor Theodore and they ended up happily married. She died in the old age home on Hydra in 2005.

James Burke had a worldwide career as a photographer, but he was killed in an accident in the Himalayas aged 49. He lost his footing on the mountain and fell 800 feet.

Anthony Kingsmill continued to paint, wrote a book about his time in Hydra, *The Rings of Moss*, and died in 1993.

Gordon Merrick carried on writing novels, mainly on gay themes. He and his partner Charles 'Chuck' Hulse (a dancer turned novelist) left Hydra and stayed together for 32 years until Merrick's death in 1988.

Olivia de Haulleville lives in the Southern Californian desert and has written books about Buddhism. Her son, Michael, is a Tibetan monk.

Sources of Quotations

Chapter v

'And now our feet...' Psalm 122

'The privilege...' Carl Jung

'The mountains...' Psalm 114

'Had I the heavens...' W. B. Yeats. 'He wishes for the cloths of heavens' [also appears in Chapter xxi]

'Set me as a seal...' The Song of Solomon, Chapter 8

Chapter vii

'Through the laurel branches...' Federico García Lorca, 'Of the Dark Doves'

'Our words must seem...' W. B Yeats

Chapter xix

'On this, pale fear...' Homer, *The Odyssey*, book 24

Chapter xx

'Lay your sleeping head...' W. H. Auden, 'Lullaby'

Chapter xxviii

'Morning sounds...' Charmian Clift, *Peel Me a Lotus*

Chapter xxxvii

'Blessed art thou...' *The Haggadah*

Acknowledgements

I have found the following sources helpful:

Max Brown, *Charmian and George: The Marriage of George Johnston and Charmian Clift* (Rosenberg, 2004)

James Burke, photoshoot in *Life* magazine (1960)

Charmian Clift, *Peel Me a Lotus* (Hutchinson, 1959)

Leonard Cohen, *The Favourite Game* (Secker and Warburg, 1963)

Leonard Cohen, *Flowers for Hitler* (McClelland and Stewart, 1964)

David Conley, 'The magic of journalism in George Johnston's fiction' in *Australian Studies in Journalism* (2001–2)

Paul Daley '*My Brother Jack* at 50 – the novel of a man whose whole life led up to it' in *The Guardian*, 23rd December 2014

Kari Hesthamar, transcript of the *Interview with Leonard Cohen*, Los Angeles, 2005 for Norwegian radio

Kari Hesthamar, *So Long Marianne: A Love Story*, translated by Helle V. Goldman (E.C.W. Press, 2014)

Aubrey Hodes, *Dialogue with Ishmael* (Funk and Wagnalls, 1968)

Aubrey Hodes, *Encounter with Martin Buber* (Penguin, 1971)

George Johnston, 'Sidney Nolan's Gallipoli Paintings' in *ART and Australia*, 1967

Ira B. Nadel *Various Positions: A Life of Leonard Cohen* (Pantheon Books, 1996)

John Tranter, *An Introduction to Martin Johnston – Selected Poems and Prose* (University of Queensland Press, 1993)

Nadia Wheatley, *The Life and Myth of Charmian Clift* (Harper Collins, 2001)

Nadia Wheatley, 'Lies and Silences' (paper given at a conference in Australia, 2002)

I am extremely grateful to the following people:

Yvonne Barlow of Hookline Books for her careful editing and for believing in this novel.

Jarkko Arjastalo (Leonard Cohen Files) and Allan Showalter (Cohencentric) for their encouragement and help.

Michele Bernier of the Musée National des Beaux-arts du Québec for sending me a copy of the painting of Marianne and Axel Joachim by Marcella Maltais (1972)

Professor Nils Roemer for sending me the film *Ladies and Gentlemen…. Mr Leonard Cohen* (1964)

Rebecca Smith for reading the novel and giving me useful feedback.

The staff at the Godolphin School in Salisbury where I have taught English for seventeen years; many of my colleagues have been kind enough to show an interest in my writing. I especially want to thank Clare Astbury for sharing with me her love of Leonard Cohen.

My children, Ben and Daisy, and their partners, Ellie and Barnaby, for their love and support.

Above all, I want to thank my husband, Dave, who has encouraged and loved me for the past thirty-five years and persuaded me to keep on writing, even when I lost hope.

About the author:

Tamar Hodes was born in Israel in 1961 and lived on Hydra and in South Africa before settling in the UK in 1967. After growing up in north London, she read English and Education at Homerton College, Cambridge. For the past thirty-three years she has taught English in schools, universities and prisons.

Her novel *Raffy's Shapes* was published by Accent Press in 2006. She has had ten stories broadcast on Radio 4 and many others have appeared in anthologies including Salt's *Best British Short Stories 2015*, *The Pigeonhole*, *Your One Phone Call*, the *Ofi Press*, *MIR Online* and *Fictive Dream*.

Tamar is married with two grown-up children and a grandson.

Lightning Source UK Ltd.
Milton Keynes UK
UKHW012224030820
367622UK00003B/898